Stepping
CAREFULLY

Jean Ponte

STEPPING CAREFULLY

iUniverse books may be ordered through booksellers or by contacting:

iUniverse
1663 Liberty Drive
Bloomington, IN 47403
www.iuniverse.com
1-800-Authors (1-800-288-4677)

ISBN: 978-1-4917-6048-2 (sc)
ISBN: 978-1-4917-6049-9 (e)

Print information available on the last page.

iUniverse rev. date: 07/20/2019

CHAPTER 1

$\mathcal{E}$arly this morning before my son Tommy stirs, I make my way down the path from the cottage to the beach with a cup of coffee in my right hand. With the other hand I cover the top of the cup to keep out the clouds of tiny bugs fluttering around. Abruptly I stop and then sniff again.

After rounding the bend in the needle-covered path to the beach and breathing-in the pungent smell of the cedars that have been here since I was a child, I stop abruptly. Suddenly I sniff a different odor, a putrid one. "Pheeewwwuuu!" I whisper to myself, not wanting to break the pristine morning silence with loud words. Then I recognize the smell. It's the stench of something decaying, the slow rotting of an animal body.

Until I reach the beach, I can't exactly locate the smell. Then I actually see the source just ahead of me smack in the middle of the path. It's nothing but a decaying fish.

Finding a dead fish on the beach isn't all that uncommon, but this one, about two and a half feet long with its gaping mouth of ferocious teeth—a pike, I assume—and eyes already plucked out by the gulls, has a stick piercing straight through its abdomen and the stick thrust upright in the sandy path. It appears to have been placed there quite intentionally. Is it really deliberate or am I being overly suspicious? I hold my nose and mutter nasally, "At least it's not a human body."

Is this decaying, skewered fish supposed to convey some sort of message? Is it meant to be a warning to me, a threat like a severed head stuck on a pole after a battle? Yet, a stinky fish is hardly something to make one shake, or shiver, or spill their coffee. Though the incident is not serious, it does show me exactly how close to the cottage someone can trespass without my even knowing that a stranger is around.

Taking the path from my father's old white cottage down to the beach is nothing unusual. It's just part of my morning ritual here at Tatterack. I feel that the beach is my own personal sanctuary, and I always try to visit it before the church, situated a block away, begins its morning cacophony of bells. The pseudo bells from the church with their freaky electronic sounds will strike the morning air with a hammer-like blow, overriding the delicate susurrations of water touching the shore.

At this time of the morning when the beach is empty, empty of people, that is, I truly believe, selfish as it sounds, that this patch of shoreline in front of the cottage belongs to me and to no one else in the world. I don't want anything to intervene between me and its special moods: the plash of water threading its way around jagged rocks or the sharp assaults on my nose, whether clean air, skunk or fish. I even wish I didn't have to share the fog with anyone else as it hovers over the water or ghosts its way between the pine tree branches. The shore and its moods have always been part of my life until marriage kept me away for several years. Now that I'm single again, the beach and my father's cottage have once again become a major part of my life.

Some mornings I find well-polished colored glass—blue, if I'm lucky—or bits of plastic, or gooey party balloons with the ribbons still attached. Those need to be dropped in the garbage pail so that the shore birds won't swallow them and choke to death. Sometimes the waves push aside the sand and pebbles to reveal a fossil, one I haven't yet collected over the years.

After finding the dead fish this morning, I set my coffee cup down on a nearby log and pull the stake with the fish still attached out of the sand quite easily. Yet, a few minutes later when I return with a black plastic bag in my hand intending to drop the fish into it,

I have to shake and beat the stick hard against a rock in an attempt to loosen the fish. But it won't slip off the stick. Instead, the huge jaws vomit up some of the fish's innards. "Yuck!" I gasp, and look away from the sickening disgorging, hoping the regurgitation won't affect my stomach. I know how easily my stomach can become nauseated.

I give up trying to stuff the fish into the plastic bag and instead scuff sand over the jelly-like innards, then carry the pole with the remains of the speared fish down to the edge of the shore where the gulls can finish it off. The strong fish odor will surely become far more potent before the pecking process is completed. Quickly, I head up the path towards the cottage not wanting to look back at the wiggling fish, which will appear, because of the action of the water, to be in a hopeless struggle to escape from the pole thrust through its belly.

Nervously I finger back my hair, attempting to tuck the sun-bleached strands behind each ear. In the first few seconds after finding the dead fish on the beach, my mind naturally swings to Tommy, my seven-year-old son, as the culprit. Isn't a stinky fish the sort of prank a young boy might think of perpetrating in order to piss-off his mom?

A bit later, when Tommy and the dog come scurrying through the back doorway of the cottage and let the screen door slam, I hold out my hand to stop them. "Halt, Sergeant Tommy! Did you leave something dead and stinky down there on the beach? Empty your shoes if you've been down on the shore."

"Haven't," my seven-year old answers after a sloppy salute.

"Haven't sand in your shoes or haven't put the dead fish in the middle of the path?"

"What fish? Is it a big one? Where?" Excitement starts him rocking from leg to leg.

I point towards the beach and Tommy slams back out the screen door again. In trying to follow, our curly-haired mutt nearly gets caught in the rapidly closing screen. From Tommy's reactions I feel certain that he isn't the one who put the fish out there on the beach.

His brown eyes didn't dance and shift, and the corners of his mouth didn't twitch as they sometimes do when he's trying to pull a "fast one." Someone else has deliberately stuck the fish and pole on the beach.

A half-hour later, I'm crouched on my knees about to begin stapling a new twenty-four by thirty-inch piece of canvas onto the stretchers. Instead, I lay my stapler down and sit back, my legs folded. It's hard to get my mind on painting when some unusual things are happening to Tommy and me lately.

Perhaps a neighbor or some stranger is behind the quirky fish incident. Who could be so upset with me, aside from a few people I've spoken to in private regarding the loudness of the electronic bells blasting from the church nearby? Can't this person or persons, whomever they are, restrain their anger? I don't want anyone to be so upset that they might take their disgruntlement out on Tommy. That wouldn't be fair. Incidents meant to hurt me shouldn't include an innocent child like my small seven-year-old son. Worrying too much about Tommy is a habit I'll probably never get over.

I can easily vegetate by the shore all day long and never get any of my art work or the cottage housework done, so I make bargains with myself, hoping to prevent my ennui from taking over. I'll say, "Leah Fleury—that's my name again since Roger and I have divorced—Leah, if you get the hated vacuum out and do the living room rug and staple the new canvas on the stretchers ready for your next painting, then you can have one hour at the beach to sit and watch the water, the sandpiper, and hunt for fossils. Then, just maybe, you can have another hour later in the day at the shore after you take Tommy for his haircut." Actually, I'm the one who needs a haircut more than Tommy, but these are lean times so I've let my thick straight hair grow. Now it's nearly brushing my shoulders.

My father was here at the cottage with us earlier in the summer but now has returned to Holland, Michigan, where he still resides in the same old cream-colored stucco house in which I had been brought up. The house looks even more dated now and needs a coat of paint. The house's age is also clearly defined by the small gas fireplace, bordered in slippery black tiles and awkwardly placed in a corner of the living room, as well as the wide oak panel door between the stair hall and the dining room.

Back in the late thirties when the house was new the extra half bath just off the den had probably been considered quite a luxury. The only brand new thing about the old house is the ten by twelve-foot glassed-in room built on the southeast side of the dining room for my mother's plants, which she attended so lovingly. Now that she is gone I use the room for my painting studio. True, my father never says a word against my using it, but sometimes he looks disgusted at the messes I leave. After all, the room had been specifically designed to please my poor sickly mother and she had been extremely neat, barely letting a leaf touch the floor before sweeping it up. Since my divorce from Roger, Tommy, and I are now living with my father.

That evening of the same day when the rotting fish was discovered on the beach, I have dinner ready and placed on the cherry drop-leaf table in the low-ceilinged kitchen when the bells from the church break forth with a rendition of *We Shall Overcome*. Resentment at the loud musical noise foisted upon us overwhelms me. Abruptly, I spring up from the table and vent my frustration by slamming a cupboard door shut which forces another cupboard door to burst open and then another and another. There is something about the air pressure behind those old warped pine planks that won't allow all the doors to stay closed at once. But nothing stops me. I slam each succeeding door as it pops open. In my frustration, I'd have gone on slamming every cupboard door in the kitchen if Tommy hadn't sprung up from the table pleading, "Mom! Mom! Stop!" He ran into the living room and grabbed my ear-plugs. "Here!"

I suppose my bizarre behavior is enough to frighten anyone not just a child. I stop slamming cupboard doors, plug my ears, and try to calm myself down. Tommy doesn't need a weird mother. He already has an eccentric, absentee Father. "Thanks, Tommy." Actually the earplugs don't help much.

At the ending of an otherwise perfect summer day, the obnoxiously loud bell music spoils everything. It blares forth like a rock concert, only it isn't Madonna or The Beach Boys—not that I would want them spoiling the ambience of the beach colony either. Our cottage and others within an area of a half-mile are assaulted with these shrill electronic renditions of hymns at least three times a day: Nine in the morning, noon, six, and occasionally even nine in the evening. Sometimes if there is a funeral service at the church or if Father Ciconni decides upon a whim to have a concert for his own benefit, we are treated, or rather irreverently mistreated, to an extra twenty minutes of electronic bells.

The taped medley of hymns, bells and instruments together, are broadcast through two prominent speakers, large as elephant ears, on the squat tower of the buff-colored brick church. I assume that a genuine bell is no longer hanging inside the square tower, although rumor has it that it once did.

I am quite appreciative of genuine bells such as those at the Bock Tower in Florida and the carillons I once heard near Philadelphia where my parents took me when I was twelve years old. I still have a pleasant memory of the dulcet sounds. The tones were clear and lovely. They carried a delicate "other worldliness" message that made me shiver and sent my imagination soaring. They were as different from the electronic bells here in Tatterack as the graceless dancing of elephants would be compared to a New York City Ballet performance.

CHAPTER 2

I was taking the dog for a walk this noon when I encountered Mr. Lumus striding briskly in the opposite direction. His small cottage was located on the opposite side of the road from my father's. All that I knew about Mr. Lumus was that he had once driven a Greyhound bus. Now that he was retired, he drove a Cadillac. Perhaps the Cadillac reminded him of driving the heavy, smooth bus down the highway. He also possessed a pickup truck, a red one so deprived of paint that it was difficult to see exactly where paint and rust met. It was rumored that his cottage was constructed of lumber taken from an old boathouse up at Genner's Point. The boathouse had once belonged to the Coast Guard Lighthouse before it was decommissioned.

As our paths crossed out on the dirt road behind my father's cottage, the church began its ten-minute bombardment of hymns. Mr. Lumus barely gave me a nod. Dispensing with polite greetings of any sort, he immediately began ranting against the electronic bells.

I took the precaution of quickly stepping aside as he spewed forth missile after missile of rancor, encompassing numerous swear words in a cloud so thick I thought I could almost see the polluted air moving towards me. I began to wonder if he were quite normal. I was positive that I didn't sound as radical or as unseemly as he did when I voiced my opinion about the electronic bells, although, when I was sure Tommy couldn't overhear me, I often became less respectful on the subject.

I suggested to Mr. Lumus, "Since you attend that church yourself, why don't you complain to Father Ciconni about the loudness."

"Oh, him!" Mr. Lumus grimaced in disgust. "He thinks he's the Pope. If I asked him to turn down the volume of the bells, he'd take off my head and roll it down the church aisle."

This vision of Mr. Lumus's elongated head wobbling unevenly down between the wooden pews was so vivid that I had to stifle a laugh. I thought he sounded a bit hyperbolic. "Surely other people in the beach community have complained."

Mr. Lumus was not smiling. "No. They don't dare. You don't know that old man. He has a fixation on the church as it was in ancient times. Back in the medieval period, the church practically ruled the small villages, and he thinks it still ought to." Mr. Lumus' voice soared in volume to span the width of four cottages. His loud verbosity made me feel uncomfortable. We were highly spotlighted out here in the middle of the dirt road where the neighbors might be able to hear every word.

"Now, now." I put my finger to my lips. I tried to calm him down before he spewed forth a second volley of explosives. "Surely other folks have complained," I said.

"They wouldn't dare! He gets even if they try." I backed up further before he spewed forth a second volley of expletives.

"He can't be quite that terrible." I was seriously beginning to have my doubts about Mr. Lumus' rationality since his voice had risen another decibel.

"He is, believe me. He's a real case…a cunning bas…."

Fortunately, no one could have heard Mr. Lumus' last word because the bells began to play a very loud version of *Let Jesus be Your Redeemer.* Personally, I thought Mr. Lumus might need it. Redeeming, I mean. He was so full of rancor.

It was difficult for me to believe that any man of the cloth, like Father Ciconni, could be as undisciplined as Mr. Lumus claimed. After all, weren't priests supposed to embody the teachings of Christ?

To me, the word "amenable" had always been how I felt about priests and ministers. My home-town minister, Dr. Denning, was a very approachable, friendly person. I even sought his advice about Tommy when I first thought of a separation from Roger. The minister, or at least that particular one, had a ready handshake and an easy smile, all part of the tool box from which I assumed all ministers and priests were equipped before being thrust out into the midst of their voracious congregations.

After Mr. Lumus had finished ranting against the little Father and began to walk away, I called after him. "Have you tried writing a letter to the Father about the bells?"

"He tore it up."

"Wait! If I discover that the decibels of the bells are too high and ought to be legally lowered, will you come with me to talk to Father Ciconni?"

"Just you and me?"

"Well, along with some other concerned people."

"If you get any." he answered with a waver of his hand, but the uncertain tone of his voice implied that the possibility of getting other people to join with me was quite remote.

So how could this Father Ciconni at the nearby church be so much different from the norm? I suspected the highly excitable Mr. Lumus of distorting the truth a bit. Most likely because he once had a personal run-in with Father Ciconni, and the disagreement had tainted his attitude. But "tainted was far too mild a term. Mr. Lumus was a pricked sausage spewing forth burning, red-hot grease.

My mind grappled with the pros and cons of taking any action at all against the bells since I had plenty to occupy me just by taking care of Tommy and working on my paintings, which were a small source of income.

On the other hand, how was I to ignore the three daily assaults on my ears, each one at least ten minutes long? If only the earplugs had helped. But they didn't.

How could other folks tolerate the electronic bells either? The tapes were shrill, obnoxious, outshouting the wonderful natural sounds that I loved so much. The electronic bells silenced the scolding of the plovers and wild ducks, even the quarrelsome wrangling of the gulls, and especially the rhythmical, splashing of the water that soothed each day of my life.

CHAPTER 3

Our once-a-summer beach colony meeting at the library was scheduled for the following Tuesday and I didn't want to miss it. There was to be an interesting lecture on the history of a town located nearby called Titusville where I had once stopped to admire the old cemetery tombstones dating back to the seventeen hundreds. Also, this meeting might be an opportunity to find out what other folks thought about the loud bell music. Not being an outgoing type of person, I wasn't sure how successful I'd be. I thought, surely everyone must be as annoyed as I was by the blast of sound coming from the church.

Before the meeting actually started and most of us were still standing around in the back of the room before taking our seats, I saw my neighbor, Mavis nearby. Being less shy with someone I knew well, I asked her what she thought about the loud music coming from the church, She smiled and shrugged, "Guess I've grown used to it."

I wanted to ask her "Why? Why should one settle for 'getting used to' something so outrageously loud, but I restrained myself from actually confronting her. Mavis is a gentle person, and so thoughtful of others. I wasn't at this meeting to make anyone uncomfortable, and certainly not my close neighbor. I turned to Mr. Hudson who stood on the other side of me to ask his opinion, but he nodded to me and walked off to find a seat before I could query him.

At the end of the meeting when we were having refreshments, I decided to speak to Mrs. Daniels who was sipping hot tea nearby, about the loud bell music. I prefaced my query by asking casually, "Do you think the church bells are a bit on the loud side?"

She nodded. "But our cottage is further away from the church than yours." She added in a whisper, "Thank God."

I smiled until she cautioned, "Be careful what you say to folks. There are big ears on your other side."

"Oh?"

"Come over here," she beckoned, and we both moved closer to the shelves where magazines were stored. "It might be better if we aren't overheard discussing the bells in front of that man, the one who was standing close to you. He's one of the grounds-keepers at the church; he also does mowing for several of the year-round homes along the shore, though why anyone should want a lawn up here, I can't imagine."

I nodded with strong emphasis, then decided it would be wiser to maintain a neutral expression. "Fake bells," I call them. Mrs. Daniels sympathized, "The bells must be dreadfully loud for those of you living so near to the church."

I nodded with strong emphasis. "That's interesting news about the grounds-keeper. Thanks for telling me." Then I asked her, "Why hasn't anyone gone straight to the Father and aked him to lower the volume of the bells?"

"I don't know. Maybe they think it's better to leave well enough alone."

"You mean people might be intimidated?"

"I mean the Father doesn't handle suggestions well."

Before she could elucidate any further on the subject or explain what she meant, we were interrupted by a man who came up to speak to her and then led her away to introduce her to his wife.

"Goodnight and thanks." I called after Mrs. Daniels.

I collected Tommy who hadn't quite finished his paper cup of hot chocolate, though I was sure he had devoured a cookie, probably even three, while I had been talking to Mrs. Daniels. "You can bring your drink home with you if you like. Did you remember to thank the lady who gave you the drink and cookies?" Tommy nodded and I urged him towards the backdoor.

Tommy and I were about to step through the outside door when Mrs. Daniels raised her hand, "Wait up a second." She sidled over to the door and whispered a few words in my ear, "Be careful what you say about the bells. The little father doesn't like to be bested, and he's never wrong."

"Oh?" I wasn't quite sure what she meant, but it wasn't likely I'd go to visit him. "Goodnight."

After opening the outside door and discovering that it was still light outside, Tommy complained in an offended tone, "Mom, what's the big hurry? It isn't even dark out yet. It couldn't be anywhere near bedtime either."

"Well, almost bedtime. You know that it stays light even past your bedtime this time of year." Tommy continued to grumble between sips of chocolate as I hurried him along.

It was only a couple of half-blocks back to the cottage, but the entire time I was occupied with indecision. Did I, or didn't I, want to put aside my daily routine of painting in order to complain to the church about the loud bells? Of course, first I had to find out if they actually were too loud. At the same time I also wondered about Tommy's welfare and how he might be affected if it got spread around the colony that I was attempting to quell the noisy bells. What if someone became so upset with me that they took out their anger on Tommy? No, I soothed myself, that wasn't likely to happen. Most people around here were more laid-back than that. I grappled with the pros and cons of going directly to the church or first visiting with other beach people and maybe persuading them to join me against the noise pollution. I didn't want to go-it alone. What would I say...no, what would we say to convince the church to lower the noise level? I was certainly not going alone.

All the next afternoon while I worked on one of my paintings, my mind grappled with the pros and cons of going to visit the Father at the church. I didn't want to go alone. What would I say to convince him to lower the noise level? First, I needed facts. I needed the exact decibels of the bells...not just a vague guess. Then, I needed to find some other people in the beach colony to go with me...people who were "outgoing types." I knew I didn't have the nerve to go alone! On second thought, I had plenty to keep myself busy right here at the cottage just by working on my landscape paintings and caring for Tommy.

Even Mrs. Daniels at the library meeting the other evening was careful not to allow others in the room to overhear what she was saying to me. I wondered. Why was the topic of the bells treated so hush-hush and abruptly dropped as though speaking about something uncouth? I started to laugh.

"What's so funny?" Tommy asked.

"Oh, look, Tommy! It's dark enough to see the moon already," was my quickly thought up reply.

What was so holy about the bell music itself? Nothing, I decided. Then why were people so afraid to discuss the loudness of the bells with the Father?

In any case, how could anyone ignore the three daily assaults of the electronic bells sweeping from the loudspeakers into their ears? Each lasted a minimum of ten minutes, but often much longer. Why were other folks tolerating them better than I seemed able to do? The tapes were shrill, obnoxious, outshouting the wonderful natural sounds that I loved so much...the smooth flow of water, the burble and splash against the shore, followed by the gentle backwash, or sometimes a pounding surf that caused uncertainty and promoted an edgy excitement.

CHAPTER 4

*U*nknown to either my father or Tommy, I had borrowed an instrument called a decimeter to test the level of noise pollution at the beach colony. I had an idea that if I could prove to other folks living at the shore exactly how loud the bells really were, I could garner more support to rid our beach colony of the obtrusive noise.

It was Enid, my dear, but outspoken friend, who taught environmental studies at Western Michigan University who had trusted me with the cumbersome old decimeter which I needed to determine just how high the volume really was before drawing others into helping me. After all, hadn't we all migrated to this wonderful spot every summer year after year for the quiet atmosphere it offered...to hear the birds and enjoy peaceful canoe rides at sunset?

When I was a freshman in college, my friend Enid and I had shared an off-campus room down below the hill on Lovell Street. I can still recall the huge Elm trees, many long since diseased and cut down, shading that street, and my weary climb up the steep hill to my classes on the older campus when the cable car wasn't working or around to the other side of the hill to the newer campus.

My second year in college was when I met Roger. Enid had bluntly warned me off. "You're right, the guy is smart, but in a viperish way."

"Oh," I claimed, rushing to his defense, "he just enjoys clever repartee." Not only had I attempted to dampen down her warning, but I had even convinced myself that Enid was a bit jealous. Looking back, I fervently wished I had listened to her advice more carefully.

Enid still lives down on Lovell Street in a big old house near where we both used to room, but recently she has become married to Dr. Harold Dremer who teaches social studies at Western University. During my visit with Enid earlier in the spring, she explained carefully in her patient teachery voice—she already knew my poor concept of mechanical things—just how to use the decimeter. "It's an older model," she explained, "but in spite of its scratched and worn looking leather case, it's still accurate."

"Thank you, dear friend." I gave Enid a hug and ran my fingers through her curly dark hair. She already knew how envious I was of her tight curls since my hair was just the opposite.

Right after my father left the cottage at the end of June to return home to Holland, Michigan, I chose a time when Tommy was off playing with his friend Stevie, who lived a quarter-mile up the curved beach, before unpacking the decimeter. Carefully I pulled it out of the box, well hidden under some shoes in the car where no one would see it during the drive North.

I wasn't ready for Tommy to know what I was about to do because he might accidentally blurt it out to someone in his trusting way. Most seven-year-olds aren't expected to understand the word "discretion." Common sense told me that it was wiser to quietly check out the decimeter readings first. What if I was completely wrong and the readings weren't as high or as dangerous as I assumed? And if they weren't too high, what leverage did I, or anyone else, have to request that the church lower the volume of the electronic bells?

Today, at noon, just as the electronic bells began to sound-off, I opened the leather case and took my first reading right here on the wide back porch of my father's cottage. The decimeter registered eighty-five. At the dirt road, which ran behind our cottage and was about thirty feet closer to the church, the meter fluctuated between eighty-five and ninety. I already knew from reading several articles on the subject of noise pollution that ninety was the point where the sound could damage the ear drums if that same noise level was sustained for any length of time. Though ten minutes at ninety decibels was not a long enough period to damage the eardrums, it was dangerous enough to provide a good arguing point for lowering the volume.

I noticed that Mr. Lumus' pickup truck was missing from his driveway so I assumed he was not at home. The Cadillac, on the other hand, was quite evident since it didn't seem much smaller than the cottage itself. In order to get a new reading on the decimeter closer to the church, I strolled as casually as possible across the dirt road to Mr. Lumus' cottage. I certainly meant to be unobtrusive about my foray into his yard, but doubted that it would go completely unnoticed. In a beach colony like this one where most of the cottages were close enough for the inhabitants to catch colds from each other, it was best to assume that someone had indeed spotted me.

Mr. Lumus' cottage was a humble abode of weathered timber, patched together. Materially, it wasn't much to show for his years of driving a bus unless unbeknownst to me, he also had another home somewhere else downstate. I once heard my neighbor, Mr. Harris, tell someone that the boards in Mr. Lumus' cottage were actually salvaged in the dead of night from the Coastguard boathouse with the help of one of his brothers. Then, the story goes, he had reassembled the wide boards on the narrow lot on the backside of the road.

After entering Mr. Lumus' yard, I again unsnapped the heavy leather cover and switched on the decimeter. The indicator rose up and up until it reached about ninety-two. Exactly as I suspected! Mr. Lumus' ears were constantly in a danger zone. Therefore, didn't it follow that the readings at the church itself, which was juxtaposed under the loudspeakers, must be even higher than the ninety decibels registered at this spot where I was standing right now? Surely then, I rationalized, if I or someone else gave Father Ciconni this new information, he would feel a civic-minded duty to lower the volume of the electronic bells rather than expose the ears of his Sunday congregation to possible deafness. I murmured to myself: I'll bet the poor unworldly man is so taken up with prayer and good works that he has absolutely no idea that the bells are annoying people in his parish.

Impulsively, I decided that I ought to get a reading on the decimeter much closer to the church. Would it be in poor taste to sneak up on the rear of the holy edifice? Possibly, but nevertheless I was contemplating doing exactly that. Immediately I began hunting for a safe passage through the large patch of poison ivy that was extremely lush between Mr. Lumus' property and the church lawn. Suddenly, a man on a throbbing mower came riding around to the back of the church. He didn't see me, so I made a quick retreat or started to when just as unexpectedly I heard the rattle-bang of Mr. Lumus' pickup truck pulling into his driveway on the opposite side of me.

Now I was cut-off in both directions. Trapped! How embarrassing to be caught snooping, especially after the bells had stopped ringing. I had no excuse for being there in the first place. Either I had to continue going through the poison ivy and face the man on the huge mower or turn around, go through the poison ivy again and face Mr. Lumus.

As I turned around, my heart was thumping as loudly as the mower noisily chewing up grass. I picked my way back again through the first half of the poison ivy. Truly, after suffering summer after summer during my youth from the blisters of poison ivy, I was far more afraid of that lush three-leafed plant than I was of the explosive Mr. Lumus.

"Ah, there you are," I said, acting as though I had purposely been seeking him out. Slowly, Mr. Lumus got out of his old dented truck and eyed me suspiciously.

"What are you doing here?" he asked grumpily.

"This," I said, taking a gulp of air to steady my nerves. "Have you ever seen a decimeter?" He shook his head.

I jumped over the last patch of ivy, walked over to him, and flipped up the leather flap to demonstrate how the decimeter worked even though the bells had longed ceased.

I pointed to a figure on the dial. "This is how high it registered right here at your cottage door while the bells were being broadcast."

"Yeah? I could have told you it was damn loud without your contraption. What did you call it?"

"A decimeter."

"You planning to tell the old grouch about it?"

"You mean Father Ciconni? Oh yes, probably." My voice began to grow louder and louder in an attempt to overcome the approaching mower noise behind me. "If I can convince some of the beach people to come with me."

Mr. Lumus returned to his truck and slammed the door shut. He muttered something. I thought it sounded like, "... he'll make you pay," or it could have been "good day," though surely that was too polite a wording coming from Mr. Lumus.

"What did you say?" Mr. Lumus didn't answer, just kept on walking away towards his cottage door. I called after him, "By the way, do you know what happened to the real bell that once hung in the tower?"

Mr. Lumus stopped and turned. His relish was apparent, "Sabotage."

"Sabotage? By whom?"

But it was too late. Mr. Lumus had already stepped inside his cottage and slammed the heavy door which shook his cottage walls. Such a strange man, I told myself. I snapped shut the leather flap over the decimeter dial and walked back to my father's cottage on the other side of the dirt road.

I needed answers. Exactly what had happened to the genuine bell years ago and why wasn't it still in use? Reluctantly, my mind drifted back in a series of mental snapshots, an attempt to resurrect the truth about the bell. But some pictures were too traumatic to resuscitate... my mother's death for instance, which brought up vivid pictures of her sad funeral. But I still thought that somewhere in that basket of memories, there might be an answer to what had happened to the bell.

CHAPTER 5

*A*t age sixteen I was a senior at Red Heart Parochial High
School, which I attended not because my family was Catholic
but because the school was considered academically good. Also, the
school was a mere mile away from our home, making chauffeuring
by my mother unnecessary. Even back then she had unpredictable
asthma attacks and often needed to stay at home and indoors when
the air quality was poor.

In that same time period, I had an after-school job in a gift
shop. The shop was only a half mile from our house so I could
have easily walked home after work. When it got dark early in the
fall and winter, my father, Erwin Fleury, a manager in a machine
shop—he was tall and robust at that time but more hunkered over
now—insisted on picking me up every single day, even if he had to
wait, which he often did. "Better safe than sorry," he always said. My
father was into platitudes.

"You're embarrassing me," I complained. "The other clerks in
the store will never treat me like anything except a teenager, not after
seeing you outside waiting at the curb every evening as though I were
a retard." It felt as though my father had the key to my freedom, and
although I knew it would be hopeless to try to break the lock, I kept
testing his resolve anyway.

My father tried to soothe me with another of his favorite phrases,
"It's what God wants... for me to take care of you." I thought at the time
that it was a meaningless assumption—that about God—because my

20

father never attended church or showed any other religious inclination. I could even have placed bets on the very next platitude that would blossom forth from his mouth and sure enough, here it came.

"Everything's going to be all right," he said, patting my knee.

"I'm sick of hearing that old chestnut." I pouted the rest of the way home.

My father's platitudes don't bother me anymore—he could spout a ton of them—though several times I have had to halt myself before using those very same worn out phrases on Tommy. Afterwards, I would laugh at myself and muse; perhaps those wornout platitudes my father used over and over again were really meant to sooth himself more than they were ever meant to placate me. Or maybe they were even a form of prayer...an asking for hints on how to bring up a teenage daughter. I wondered if I was a typical one and decided that I probably wasn't. Who wants to be just like everyone else?

The cloisterism and the predictability of home life fairly spun me into reverse mode... and into Roger, whom I met at the university. Roger looked medium in every way: medium brown wavy hair, medium height, about five-eleven, and brown eyes, also medium in shade. In appearance he could have been the model for a well-adjusted American youth. Because of this boyish, fresh out of the mold appearance, people, including me, misread his character until later when they became all too aware of his sarcasm and his smart-assed manner, and especially in my case, his possessiveness.

At the time, I was just seventeen and my own self-esteem was elevated loftily by being the object of Roger's interest and what I perceived to be his brilliant mind. I still think he has a clever mind, though slightly skewed. I had a keen thirst for attention back then... not fatherly attention either.

"Baby," Roger once said to me, "you're thoroughbred stock and I plan to keep you in my paddock." Roger lavished me with compliments usually dressed in sarcasm. I knew he wasn't playing the part of a traditional suitor, but his backhanded compliments made me feel important just the same. Somehow I simply overlooked the small pricks of criticism that were well disguised as humor. Roger's parents were deceased, but he had an Aunt Lucy whom we visited often in Grand Rapids because we both liked her so much. Roger and his Aunt Lucy slung witticisms and insults back and forth faster than a tennis ball over the net but never ended up angry. In fact, they often kissed each other goodbye at the end of their visit. If tickets to their conversations had been sold, it would have been worth the price of a game just to listen to the two of them. I still visit his Aunt Lucy whenever I can.

In college when I overspent my allowance and found myself broke and hungry on college vacation outings to Daytona Beach or San Antonio, Roger came through with a few dollars to tide me over. "Here," he'd say after handing me ten dollars, "Have a ball." I was always in debt to him, which—had I realized it—put me even further under his influence. It didn't take a great deal of pressure for his smart-tongued, verbose personality to inundate my yet to be jelled one; shamefully, I followed his ideas like a mesmerized bird.

Three years later, when I next visited Tatterack and the cottage in the beach colony, Roger and I were married and Tommy was barely two years old. That's when I noticed the lack of a genuine church bell, but just barely, because I was happily distracted by Tommy and his need for love and attention, and usually a change of diaper.

Now my recalcitrant memory finally coughed up what I wanted to recall about the church bell in the tower. It was during one of those visits to the cottage when I heard the wild rumor about some boys— no one seemed to know exactly who they were, or if they did know, they kept mum about it—who decided that the bell rang far too early in the morning—eight o'clock—for a vacation resort. The boys, or so the story goes, had somehow gotten inside the church tower at night and cut the ropes on the bell. According to Father Ciconni, the bell cracked when it fell and hit the bottom of the tower. That was the rumor. After the damage was verified by the Father, the people from town blamed the beach colony, insisting that the boys who wrecked the bell were a disreputable gang from the colony.

Could Father Ciconni be wrong?" I muttered, as I brought my mind back to the present. "Was there any solid proof?"

Five years later, the square bell tower was still empty, as far as I knew, and two big loudspeakers were perched like evil horns on the outside of that same brick edifice. Did all that electronic equipment cost less than forging a brand new, beautiful sounding, bell? Or had someone persuaded the Church Board that religious music, wafting through the ether four times a day, would be so persuasive that it might double the church's congregation and ultimately the church's coffer?

That conclusion was sheer conjecture on my part…an allegation which sounded suspiciously unchristian. Maybe I should be struck by lightening, but I think the loud bells constantly blasting through the cottage are already fulfilling that punishment. During my subsequent lobbying against the bells, someone told me that Father Ciconni had actually stood in his pulpit one Sunday and proclaimed: to his entire congregation that "…those people against the church's musical tapes would bring down upon themselves divine punishment."

Obviously, the loud concerts blasting through our cottages were already doing the job for Him. Punishing, I mean. Later in the summer, I was the one who needed *saving*… but it wasn't quite clear from whom.

CHAPTER 6

A s I cleaned the acrylic paint from my brushes under the kitchen faucet, I explained to the dog, an avid listener because he was under the mistaken impression that he would be given one of those milk bone treats. "If I had a lot more guts, I'd rappel up the church tower and put the two loud-speakers—those aimed in the direction of the beach colony—out of commission." I didn't know even the rudiments of rock climbing, much less sheer brick walls, but that didn't stop my fantasy. The dog wagged his tail encouragingly, so I jabbered on: "like one of those jewel robbers, I'd dress all in black, looking svelte, and wait until midnight to do my heroic deed."

If Roger, my former husband, could listen-in on my ranting and my determination to do something about the loud bell tapes, he would laugh snidely. Roger thought he knew my nature thoroughly, claiming it was as ingrown as a toenail and assuming that I would scold and fume awhile and then drop the matter of the noise pollution. It was true that I had no intention of coolly confronting the Reverend Father at the church all by myself to state my case against the loud bells. No, definitely not by myself. I considered myself an egalitarian but certainly not one of those outgoing activist types who protest loudly for this or that good cause and hold up signs at street corners.

Assuredly though, I thought, if I informed a few of my neighbors about the high decibels, which I had just verified by using the decimeter this past week, they would all fuse together and come to my aid just as people with "like" interests were generally inclined to do. It was rudimentary. I would be the solder or hot glue and together we would all rectify the problem of the obnoxiously loud electronic bells. It seemed like a very straightforward, simple plan to me.

Out loud, I cautioned myself, "Now hold on a minute. You are about to make a big detour. Contacting a large number of beach colony people will take up a huge chunk of time." Selfishly, I realized how it would severely cut back on my easel painting and my privacy. Then there was Tommy. "What will I do about him?" I asked myself. I couldn't just leave him all alone while I traipsed from cottage to cottage for signatures. I felt a sudden weakening of my resolve. Just then the dog began to bark and cut short my on-again, off-again, fantasies about quelling noise pollution.

I looked out the kitchen window and spotted Mr. Harris, my neighbor from the cottage on the west approaching my back porch with a covered dish in his hand.

I walked outside onto the back porch and he called out, "Hello. Mavis sent over these strawberries. We got carried away and picked far too many down on the Pruvis's Farm near Traverse City."

"Ummm lovely, thanks. She must be making jam."

"Indeed. There is a colossal mess in the kitchen...stickiness all over the place. I want nothing to do with her domestic traditions."

"But you'll savor the jam on your breakfast muffins."

"Absolutely."

"Thanks, Fred... I mean Frederick." I remembered just in time that he preferred to be called Frederick. He had spent six months in England as an exchange professor teaching a course in English literature, and ever since, his speech has reeked, stronger than garlic on one's breath, with a British accent plus his need for a more formal, longer title such as Professor Frederick Martin Harris II. I presumed it was meant to convey the impression of a superior university education such as Oxford, because thats what he allowed his new friends to mistakenly believe. In actuality he had graduated from Ohio State. For some reason his pride needed that Oxford deception to boost his ego.

"Met any grizzly skunks lately?" I asked, keeping a straight face.

"You be nice or maybe I won't give you these hard-picked juicy berries." Fred thrust the bowl of berries behind his back.

I laughed, remembering the humorous incident when the strawberries Fred loved so much had been filched right out from under his nose by a baby skunk darting up on his cottage deck one evening as he and Mavis were eating. Of course, the way Frederick told the story, it came out sounding more like a ferocious bear had accosted them rather than an innocuous little skunk that he had been afraid to scare away even to save his precious strawberries.

"Sorry. I couldn't resist ribbing you. Frederick. I quickly decided to take this opportunity to test Fred's opinion. "Frederick, I was thinking about going around the neighborhood asking people to sign a complaint against the loud church bells and maybe also to gather a number of people to speak to Father Ciconni over at the church. Would you be willing to join such a group?" Fred didn't answer immediately.

"The bells are bloody loud all right," he admitted in his carefully practiced British accent, "and I certainly wish we had more control over our beach colony environment. But lovey, don't you think life is too short to get so upset over something like that? Besides, there are lots of things that need fixing in the world. There are greater, needier causes."

"Oh, I agree," I hesitated and then countered, "but usually we aren't in a position to do anything about most of them except to donate money, but noise pollution is something we can eradicate." Suddenly I recalled Mavis telling me about Frederick's high blood pressure. Maybe emphasizing the connection between noise pollution and stress would have more clout. "Did you know that a person's blood pressure actually goes up when exposed to noise pollution?"

"Indeed?" Frederick assumed an air of dignity and refused to discuss the matter any further except to say, "I'll think on the merits of the cause and let you know."

That probably meant he would discuss it with his bridge club members. I called out as Fred retreated. "Please thank Mavis for the berries."

Frederick's point of view irritated me more than it dampened my enthusiasm for eradicating the noise situation. Maybe if I had been far more mentally alert and told him exactly how high the decimeter readings were, he would have been more impressed, more amenable to the idea of doing something about the problem. Still, if someone like Frederick, with his higher ideals of keeping the beach a quiet, private place, wasn't interested in lowering the volume of the bells, would anyone else? "Oh, fiddle," I grumbled," Anyway, I suspected Fred's ideals were nothing more than a tissue-thin façade.

CHAPTER 7

"Oh, Leah," my friend, Enid sighed on the phone that evening as she tried to verbally kick-start my enthusiasm for thwarting noise pollution, "nothing gets accomplished by sitting back and allowing the status quo. If somebody doesn't do something about those loud bells up there, everyone will go on listening to the crassness of that artificial sounding music every summer for the rest of their lives. Do you want that?"

"No," I nearly shouted.

"Well then," she urged me on by making me feel like a slacker, "just give it that good old college try. Don't forget to tell folks that your crusade against the bells isn't only about the damage to their ears but that noise influences the entire physiological and psychological makeup of a human being."

Keeping Enid's advice in mind, though I doubted that I would remember all those words beginning with *phy* and *psy,* I primed myself like a rusty pump by first making a list of the reasons why my neighbors should be concerned over the electronic bells. Near the top of my list, right after high decibels that might damage the listeners' ears, was the fact that taped bells didn't sound as authentic as one genuine bell.

Furthermore, I could remind cottagers, if by chance I spoke to them, that we had no way of clicking off the electronic music from the church as we did with a television program. I thought that was completely unfair, undemocratic. In this case, the loud tapes were no better than a advertisement for just that one church's denomination.

After going over those points in my head once again, I still wondered if anyone would consider them salient when used against a supposedly holy institution. Would I be called unchristian? Perhaps I should simply tell people how the needle on the decimeter had quickly swung up to ninety. Why should any other argument be necessary as an inducement for a signature on a piece of paper?

There was no doubt that I, myself, was completely incensed against the noise intrusion that was spoiling my summers, but I seemed to lack the courage to push myself to the point of canvassing for signatures. Being the type of person I was, someone who avoids assiduously large gatherings, clubs, and parties, how was I to gather up enough courage to go and knock on the doors of mostly strangers? I shivered and shrank inside my sweater just thinking about such an outgoing endeavor.

Two more days pass and still I procrastinated. Then something occurred that flooded me with anger and finally swept me into action. The church introduced a brand new, never heard before, electronic tape. The bell music split the pristine quiet morning with its shrillness, even before I had finished my first cup of coffee or had a chance to visit my personal sanctuary, the beach. It was the longest medley of hymns yet played and also the loudest. Even the dog noticed the difference and let out a long mournful howl. "Wow!" Tommy exclaimed. "That was sure loud. Why don't they try a little rap music instead?"

I groaned and didn't answer Tommy. The church's new tape was like one of those cattle prods to my nervous system. It produced a whammy of a shock and a shock was exactly what it took to get me started.

Reluctantly, I turned away from the lovely view of the ruffled water in front of the cottage and forced myself to ignore the lacey bubbles as they piled-up on the shore.

I planned to make my first stop at the Kramer Cottage because that was the ninth one in an easterly direction from my father's. I had previously reconnoitered and discovered that, depending upon the particular direction of the wind, the electronic tapes were loudest all the way from our cottage up to about the ninth cottage in both directions, east and west. The sound diminished to an acceptable level after that. Certainly, I thought, the people living in those cottages where the noise was the most deafening were the ones I could probably count on for help.

My former husband, Roger, had he been around, would have been great at persuading people to sign my protest. I could imagine him combining both charm and witticisms as he went from cottage to cottage. Men particularly liked his wisecracking quick wit until that same wit began to take bites, like tiny nicks of a razor blade in their feelings.

The names of most of the people living in the cottages nearby were familiar to me, but I didn't really *know* the people, their personalities, their church affiliations, or their foibles. Roger would have said, "Aha, Lee—ah!" He always spread out the syllables of my name thinking it was funny—"it's your own fault for not being more sociable like me." I had fruitlessly argued back that I didn't come up to the cottage on vacation to play bridge or hold beach parties. I came to see the waves pummeling the shore, to paint pictures, to listen to the birds and enjoy quiet reading in a beach chair—well, actually not so quiet with the electronic music and the proliferation of jet skis.

Actually, I had set yesterday afternoon as the starting time for the canvassing, but like the racehorse at the gate, the one who backed up and tried to dump his rider, I kept balking and finding excuses. My khaki pants seemed too rumpled so I changed them. Then I couldn't find my notebook and argued with Tommy who didn't want to tag along with me. All of my excuses were flimsy, nothing more than the usual reluctance to face up to strangers.

It was finally decided that Tommy and his dog were to stay near the back porch of our cottage while I was gone, so that Mrs. Harris,

Mavis, my close neighbor on the west, could glance out her kitchen window from time to time and check on them while she continued to make strawberry jam. And of course, I would never be further away from Tommy than one and a half blocks. With my cell phone in my pocket, I felt relatively confident that Tommy would be safe.

Mrs. Harris, quite unlike her husband, wasn't in the least prone to putting on airs. She was the relaxed sort. It seemed as though she purposely aimed for the opposite image from her husband's attempt to behave like a proper British professor. As opposed to his formality, her conversations were sprinkled with homespun phrases and her outlook on all subjects, except maybe her garden, were placid. In her striped woolly sweater she could almost be likened to a mature cat, able to adapt herself to a hard rock or a comfy sofa—as long as it was large enough to hold her ample body. Unlike the cat, she was no longer quite so curious and much less interested in anything too controversial.

As I left to solicit my first signatures, Tommy was making his own noise pollution, engine noises, as he played with his trucks in the edge of my flower garden. "Now remember, Tommy, you are not to wander off. Promise?" Tommy nodded but didn't stop his engine noises as he pushed a red dump truck up a dirt hill headed for the Hosta plants. My parting words were: "Please don't kill that Hosta plant."

"Urum rum rumrummm," was all I heard in response.

CHAPTER 8

Like so many other cottages along the beach, the Kramer cottage had been kept in the family and passed on down, so that now there were the elderly Kramers and the younger Kramers, sharing the cottage along with their children. I knew the younger Kramer family only well enough to nod if I ran into them at the post office or church... at least I thought they attended the same church as Tommy and I.

This particular cottage, like Mr. Lumus's, though much larger and not in the least crude in appearance, was situated on the inland side of the road. The cottage looked a bit top heavy on the east end where the new addition had been built over the garage. I guessed it was probably an extra bedroom to accommodate the growing number of grandchildren.

Most cottages didn't have doorbells, so I lifted my hand to knock, but even before my hand touched the door, it opened, as though sucked-in by the bevy of children I saw standing just inside. There must have been at least seven. Mrs. Kramer invited me to come inside, but as I attempted to enter, the children, all wearing colorful bathing suits, blocked my way and then scattered across the dirt road to the beach.

"Stay out of the water until I get there," Mrs. Kramer called as a warning to the children and then turned back to me. "Great beach weather we're having," she said to give our conversation a sociable boost. She was dressed in shorts and a sweatshirt; her hair was hidden by a blue scarf and topped by a cone-shaped straw hat with a visor.

"Yes, very nice weather." I tried to swallow my nervousness and rushed straight into my little prepared spiel. "Mrs. Kramer, don't you find those electronic bells from the nearby church terribly loud?"

"Oh? Are they electronic? Anyway, we don't mind them."

I was flummoxed. I hadn't actually prepared a rejoinder or any argument at all if faced with negative replies, so I cleared my throat, which tension had suddenly clamped shut. "Kahumm…they are terribly loud at our cottage. We are situated even closer to the church than you are. I'm hoping to gather a few people to join me in asking the church Father to turn down the volume of the bells. If someone isn't able to go in person with me to visit with him, then they can sign this complaint instead." I held out my blank sheet of paper, but Mrs. Kramer ignored it. Instead, she repeated, quite concisely, as though my hearing might be at fault. "No, we don't mind the bells at all."

Since her hand was still on the open door, I guessed that I was expected to exit quickly. Lamely, I added, "If you change your mind, let me know."

"Oh, I won't change my mind," she said, her tone still cheerful yet showing a touch of impatience to be leaving. "Excuse me, I must get over to the beach to watch the children."

I felt schoolmarm dismissed and wondered how I could get myself out of sight gracefully. I wasn't long in doubt because Mrs. Kramer passed me and crossed the street before I could open my mouth again or even call out, "Nice meeting you." It was almost like standing on a podium lecturing as the audience walked out of the room. Outside on the porch facing the road, I tried to appear undaunted, instead of abandoned, in case a neighbor was watching me. I felt like an idiot, first class.

Maybe the Kramers weren't from the church up in the village that Tommy and I attended afterall. Perhaps they belonged to the church from which the loud music was emanating. If so, what a faux pas on my part! Instantly, I wanted to flee down the road to Fleury cottage and escape back into my painting routine. I wanted to give up the whole troublesome idea of thwarting noise pollution after just this one small effort.

CHAPTER 9

*T*here was no answer to my knock at the second cottage, the yellow one on the waterside of the road where brown and blue striped towels flapped on the clothesline day after day. In spite of the towels, the cottage looked empty. Maybe, I laughed to myself, the owners were "missing at sea?" Actually, no one could imagine how relieved I felt to have an excuse to pass up just that one cottage.

The following cottage drew Beatrice Tullman to the door. I knew her a lot better than most of the people along this end of the beach because she and my mother had once chummed around together in their college days at Michigan State University. Beatrice was at least thirty-five or forty years older than I...just about my mother's age... if she had lived.

With a cordial beckoning, Beatrice invited me inside her cottage. Her living room bore no resemblance to a cottage at all. It looked more like a suburban living room with thick beige carpeting, several upholstered chairs, also in beige, TV, and plaster walls. I was not used to such refinements in a cottage and walked carefully across the springy deep carpet.

The majority of places along the beach were more like my father's cottage replete with hand-me-downs from winter homes: throw rugs that didn't match the color scheme, rockers that took up too much space, lamps with chipped bases, and also—almost as solid as any piece of furniture—the accumulated smell of a structure located next to a large body of water with no central heating to ward off the darkness that had gathered during the winter. I had grown accustomed to that smell in my father's cottage, a combination of pine and musty odor striking us when we first opened the family cottage each spring.

Beatrice's cottage smelled of new carpeting chemicals and nothing more. Not a bonafide cottage smell at all.

The interior walls of my father's cottage were of beaded boards, heavily varnished, making most of the rooms, except the upstairs bedrooms, dark and somber. Beatrice's were painted pale yellow and I especially liked that cheerfulness. Personally, I thought we had enough gloom inside of us without having it on the walls as well. At least my father's cottage had a white exterior in common with Beatrice's, though his cottage was larger and had a Victorian farmhouse appeal, while Beatrice's cottage had once been a tiny two or three room bungalow before a room was added downstairs and then a whole second floor. It no longer resembled its humble beginnings, nor did it resemble any particular class of architecture.

Beatrice was well known by everyone at our end of the beach, and also Sid, her late husband. He had been a sociable fellow who spent many of his mornings visiting nearby cottagers. I knew he had passed away during the summer before this one.

"Sit down anywhere." Beatrice made me feel comfortable and welcome, though I sank too deeply into a chair just as I had sunk into the carpeting seconds before. This time I decided to slide more diplomatically into the subject of the electronic bells instead of my former pounce into the subject as I had done at the Kramer cottage. "How was your winter?" I asked sociably.

"Oh, it was a mild one compared to other winters. It's lovely here most winters, you know. When the sun hits all that white ice out there, it gives off shimmering color. It's as spectacular as a field of Northern Lights only on the ground instead of up in the sky."

"Do you have any trouble driving out in winter?"

"Oh no, the roads are kept well plowed. What brings you here today, Leah?"

So much for being subtle and easing into my subject, I thought. I told her about the high decibel readings of the electronic bells. "Not exactly quality music either," I added. Beatrice nodded in response and I thought to myself; *here at last is someone who agrees with me.... a fellow being who has the taste to discriminate between mediocre and good quality music.*

"Much too loud." I insisted.

"Not the best there is to offer in bell music," Beatrice acknowledged, as she dropped her solid frame from an upright standing position straight down into one of the bulky chairs.

"Then perhaps you'll join me in speaking to Father Ciconni about the high decibels I recorded at Mr. Lumus' cottage. Though it was only ninty-two at that cottage, it must be much higher at the church."

"Before I answer your question, let me tell you something about this town." She began to arrange her long green skirt as she crossed her legs, but the right leg kept slipping off her left knee, so she gave it up and sat with her legs sprawled apart and the skirt modestly draped between them.

I settled back in the chair, built for someone with a long torso and long legs, probably Sid her late husband, and listened. Beatrice leaned forward and looked around furtively, as though about to divulge some dire prediction or family secret. I was disappointed by her attempt to stall me.

Beatrice had lived in the beach colony many more years than I, so naturally I was more willing to give her the benefit of my attention and respect, though I was anxious for her to reach "the point" of her deviation from the subject matter. I assumed it was some trivial thing she wanted to get off her mind. Now that her husband had passed on, she was probably lonely and just wanted to detain me as long as possible for my company. Maybe she simply needed someone to filter her thoughts through, or something new to fill up her time.

"This is really a small town when the summer residents, people like yourself and the tourists, leave in September. Just about a thousand people or perhaps a few more, live here in winter. In this snow-blanketed, white landscape, people tend to tighten ranks, as though they needed each other for warmth. They become more closely knit. If you get their backs up about something like those church bells, they will take it very personally. No telling what might happen."

"What do you mean?" Suddenly I was quite alert. Why was Beatrice being so mysterious, I wondered. She should be more specific and come straight to the point, if there was one.

"In winter there are fewer tourists or beach people around to dilute the opinions of the locals attending that church that broadcasts the loud bells, so I get a more accurate picture of local feelings."

I interrupt again, "But you don't attend that church yourself, do you?"

"No, but in spite of that, I do get a more accurate picture of the local opinion when the cottages are closed and beach people have gone to their winter homes. To put it indelicately, the locals don't appreciate out-of-towners interfering in their church or civic affairs."

"But I *am* from this town," I protest "and from this state. I've been coming here to Tatterack for nearly twenty years. My father pays high taxes here…at least at a higher rate than in Holland, including school taxes even though we have never used the schools."

"Even so, you are still considered an outsider. Some folks are prejudiced and well… things happen…. if people get down on others."

"I still don't understand. What could happen to me?"

"If you complain about the bells, I'm afraid you'll have many of the villagers angry with you because as I just told you, the majority of citizens attend that particular church denomination where the bells seem so loud."

I can't believe what she is telling me. It's a warning-off even before I have begun to explain what the high decibels could do to people's ears and bodies. I smile sardonically, "Sounds medieval. I hope they don't still lynch people around here." I started to smile but changed my mind after looking at Beatrice's somber face.

"Anyway," I continued, "I'm not talking about having the bell tapes eliminated... not done away with completely, no nothing so radical. I just mean asking to have the loud volume reduced and the length of the bell concerts shortened if possible. Of course, I wouldn't mind having a better quality of music as well. Why should anyone object to that?" I pause and look carefully at Beatrice's face again. She still wasn't smiling; her expression was deadly serious. "Besides, what could anyone do to me?"

"Just make your life rough in various ways. Give you slow service when you need something fixed or need to have your water turned on in the springtime. They know you can't do without water. And remember, your father's cottage is empty and vulnerable during the winter."

"Some cottages do get broken windows."

"More than that."

"Anyway, people wouldn't single me out as the prime complainer against the bells if I got several other people to go along with me to discuss the problem with Father Ciconni."

"That would be smarter. . .if you can." Her tone of voice dragged heavily with doubt. "But anyway, the news that you are the instigator will leak out somehow. Everyone in this town is related to someone else. Mr. Purdue, living in the third cottage west of here, has several brothers living in nearby small towns. Gossip ebbs and flows between relatives and mixes very much like the currents out here in the Straits." She gestures out the window at the yellow and green water sparkling in the sunshine. "I don't want to overly alarm you, Leah, but you'd be wise to think it over."

Beatrice meant to be doing me a kind favor, so I felt obligated to respond in like. "Thanks for your concern." To myself I decided that what she had just told me was an exaggerated opinion, mostly nonsense. Her failure to come right out with some facts or examples of the town's culpability, irritated me. I decided that she was being mysterious without cause. Maybe Beatrice was just one of those overly fearful people. Yes, I assured myself, she was exaggerating. Still, I conceded that Beatrice, having lived here occasionally throughout the entire winter, knew a great deal more about the local point of view than I did. I wondered if she had actually overheard gossip about past retaliations?

"Then you don't think it's prudent for you to sign your name to this protest or go with me to visit Father Ciconni?"

"No, I'd better not."

I scrambled forward in the deep chair and said my polite good byes.

This visit had turned out to be another letdown. I had promised myself that I would visit four cottages, but now I felt discouraged after just two. Not that Beatrice had frightened me unduly with her dire predictions. Well, to be truthful. perhaps just a bit. Probably I was grasping at *any excuse* to cut my canvassing short and get back to my painting.

"Shirker," I chastised myself out loud. I looked at my watch and discovered that I had been gone well over thirty minutes. It was time to check up on Tommy. I realized that I was using Tommy as my prime excuse to quit this thankless signature gathering for the day.

As I headed back towards Fleury cottage, I passed a curved driveway with a half moon of lush flowers. There were hollyhocks, delphiniums, yarrow, and roses, between the cottage and the road. Should I stop, I wondered? I hadn't managed to get even one signer thus far—nor even a promise from someone to go with me to speak to Father Ciconni in person. My morning seemed like a complete waste of time.

Why not try just one more cottage before quitting? Then, I told myself, if you don't get a signature here, you'll have an even better excuse to give up the whole project right today. My thoughts turned to Enid. I knew she would be disgusted with my lack of courage. When she decided to accomplish something, she hung on with a bulldog's jaw until it was completed. "She would be deeply disappointed in me if I gave up so easily."

I stood in the road looking up at the large white cottage in front of me and at the lovely flower garden. The new owners, whoever they were, had just moved in last summer after renovating the old place. Attached to a post was a carriage lamp embellished with Victorian curlicues and beneath it hung a swinging sign stating *Summer Place* in large gold letters on a blue background. At least that's an appropriate name. How astute of them, I stated to myself a bit sarcastically.

Some cottages along the shore had Indian names like *Oconowee* or trite ones such as *Bide-a-While.* Other names played upon the owner's name, *Button-Inn,* for example. My father's cottage was called *Fleury Place* because that was our exact name. I recalled how my mother had laughed when my father hung up the sign next to the driveway. "The name," she protested, "if misread, sounds a lot more like *Fury Place.* Everyone will think we're always in a cat-clawing rage."

On the bottom of the blue sign facing me right now, was printed in smaller letters the name: Sjoberg. I knocked, and watched through the long oval glass in the door as a man appeared. He wore a business suit, odd apparel for a relaxed beach resort. His neatness prompted me to glance down at my own feet. Had I mistakenly worn the old sneakers with holes? No, but just the same I felt very unkempt, so I tried to neaten my hair by drawing it behind my ears, a typical self-conscious mannerism. Again, I glanced up at the man's blue eyes and felt a bit chilled. Perhaps he was disturbed at being interrupted so close to lunchtime?

My second impression of the cold-eyed man on the other side of the Victorian glass door, was that he seemed on the sturdy side, and about a head and a half taller than my five foot five inches in height. Not that tall. Weren't all Scandinavians supposed to be thin and sinewy? Certainly the name, Sjoberg, suggested the countries of Norway or Sweden or even Denmark. His hair was kinky, reddish-blond. His mustache, also tinged with the same red-blonde, appeared very sparse, as though it had just given birth on his upper lip. Again,

I glanced up at his blue eyes through the door and felt a deep chill. I began to turn away when his expression changed to a smile... a teasing type of smile.

"Please don't run away. I only bite dogs."

CHAPTER 10

As the man opened the door, I saw the gelled coolness of his blue eyes rapidly move up the temperature scale to a questioning friendliness and I felt myself responding. A pleasurable swish begins moving up my spine. The rapid change leaves me slightly disorientated. My legs feel a bit unsteady as I look towards the man, so I watch his face instead of my feet, and that's when I stumble, not too gracefully. Not gracefully at all.

I did catch myself before actually falling down, but even so, the man had the nerve to grin widely, as though my wobbly misstep had been affected by his manly presence. Immediately, I told myself to be wary. After my disappointment over Roger, my former husband, I hadn't felt or wanted to feel any sparks of interest flying between me and any man...positively none.

"Hello, come in." he said. "You're one of my neighbors I assume. I've seen you bicycling up the road with your little brother."

"That was my son, Tommy," I corrected him. "Is Mrs. Sjoberg in?"

"Yes, you've caught her *in* for a change." He laughed, as though taunting his wife for her busy schedule. "You want to speak to her?" I nodded, and he called out, "Mother?"

Oh, I thought to myself, not his wife, his mother.

"In here, Peter," a woman's voice responded. To steady my legs and stall for time after my stumble, I wiped my feet carefully on the mat just inside the door and muttered something predictable to fill-in a blank moment. "I admire your garden out there by the driveway"

"That's my mother's project."

The man, who I now realize must obviously be Mrs. Sjoberg's son and not her husband, beckons me through the archway on the left and into a large room two stories high with a balcony along one side of the second floor from which there are doors, bedroom doors I assume. I gaze around at the expanse with unconcealed admiration on my face. His mother is sitting at a writing desk situated behind a wicker sofa. My eyes quickly swing to the huge fieldstone fireplace, twice the height and width of the one in my father's cottage. At one end of the room stands a tall glass curio cabinet. I have only a second to glance at the contents, which consist predominantly of model sailing vessels, large and small.

Mrs. Sjoberg appears to be in her early sixties. Of course, it's only a guess. Her petite form is obviously a bit thicker at the waist where the slacks and linen shirt come together.

"You must be Ms. Fleury?" She arises from the desk with her hand out. How relaxing it feels to be greeted so graciously. Her voice is brisk, typical of a personality that thinks and speaks in energetic spurts. Apparently, she is someone quite adept at making others feel comfortable and welcome; someone who can face all kinds of social occasions with aplomb.

"Oh no, my mistake," she continues. "That's not your married name."

"Yes, you were quite right," I assure her. "I am Leah Fleury. It's my maiden name which I use now that I am no longer married."

"Well," said Mrs. Sjoberg after I have explained my mission and shown her my sheet of paper minus any signatures, "I don't think any church has a right to advertise itself so blatantly as that one does. It takes away our freedom of the airwaves. And it *is* loud, though not as loud as it must be at your cottage since you are so much closer. I'll sign, but I can't promise to go with you to see the Father at the church because I'll be gone for a couple of weeks starting this coming Sunday. I'm driving down to Ann Arbor for a class reunion and then on to visit my cousin in Cleveland. This is my son, Peter, whom you've already met."

Her son joins us near the desk. "Nice to meet you." Again his eyes scrutinize me carefully and I try to avoid looking into his face directly so that I can avoid that unsteady feeling that seems to affect me. Just as Mrs. Sjoberg is about to scrawl her signature on my paper, her son leans over her at the desk and frowns as though he is about to dissuade her. Then he smiles. "Are you a member of that church?" he asks. I notice that one of his eyebrows cocks up slightly. It occurs to me that he might be teasing again, though my choice of religion is hardly a subject for teasing or anybody's business.

"No," I answer, fixing him with what I hope is a challenging stare. "Not all the Irish are Catholic. Up here in Tatterack Tommy and I attend the Presbyterian-Congregational Church. You just asked me the very question that I refuse to answer in blank spaces provided on all the official forms and documents."

He looks amused, even cheeky. "Because it's nobody's business?"

"Exactly," I nod.

"So how do you fill in the blank space beside the question about race?"

"Ghost," I answer with a serious expression.

"Serves you right, Peter, for teasing." Mrs. Sjoberg laughs and hands the paper with her signature back to me. In a more serious tone, she asks, "You do understand what you may be getting yourself into? People are very sensitive when their church is criticized whether deserved or not."

Not another warning, I think, and resist letting out a huge sigh.

"Mother, she's not attacking the church, just the loudness of the electronic bells."

"Same thing... or at least the priest and congregation will think so."

"Mrs. Sjoberg, it's the volume of the artificial bell music I'd like to lower, though of course I'd dearly love to change their choice back to a genuine bell as well."

"Why not ask to have it eliminated altogether? It's rather poor quality sometimes and far too lengthy."

Abruptly, Peter, still hovering nearby, asks: "How old is your son? I believe you call him, Tommy?"

"He's seven years old and that reminds me it's past time to get back to the cottage and check-up on him and the dog. It's been nice meeting you both."

Peter Sjoberg follows me to the door, so I guess you don't spend a great deal of time up here at your mother's cottage or I would have seen you before."

"I'm usually here on weekends and some vacations. It's a short trip up from Allegan in lower Michigan."

I turn back towards the hallway arch and call out, "Thank you, Mrs. Sjoberg."

"Good luck with your project," I hear her reply as her son opens the outside door for me. At that exact moment Tommy comes hurtling up the driveway. He stops, gasps, and takes a breath.

"Mom! I've been looking all over for you. Pillage ran off."

"Pillage?" Mr. Sjoberg's eyebrows rise up in a bewildering frown.

"The dog," I explain. "Which way did he go?"

"Up the old railroad track after another dog. They disappeared into the woods, so I came back."

"Tommy, I've told you again and again never to go up that track without someone being with you. It's too isolated."

"I didn't go far, honest. Please, please Mom, can we go get the car and hunt for him?"

"All right, let's go." I turned to head west up the road towards my father's cottage.

"Why not use my car?" Mr. Sjoberg offers. "It's right here and lots quicker. Come on, Thomas." Before I can stop him, Tommy has climbed into Peter's silver Mazda and begins beckoning frantically to me.

"Hurry up, Mom!"

Mrs. Sjoberg calls from the doorway, "Hope you find him."

We drove the six or seven blocks to where the old train track used to curve north, but we headed south. In the opposite direction, the track had once curved through the woods towards the town, past the round house, the depot, and then straight to the ferryboat dock. At that point the train cars were separated and pushed onto the ferryboat to make the trip across the water to the Upper Peninsula. Now, everything had changed. All that remained of the old track system were cinders and occasionally a few rusty encrusted spikes. The rails and ties had been hauled away years ago.

"Tommy," Mr. Sjoberg asked as we drove along, "how did your dog get that unusual name?"

"Oh, he sorta got into stuff."

"Sort-of?" I groaned in mock despair. "He ravaged the house when he was a puppy. He pillaged it like a whole army." From the back seat, I could see one corner of Mr. Sjoberg's mouth curve upwards, but in deference to Tommy's feelings, he didn't laugh out loud.

We drove a short distance down the track until the trees brushed the car on both sides. Tommy flung the car door open and began to call, "Pill, Pill! Come boy, come!" We followed Tommy on foot for at least a quarter-mile. Pillage wasn't anywhere or rather he was somewhere but not here. Mosquitoes were here, though, and they didn't need to be called.

"He'll show up." I tried to reassure Tommy who was looking more and more dejected. "Remember, it's not the first time he's run off after another dog."

As we returned to the car, I happened to be walking behind Tommy and Mr. Sjoberg. It was exactly then that I noticed Mr. Sjoberg's slight limp and that his right shoe had a thicker sole. I wondered if his shorter leg was the result of polio or if it was a birth defect? I was curious about it, but naturally I didn't ask. It seemed impolite and much too forward to broach a question like that. After all, I was a complete stranger to him.

Mr. Sjoberg suggested that we drive another half-mile to an intersection where the old railroad track once crossed near the main highway and I agreed. Again we all got out of the car and called Pillage's name. Finally, after no results, Mr. Sjoberg drove us back to the beach colony and let Tommy and me out at the head of the driveway to my father's cottage.

"Call on me if you need any more help. I'll be around until late Sunday afternoon."

"Thanks, Mr. Sjoberg. You've been very kind."

"Peter," he rejoined. "Call me Peter." He waved goodbye, backed out, and drove off.

Mr. Sjoberg left me with the comfortable feeling of having a friendly presence living nearby, except of course he wouldn't be around very often.

His sharp blue eyes with feathery red-blonde lashes seemed to give no hint of interest in me personally, except for that initial scrutiny that had done quite unnatural things to my legs. Perhaps I was imagining it, yet his eyes sent a message telling me that if he promised support to someone, support was what they would get.

Immediately following my profound, though yet to be proven assessment of Peter's reliability, I hastily ridiculed myself: Oh my, aren't I the all-knowing! I was hardly an authority on the subject of character reading. After what had transpired between Roger and myself, how could I ever again be positively certain of accurately interpreting anyone's character? Hadn't I felt this same comfortable, reliable belief about Roger? Yes, at first, but I was inexperienced back then. Now, I told myself, I was far more mature.

My character had begun to develop a spurt of independence that summer when Tommy was still a baby. My perception of Roger's character became enlightened and far more realistic. I might still be in his paddock as he had joked, but—I laughed to myself—he could no longer put a halter on me. His sarcasm seemed to accelerate with time and it contaminated any remaining affection I felt for him. I grew less and less respectful of Roger and far more confident of my own direction. At long last I thought of myself as a separate being from Roger as I became further immune to his influence.

My doubts had increased with each year of living with Roger. I never knew when Roger's witty-viper mood might strike, but I soon learned that I would be the butt of his weird jokes about wives and their ineptness. My character might get trashed at the annual attorney's dinner, or at our friends, the Bassets. A couple of years into our marriage I learned that if there was no other fodder for Roger's jokes, then he would use me. Even after we separated, I was too readily available. I reminded myself often that it would be wise to never, never forget the reasons for our separation. I still tended to have insecure feelings when associating with people, especially men.

Today, after Mr. Sjoberg drove us back to the cottage, Tommy scuffed his old sneakers towards the beach and I followed. I knew exactly how badly he felt about Pillage. I had gone through the same sadness and feelings of loss when I was growing up; however, my sorrows had been over a series of cats that got killed on the street in front of our house.

Naturally, I didn't plan to go back to my door-to-door canvassing, not again today. This was a time to be with Tommy and give consolation if Pillage didn't find his way back home. The bell problem could wait since it had already waited a long time. Anyway, I hated the knocking on doors like a sales woman, a very unsuccessful one at that. Truly, I wanted nothing more than to give up the canvassing altogether.

That same afternoon as I stood painting at my easel in my upstairs bedroom, I thought about all the dire warnings Beatrice's conversation had pressed on me. The experience of talking to her had weakened my resolve and put tentative thoughts in my head of setting the bell project on a high, high shelf out of reach forever. It seemed like a perfectly logical decision. Then, the usual six o'clock bells shrilled forth, but this time in funeral-like dirges to cast gloom out over the calm blue-green water. The invasion of sad, disruptive music called forth dark thoughts so I instantly stopped painting. Spurts of anger inundated me all over again.

How could I do anything creative like painting with that ugliness assaulting my ears? What church had the right to impose its noise on anyone whenever it chose without first getting the people's consent? Yet I could almost hear some of my old bible class friends saying, "Who else has the right, if not God?" In my imagination I countered their words: If God ran the church in Tatterack, he would have better taste in music. Anyway, forcing things on people wasn't God's method... it was a people-method... or rather a Father Ciconni method. Tomorrow I vowed to go on with the door-to-door canvassing.

A few minutes after dinner—one in which Tommy barely touched his favorite pizza because he was constantly jumping up from the table to look out the door—Pillage came trotting along and plopped himself down heavily on the back porch. With tongue hanging out and mouth drooling, he looked like the saddest of old clowns. Tommy was elated. He banged through the screen door to hug Pillage. I took the dog's water dish out to him and as a token of my welcome home indulged him by giving him a slice of pepperoni from my pizza.

"Pill has probably been through whole patches of poison ivy this afternoon, so you'd better go inside and thoroughly wash your hands and face with yellow laundry soap. But first take Pillage and tie him up in the yard.

"In a minute." Tommy stalled, lying down beside Pillage on the porch.

"Right now, old chap, and then come inside and help me dry the silverware… after you've washed."

With Pillage's return, our day ended on an upbeat, happy note. I wished I could have claimed the same for all the following days.

CHAPTER 11

*I*n my trek from cottage to cottage for signatures against the loud bells, I had at last the good fortune to find one person, a Mr. Delbert, who promised to go with me to visit Father Ciconni. Mr. Delbert was an elderly gentleman who walked with a cane, his steps slow and his balance precarious. He lived in the fourth cottage east of my fathers. All summer long his little cottage burst with a constant barrage of relatives. I suppose they were married sons and daughters with their numerous children.

It seemed to me that when I was growing up and spending summers at our cottage, my mother had exactly the same situation as Mr. Delbert... too many visiting relatives. She certainly wouldn't have called it a problem though, but I, going through a shy period, often escaped the deluge of aunts and cousins that came to visit us. I'd mount my bicycle and stay away half the day. Most of the time, I would return to the cottage around five o'clock, just in time to set the evening dinner table for my mother.

I thanked the bent over Mr. Delbert profusely and shook his knarred, arthritic hand because I was so grateful for his support. Here, at last, was another person who not only agreed with me regarding the loudness of the electronic bells, but was actually willing to go with me to face Father Ciconni at the church, along with Mr. Lumus of course. Now all I needed, I told myself, was a couple more people to go with me to visit the Reverend Father and I could phone the church to set up an appointment. I began to feel easier, more confident. It took just that one success and Mrs. Sjoberg's signature to give me the impetus to face a long string of strangers in the beach colony.

The next cottage I visited, was called "Nestle Down." The name sounded cozy and peaceful, exactly the sort of name for a newlywed's retreat or a retirement cottage. I pictured a young couple spending their honeymoon getting to know each other without the world intruding. It was a lovely romantic daydream.

On the back porch was a worn wooden carousel horse with a damaged foot and the once colorful paint mostly worn off. Obviously it was an antique. Before I knocked on the door, I couldn't resist running my hand down over the satiny wood of the horse's haunches and then down one leg. My hand abruptly stopped when it reached the rougher, broken wood of the split foot. It seemed to be the only flaw in the beautiful faded horse. Naturally my mind easily swung from the split foot of the horse to the unknown reason for Peter's built-up shoe and his limp. I hadn't heard anything further from Peter since out first meeting, but I hadn't expected to either. I wasn't exactly yearning for male companionship in my life anyway, other than my best boyfriend who was naturally Tommy.

Though it still rankled against my more reclusive nature, I was beginning to feel less shy about knocking on strangers' doors. Still, out of a total of nine cottages in the easterly direction I had found only Mr. Delbert and Mr. Lumus, who were willing to face Father Ciconni.

"Mr. Lumus is a sure thing," I muttered confidently, as I turned once more to take a last look at the carousel horse and its damaged foot before a young woman stepped through the door. Immediately, I asked, "Is the horse for sale?

"Yes, absolutely, she answered, quickly glancing behind her at the cottage door.

Surprise, surprise, I thought. I doubted that I could afford it since it was obviously an antique. "How much are you asking for it?"

"Ninety dollars." Again the woman looked furtively behind her at the cottage door.

The price was a steal, though I could ill-afford even that price. "Sold!" I smiled, thrilled at the bargain. "I'll just run back to the cottage for my checkbook. I'm Leah Fleury."

"Yes, do hurry."

"Be right back." Before I could walk away, a young man came hurrying through the door. Probably he was the other half of this romantic twosome I had dreamed up in my mind.

"It's not for sale," he stated irrevocably, as though he had overheard me talking about the hobbyhorse right through the closed door of the cottage. I looked from the man to the woman not knowing whom to believe.

"It is!" the woman countered. I waited.

"It isn't," he counterclaimed.

"It belongs to me, and if I want to sell it, I will."

"It's an antique, you dunce! It's been in your family for over a hundred years."

"Don't you dare call me a dunce!" The young woman tried to slap his face.

He seized her by one arm and, none too gently yanked her through the cottage door. Hurriedly, he turned towards me and apologized. "Sorry. She's always trying to sell that horse. That's why I keep it chained."

"It's just an old piece of wood," I heard her shout from inside the cottage.

So much for my romantic ideas! Dazed by the last few minutes of marital drama, I walked away, completely forgetting why I was there in the first place. It sounded like a rocky marriage similar to mine but for a different reason.

CHAPTER 12

The clouds piled up into huge angry billows above the opposite shore the next morning. The Straits itself had completely flattened to dull gray, a mirror image of the sky above. There was an ominous stillness just before the storm broke, and the cottage became so dark that I had to give up painting. I heard Pillage's toenails clattering on the wooden stairs as he rushed up and crawled under Tommy's bed. Even I felt the nervous tension brought on by electricity in the air. "Tommy?" I called downstairs. "Can you pull the porch furniture back further so it won't get soaked?"

"I, I can't. Did you see the lightning?"

I could hear the shakiness in his voice. "I'll be right down." I put my brushes soaking in the jar of water and hurried down to take care of the porch furniture and to be with Tommy. He was clearly frightened but didn't want to admit it.

During the worst of the bad storm, Tommy and I huddled on the sofa with our feet up off the floor, and tried to concentrate on a game of Chinese checkers. As the thunder boomed, I wished the lightning would strike the church tower where the loudspeakers were positioned. "What a mean, small-minded wish," I told myself. Still, I failed to feel terribly guilty. Anyway, what good would it have done if the speakers were struck by lightning? The church would immediately solicited money from the congregation to have them repaired.

The rain left puddles of mud in the dirt road and a dreariness in my outlook. It wasn't the right sort of attitude to approach people about anything, much less the electronic bells. I had a hard time talking myself into further canvassing. Why not be satisfied with the two people who had already agreed to go with me to visit Father Ciconni, Mr. Lumus and Mr. Delbert? But my common sense argued: Those are people living east of the church, not west. I also needed signatures from west of our cottage along the shore in order to convince Father Ciconni that people in both directions were affected by the loudness of the electronic music. I reminded myself that in actuality I had gotten only one signature, Erma Sjoberg's.

After lunchtime, the rain ceased and the sun, still shadowed at times by hustling clouds, ventured forth. Tommy went to play with Stevie who lived half way up the crescent of the beach. I assumed the boys would play games inside since it was still so wet outdoors. But even if they played out by the water, I wasn't too concerned. All up and down the shore, the water was very shallow. In most places adults could wade out over one hundred feet before getting wet above their thighs. As soon as I verified with Stevie's mother that Tommy had arrived, I resumed my canvassing.

The air after the storm, newly aerated, was saturated with the clean smells whipped up by the frothy water. Back behind the cottages on the dirt road the smells were of the more earthy type from puddles holding plump drowned worms and even a frog or two. As I walked past the open gaps between cottages, the freshening breeze straight from the shore touched my face and also caused the white pine trees along the road to bombard my head with sprinkles of water when I least expected them.

I knew that another elderly couple, the Prangs, lived in the third cottage west of me. Though I assumed they were a poor possibility for signatures, I decided to stop there anyway on the chance that I might be wrong.

At the door I was surprised to be met by a woman in a wheelchair. "Come-in," she smiled and maneuvered her chair deftly out of my way. I stepped into a dark, unaired cottage. It smelled of too many bodies huddled up inside a closed area for weeks at a time. That plus a medicinal odor made me conclude that the windows were never opened to let in the warm sun and the fresh air. I was most uncomfortable inside and hoped to make a hurried get-away.

As my eyes grew accustomed to the dimness, I began to notice details. The room was full of whimsical things: a carved wooden cow in red and white with a sharp rump and exaggerated udders, baskets made of brown gnarled roots, and above the cobblestone fireplace, a small piece of driftwood in the shape of a fish. On the table were three vividly painted dolls with wooden sticks for arms and legs. I looked around expectantly and spotted a man who was standing as still as the little wooden dolls, but came to life with an abrupt and pleasant, "Hello. You like the wooden cow?" He must, I assumed, be her husband.

"Very much. It's unique. Is it from South America?"

"Brazil...one of my trips before retirement."

After I had introduced myself and finished explaining why I had come, Mrs. Prang immediately claimed, "I'll sign." Wonderful, I thought. She was just about to wheel her chair over to the table where I had laid the nearly empty paper when her husband spoke up.

"Maude, maybe you shouldn't... just to be on the safe side."

"Why not?" Surprise raised her voice to a quarrelsome pitch. "I certainly agree over the bells. They are intrusive; I'd prefer to hear the lake water and even the crows." I watched her husband move over closer to her and whisper something in her ear. With her hands on the wheels of her chair, she deftly swung herself around to face him. "Oh, I hadn't even thought about that... do you really think it might make a difference in selling the cottage?"

"Maybe. Why take a chance."

"You're thinking of selling?" I inquired in surprise. Both of them nodded. "I'm sorry to hear that. You've been coming here to the beach for many years, haven't you?"

"Yes, a long time... almost fifty years," Mr. Prang answered with a hint of sorrow in the tone of his voice. "My parents summered here for thirty years before that, but now the taxes are getting too steep for folks like us living on a small retirement fund. I'm probably exaggerating the church's influence, but just the same, Maude, maybe you shouldn't sign."

Maude hesitated and then turned her wheelchair back towards me. "I'm sorry, my dear, not to be able to help you out." It was her husband who let me out the door. "Good luck," he called after me.

"Thanks for your time," I answered, trying not to sound too disappointed.

Now I was really in a quandary. Did the church have some kind of hold on people, some leverage that I didn't know about? Could a church wield so much power and generate so much fear, or were these people just being overly cautious, afraid that if their name got bandied about as a signer of my protest, that a family of that particular church denomination would be prejudiced against buying their cottage?

Already today I felt discouraged and yearned to quit this door-to-door trekking after just this one cottage. Actually it was only a few yards from one back door to the next, but I walked those few yards as slowly as I could, my mind dragging and trudging as much as my feet. I literally scuffed from one bunch of wild carrot blossoms along the road to the next clump of blue chicory. When I looked up, I noted Peter's silver Mazda passing me. We both waved; then up the road a bit he stopped the car and backed up. Through the open window he asked, "Did Pillage ever come back?"

"Yes, right after supper that same evening."

"That's good news. I wonder if you and Tommy would like to go sailing this afternoon. I could use a crew."

I knew that his need for a crew was a hastily thought up excuse because I had already observed his little boat at its mooring just off the beach. The boat was only an eighteen-foot day sailor and could easily be handled by a single person. Mr. Sjoberg was just being gracious by making it sound as though Tommy and I were needed. But his little social fib didn't matter in the least to me, because my mind had already developed a picture of Tommy's excited face as I told him about the pending boat adventure.

"Thanks and yes. What time?"

"Anytime now. It's best to get out on the water before the wind dies down or shifts which it often does around four o'clock. Just come up the beach as soon as you're ready. Wear a bathing suit or clothes you don't mind getting wet."

I nodded my agreement and hurried towards the cottage where Stevie lived. I needed to tell Tommy the good news and bring him home to change into his swimsuit. A sail would be a wonderful treat for him as well as for me. I needed a little diversion. What a relief it would be to sweep my mind completely clear of the bell problem for the rest of the afternoon.

Immediately afterwards, I cautioned myself: Leah, you need to be wary. Yes, I dutifully warned myself, I will construct a wall of reserve against allowing Peter to undermine my common sense. There will be no repeat of that weak-legged silliness, which had affected me on the day when I first met Peter. I recalled with a shiver my reaction that day. Did Peter feel that same connection? What if the feeling had been mutual?

CHAPTER 13

*P*eter in a bathing suit definitely looked as though he could shed a few pounds, though his chest, arms and legs looked muscular—except for the pathetically thin ankle on his right leg, which drew my attention immediately. I, on the other hand, after looking at myself in the mirror back at the cottage, had dubbed my reflection: Leah-the-lanky. I thought my curves weren't curvaceous enough, though I was indented nicely at the waist. I was one of those really healthy looking women with my only claim to beauty being a remark a friend graciously made, "You're the Ingrid Bergman type. Remember her?" I barely did... just from old movies on television. Of course, I wanted to believe my friend.

Over my two-piece striped bathing suit I had added a long sleeved white shirt. Also to thwart sunburn and freckles, which both Tommy and I were prone to, I smeared on gobs of sun block cream. With all that goop spread heavily over me plus the red striped bathing suit, I probably resembled something closer to a greased barber's pole than a sexy woman.

When we first met Peter on the beach in front of his mother's cottage, Tommy observed, "You shaved off your mustache." Then he further informed Peter, "My mom doesn't like mustaches." I pretended to be swept away by the beauty of the horizon instead of listening to Tommy's frank remarks.

"That's interesting," Peter commented lightly. I could feel him looking at me and I wanted to shrink inside something after hearing

Tommy's unflattering remarks; however, a bathing suit doesn't leave any room inside to hide.

"Sorry about the frankness," I apologized to Peter for Tommy's behavior, wishing it would be considered good parenting to yank Tommy out of sight somewhere and give him a heavy swat on the behind.

"It's all right." Peter grinned good naturedly, "The mustache was too faint to have the suave impact I intended."

I didn't venture my opinion on the mustache, but to myself I recorded a much more important fact: Peter had a nice sense of humor.

As he loaded the cooler and sail bag into the dingy, I observed that Peter's gait seemed more uneven without his special shoe. His bare foot below the stalk-thin ankle looked normal in size. Polio, not a birth defect, I deduced, then wondered how that could possibly be. All children, and even those before me, had been given the polio drink. Polio had been eradicated, hadn't it?

"I'll take the cooler and sail bag out to the boat first, then come back for you and Tommy." I nodded that I understood and a few minutes later watched Peter set the cooler carefully on the deck of the boat just inside the coaming and throw the bag into the cockpit before returning to the warm sandy beach. From observing the flag on the nearby flagpole I saw with relief that the breeze was from the west and steady, not the gusty wind I had encountered right after the storm earlier in the day. Nearby, between the Sjoberg cottage and the water, I spotted a small patio of natural limestone slabs topped by a graceful gazebo with a pointed roof. It cast lacy shadows across a metal table and several chairs.

As Peter rowed Tommy and me out to the little white day sailor, I noticed for the first time the name of the boat painted on the stern: The Wench. I wondered just how much of the owner's character the boat name reflected. Was it a further sign of Peter's humor, of which I had already had a glimpse, or did it mean that he thought all "women"—not just boats—were of no higher caliber than a wench? I recalled some of the dictionary meanings: A peasant, a female servant, or a prostitute.

"What made you choose that particular name for your boat?"

"Oh, that." Peter looked chagrined. "Well, this boat, she is constantly siphoning off cold cash towards repairs. Her mainsail pulled a grommet last summer, and the summer before that, her jib split. Also, the boatyard rates have gone up for hauling her out at the end of each summer and boarding her all winter. So she's a money waster or prostitute of sorts. Think I should change the name because of women's lib?" I nodded in answer. "Give me some good ideas for a name and I'll consider changing it."

Soon after we climbed on board, Tommy was sent by Peter to unhook the buoy, because his small body fit so well under the flapping jib. Though tall for his age, Tommy has always been like a thin pretzel or a beam of light. He could hide behind skinny trees or in shallows in the back of a locker on a boat, all the places he used to hide when he was younger.

Peter called out to Tommy, "Always use one hand to hold on to something when you're on a boat to keep yourself from falling overboard."

"But what?" Tommy asked.

"See that heavy wire in front of you that the little sail is attached to? Grip that wire with one hand and unhook the buoy with your other hand."

"OK." Tommy called back.

Peter placated my worried look with his aside, "It's very shallow here…only about two and a half feet deep."

"I'm OK, Mom," Tommy called back to me from the bow. "Besides, I've got on a life preserver. How come you don't have to wear one?"

"Because you are doing hazard duty, Tommy, and I'm not."

"What's that?"

"In the navy," Peter explained, "if you volunteer for a dangerous task, it's called 'hazard duty' and you usually get paid extra money for doing a job like that."

"Do I get paid?" Tommy asked eagerly.

"No, Tommy, you're not in the navy." Thank goodness, I added to myself. Tommy slithered back to the cockpit on his stomach, adapting to the sudden movement of the boat as though he had suction cups on his fingers.

I felt instant relief when he dropped into the cockpit beside me. I struggled into my own life preserver. Peter had already donned his. I could see the curly hair on his chest escaping around the buckles, and I felt a sudden urge sweep over me, a most unwelcome one, to touch the red-blond softness.

We headed into the wind and Peter raised the mainsail. Then he adjusted our heading to slightly off the wind in a northwest direction. Suddenly, I found myself grabbing for support; I had forgotten how radically a sailboat could heel.

"Here," Peter took my right hand and moved it onto the tiller, "hold the tiller for me while I adjust the centerboard to a lower position. Use St. Hellena's Island over there as a bearing. That's right. Just don't let the wind spill from the jib and main sail."

Reluctantly, I gripped the long tiller stick and tried to keep the bow pointed towards the island Peter had pointed out to me, but the boat kept veering first to a point just to the starboard of the island and then back again to the port side.

"I can't keep it steady."

"You're doing fine. Here, I'll take the tiller now. You can help me by taking that jib line and giving it a yank to release it and then pull it in an inch or so more than it is already. Good. That's about right. See how the fluttering in the canvas has stopped?"

We slipped along through the water and soon passed the heavily wooded point of land to the south of us. I gulped in the watery, pine-rich air and sighed. The cloudless sky, the clean air, and our new friend, Peter, all induced a temporary amnesia, a relaxing of my concerns over the bells and even calmed my worries over the future and how to take care of Tommy. Between Tommy's constant questions about how to sail the boat, Peter and I managed to exchange a few basic vitals about each other.

"Where do you work in Allegan?" I asked.

"My friend, Matt Liang, and I own and manage a small pharmaceutical company. And you?" Peter asked.

"Tommy and I live in Holland with my father, but I may end up wherever I can find a permanent job." In a further exchange of information, Peter and I discovered that we had both attended Western Michigan University. Peter, however, had gone on to graduate school at Northwestern and also attended classes at the Ferris Institute. Tommy often interrupted our conversation with a "what's that called" type of question which Peter answered patiently. Later, he played a game with Tommy by pointing at a fixture or some portion of the boat, such as the boom, and asking Tommy to name it.

"Does your father come up to the cottage often?" I asked.

"He's deceased. Automobile accident six years ago."

"Sorry." Peter acknowledged my sympathy with a nod.

On our return heading the wind was behind us. "We aren't moving at all," Tommy claimed.

"Look behind the stern, Thomas."

"Wow! Mom, look back there at the water."

I could see the long trail of green bubbles strung out behind us and actually heard the singing, the voice of the boat's hull as it appeared to cut like a knife through the water.

"Had any luck getting signatures against the loud volume of the bells?" Peter asked.

"No, not many. I have just your mother's and one other so far." Then I told him about the Prangs and their dilemma over selling their cottage.

"Oh, I doubt they need to worry. Still, people can get pretty heated up sometimes to the point of retaliation. You especially need to be careful."

"Why? Surely rational people are smart enough not to start a vendetta against me over something so blatantly wrong as loud electronic bells."

"Oh, you can count on people being civilized up to a certain point, but after that...." Peter shrugged. "It seems like evolution hasn't gone quite far enough."

"At least not the behavioral evolution," I added. "I think about giving up the canvassing, then those shrill sounds run through our cottage like a noisy truck on the highway and at the exact same time completely muffle all the wonderful natural sounds, the very reason I've always loved coming to Tatterack. I wonder why any church has the right to impose itself on others in such a boisterous, unreasonable manner."

"Just think of the way the church imposed itself on people in the past. It ruled peoples' lives more surely than the monarchy. In fact, the popes were deemed far more powerful than the monarchy."

"Oh yes, if this were the dark ages, I'd be burned at the stake as a heretic for stirring people up against the church."

"If things get too tough and you need a place to hide away from the church's slings and arrows, you can run to our cottage. We have a nice big safe closet waiting for you, just like those priest holes once found in castles back when the English monarch, Henry VIII, repudiated the Catholic Church."

I laughed at the idea of Tommy and me hiding out. "How ironic," I exclaimed, "those holes were for the Catholic priests to hide in, and if I should need to hide in one, it would be for exactly the opposite reason...to escape a priest...or rather Father Ciconni."

"Getting cooperation from Father Ciconni may be quite a challenge. From what I've heard, he can be a bit staid, rather un-obliging at times."

"That's exactly what Mr. Lumus said, but in a much less refined manner." I told Peter about Mr. Lumus's ranting and ravings. "I myself went to a Catholic parochial school for several years, but I don't know that much about the church's inner workings except that they have confessionals and believe in a great deal of ritual. Do you understand why they keep claiming that their church is the only true church?"

"Perhaps because one of the Roman Emperors, Constantine, or so it's claimed, incorporated Paul's beliefs, and Paul, as you know, had been converted to the Christian belief."

"I'm not a historian, so I don't have an answer. Sorry." I thought early Christians meant to break away from the other religions."

"Actually in some instances the Christians did have titles when they were first getting organized. You see, they didn't think of themselves as distinct from Judaism, which had rabbis and priests. Later, that changed. Also, early church teachers were often married men and women unlike the celibates now in the Catholic Church."

"The way I feel about it is that God did not appoint any one religious group over another to spread his message."

"Very catholic of you."

"Pun away," I smiled. "You seem to know a great deal about Religion."

"No, not really." Peter shrugged and looked quickly away from me. I watched his eyes wander to the flapping pennant at the top of the mast to check the direction of the wind. "I've heard that Father Ciconni is near retirement age, so there is at least some hope for you and the squelching of the electronic bells."

I didn't really absorb Peter's last remark because I was wondering—suspiciously, I'll admit—how Peter knew so much about Catholicism. Maybe he had taken a Comparative Religion class at the university or a bible study course of some kind. At the time, I didn't dwell on the idea very long.

It was difficult to think too deeply about anything of a serious nature right now because the sailing and fresh air seemed to mesmerize me. They lulled me into reiterating to myself one of my father's favorite phrases, "Everything is going to be all right." How happy and relaxed I felt. Here was Peter's affable personality and Tommy's keen interest in boating finally being fulfilled. I trailed my hand lazily in the water and watched the sun touch the crest of each ripple, then split the slivers of light into thousands of tiny factions which went darting off in every direction.

"By the way," Peter drew me out of my soporific, relaxed state, "I might not come back to Tatterack until my mother returns two weeks from tomorrow. After that I'll come every weekend. Near the end of August I'll stay up here a week for more of my vacation."

Since this was only the second time of meeting between Peter and myself, I immediately questioned why Peter was carefully outlining his plans for my benefit? It was thoughtful of him, though he certainly had no obligation to inform me of anything since we barely knew each other. Yet immediately I found myself speculating; maybe all along he's been counting on seeing me again.

We were already near the mooring when Tommy teased, "Can we sail again when you come back?"

"Absolutely, Thomas. It's a promise…if it isn't too windy or completely calm. We might take your mother too, if she behaves herself."

"Thanks, guys," I laughed, "for including me." A warmth of pleasure stirred inside of me at the thought of seeing Peter again. I hoped the anticipation didn't show too brightly on my face.

CHAPTER 14

That evening of the same day when we had gone sailing with Peter, the water was unusually calm so Tommy and I decided to take the canoe out. Even the lapping sounds of water against the beach were light, like whispery breathing in a distant room. Tommy and I paddled nearly two hundred feet straight out to avoid the shallow rocks and headed east for a short distance, then west again into the glow of the lowering sun. When we were opposite the cottage once more and heading in towards the beach, I saw Peter standing there on the shore watching us. Immediately, I felt that unusually pleasant, yet upsetting *what's happening to me* sensation. It was that same sensation I had tried to thwart when I had first met Peter.

Peter pulled our canoe further up on the sand so that Tommy and I could step out without getting our feet wet, though mine already were.

"I don't suppose you'd offer me a canoe ride in exchange for that fine sailing we had this afternoon, would you?"

"Oh, I think that sounds like a fair exchange." I sat back down again in the stern. "You may have to do a major portion of the paddling though. My arm is sore. Tommy and I don't do this often enough to get our muscles into shape." Of course, Tommy immediately negated my claim regarding his arm power by pushing up his sweatshirt sleeve and showing off his muscles.

I waited for Peter to ask for the stern seat as Roger had always done, probably because it made him feel more in control. Peter, however, simply picked up the shorter paddle and said nothing about exchanging seats.

"I'll push you off," Tommy offered, but I doubted that he could with Peter's weight in the canoe. Peter may not be six feet tall, but he appeared to have the muscular physique of a boxer.

"We'll both push off," Peter said diplomatically as he removed his boat shoes and tossed them further up on the sand."

"Tommy," I cautioned, "you stay right here on the beach until we get back."

Tommy's retort came more as a challenge to my order than a question. "Right here on this very exact grain of sand?"

"You know what I mean, young man. Somewhere here on the beach where I can see you." Soon it would be dusky out and I didn't want Tommy to be alone inside the cottage where I couldn't keep an eye on him. What if some stranger should knock on the back door which I was unable to see from the water, then force his way inside?

Peter and I cast off. The water had become glassy, reflective. Every movement of our paddles was duplicated by a mirrored shadow in the water. The air was so still that one could hear the thud of a screen door and occasionally a cough coming from people on shore. We paddled quietly and then stopped to watch the sun, all red and gaudy as a circus performer, appearing to dip below the water. Soon the colors of the sunset infected the nearby clouds with brilliant pinks and lavenders, strong as a dye dropped into a vat… the sky being an endless vat.

Peter, sitting so straight in the bow, occasionally turned slightly to converse with me in a low tone so that his voice wouldn't carry across the water to shore. "I've enjoyed this weekend here at the beach more than usual because of you and Tommy."

"Thanks," I acknowledged his compliment. "It's been great for us too. Tommy hasn't stopped talking about his sailing adventure since this afternoon. He even insisted on calling his grandpa on the phone to tell him all about it." I purposely kept my voice neutral, noncommittal sounding. Being with Peter this afternoon had been nicer than I wanted to admit, not just the sailing experience but also Peter's affability and now my admitting to myself that perhaps I really had made a new friend. Nevertheless, I had finally learned from experience to be careful and not show too much enthusiasm in any man after my imbroglio with Roger. I was bitterly aware of my own culpability in having unwisely chosen him as a mate. It wouldn't happen again. No, not ever. Anyway, I wasn't actively seeking a husband or even a boyfriend. Quite the opposite.

Many times I have asked myself: Why are women like me so easily duped, letting ourselves be blindly wrapped in love compliments like a spider wrapping its victim, until we succumb. Only those of us who were stupid and naïve, I told myself. Fortunately, I did regain most of my equilibrium and good sense. I was just a little "spider shy" that's all. It wouldn't happen again, not ever.

At the very beginning, Roger's cutting remarks took place only in the privacy of our home. They were simple innuendoes such as: Hello, wife of my 'maybe' son, or will we need Mother Teresa tonight to save the lamb chops? Those remarks were often delivered as Roger came through the door after working in his legal office. At first I ignored his quips as mere buffoonery and a chance for him to unravel at the end of day. I rationalized his remarks as an example of tasteless humor. I kept telling myself that perhaps Roger should have been a stand-up comic… there were plenty of bad ones on television. Later, his jokes and sarcasms became more public; it was on those occasions that I began to dread attending public functions with him.

Could there be another Roger in Peter? I gave a shrug of dismissal. No, I couldn't see Peter using Roger's sly, clever sarcasm. But there were other kinds of cruelty just as hurtful, such as brutish physical behavior, or the silent treatment to bring a wife into line. I'd even heard about men who wouldn't let their spouses handle the checkbook because they wanted to make sure the wife stayed subservient. I was never going to let myself be drawn into any circumstances like those. Marrying again was definitely not something I wanted to think about at all. It was an institution I had worn before. Marriage wasn't as simple as putting on clothes and discarding them when they got too tight and uncomfortable.

In my head I could hear exactly what my former husband, Roger, might say if he should hear about my new acquaintance, Peter.

"Next you'll be inviting this new guy to dinner just so you can have some companionship which your age and hormones yearn for."

Piss off, I told the imaginary voice. I'm not going to make any advances of any sort towards this man. Anyway, I'm busy with the noise pollution project and my painting. I don't need any distractions. It's a good thing that Peter, paddling the canoe in the bow, didn't look around at me and read the prickly thoughts passing through my mind.

After we regained the shore, turned the canoe over on the sand, and with Tommy's help deposited the paddles and life preservers inside the small shed, which stood behind the cottage, Peter asked me if he could see some of my paintings.

"Sure, I'll be glad to show them off but it's really a bit too dark now to see them properly. Our cottage lamps are too dim." My father was frugal about light bulbs though he was generous in other ways.

"The pictures need to be seen under good lighting. Perhaps when you come back." I assumed that Peter like so many other people was simply being polite in asking about my artwork.

"I'll hold you to it. Goodnight."

"Goodnight," I answered. Even after Peter had gone and Tommy was getting ready for bed, my mind went on speculating about a man like Peter. Was I to presume that as a scientist, Peter's life would be bent only in that confining direction and that even outside of his profession everything would be based on scrupulously accurate facts and only facts? Was his desk absolutely tidy with his pencils lined up properly? What if Peter was the type of person who didn't allow himself flights of fancy...someone who even lacked imagination? I wondered if he were the sort to let his mind venture off the path of reality and into unknown territory as I often did? Roger had plenty of imagination, but all too often it was twisted in the wrong directions.

Later that evening, I took Pillage out to the road for his last peeing of the day before letting him into Tommy's room for the night. I was ashamed to admit that my thoughts that evening were mostly depressing, of how time would proceed so ploddingly and dully, until Peter returned two whole weeks from now.

I had so carefully set up a roadblock in my mind against any further fraternization with men, yet Peter and his quite open acceptance of me as a new friend had sneaked right past my carefully built-up barriers. Now my days at the beach colony would feel a little less interesting while he was gone. Well, I told myself, you'll just have to get over it. Anyway, you were getting along just fine before you met Peter.

CHAPTER 15

Tommy and I attended the Sunday morning service at the village church in Tatterack, which served jointly for both Congregational and Presbyterian denominations. The interior of the church strove for a contemporary appearance with the use of mellow wood and more clear glass windows than was usual in many churches. On this particular morning the windows behind the altar let me glimpse the leaves on the trees, mostly yellow and red, turning their backsides to the wind.

This was to be my last church attendance of the summer, though I didn't realize it at the time. Tommy had gone to the earlier Sunday school and both of us attended the main service. At this point I was still fairly sure that giving Tommy a good basis for living in a moral way—besides my setting a good example—was through the church. If Tommy should also meet some new friends in Sunday school or some buddies from the summer before, that would be an added bonus to the main purpose of attending.

Convincing Tommy to spruce up for church was a tough chore after our relaxing beach life of shorts and broken down athletic shoes. Not that either of us dressed up greatly. I wore a skirt for a change instead of slacks plus my white blouse, the one with an eyelet collar, and Tommy wore long trousers with a sport shirt. I was unable to talk him into the leather shoes so his appearance was incongruous due to the clumsy, stained Nikes showing beneath his pressed trousers. Nevertheless, Tommy looked handsome to me. He had Roger's widely set intelligent eyes but fortunately not his mouth that always thinned to a mere dash-line when stretched into a smile. Tommy's mouth, even when not reacting to humor, had a happy swoop-up at the corners, a bit more like his grandpa's.

A picture of Tommy when he was four years old flashed into my head. In it he wore his Sunday school outfit of checked coat and matching cap, white socks and shoes. How many Saturday evenings had I polished those little white shoes in preparation for our usual hour of worship?

Today in church, I looked around at the congregation and asked myself: What if those very loud electronic bells had emanated from this particular church, the Presbyterian-Congregational? My curiosity went into gear and I wondered if either that man with the white hair and the military posture sitting in front of me or the woman at the end of the next pew in flowered poly would have tolerated the electronic bells as passively as the people I had encountered in the beach colony? Of course, I wasn't about to go and query them right there in the church. I suspected though, that they would have been disinclined to make waves in the community over the loudness of the bells, just as the beach people were.

It was a cloudy Monday afternoon when I resumed my canvassing by stopping first at the Bingham cottage, a small gray bungalow with a glassed-in porch facing the water. There were several just like that one along the shore and probably built by the same contractor around nineteen hundred and nine or a bit later.

Mr. Bingham, a wiry little man, opened the door and appeared reluctant to let me inside until I told him I was a neighbor living nearby. The room was heavily decorated with patchwork quilts. It almost made me dizzy as my eyes swept over the various patterns. Some were all plaids and some were done with black and white pieces reminding me of a checkerboard game.

Quilts were everywhere. I saw them on the sofa, the chairs, even on the walls in place of pictures, plus an old one rolled up on the floor near the door. I presume it was meant to keep out the drafts in winter. The Binghams were another couple who lived at the beach both summer and winter.

"That quilt is lovely," I said in admiration, gesturing towards the one on the wall made up of random scraps of material in greens and blues, sea colors, my favorites.

"It's only leftover scraps, Mrs. Bingham sighed, as she continued to cut out even more squares of material on a card table set in front of her.

"I assume you made all these fine quilts yourself?" Mrs. Bingham nodded but didn't offer to enlighten me on the subject, so I hurried on to explain my reason for visiting and why I wanted their signatures or their presence when I went to visit Father Ciconni. When I had finished my explanation, there was an ominous silence.

Quickly, I tried to fill the blank space with an explanation. "People, like myself and others such as Mrs. Sjoberg from Florida and the Donnerts from Nebraska, who drive or fly long distances to enjoy the special characteristics of this place, would prefer quietness. It's what we all came here to enjoy. Wouldn't it be better if the electronic tapes just played a simple ding-dong instead of..."

With a thud, Mrs. Bingham dropped her heavy scissors on the table and stood up to interrupt me in a whining, half angry voice. "I am surprised at you trying to trash the bell music! That music is the most cheerful sound around here in the middle of winter when most of the cottages are shuttered up tight and no human being is in sight except the man who plows the road. Things get pretty empty and bleak around here sometimes and then the bells ring out with their cheerful hymns and swish away the gloom." Her face shed its angry expression and emitted a glow of blissfulness.

Immediately after her little ode to the bells, Mr. Bingham stepped forward and said in a menacing tone of voice, "If you don't like the music or it's too loud for you, why don't you just pack-up and leave?"

For a second his accusing words cut into me deeply. Then my Irish temper rose to the surface. "I've been coming to this beach for most of my life. It's my summer home as much as anyone else's."

"Anyway, we're not signing nothing." Mr. Bingham said and he gestured for me to leave. I did, and he slammed the door behind my back. I was shaken. No one I had visited before had been so rude. No one had reacted with such open vehemence, and no one before had given me the feeling of revilement. Discouraged, I headed straight back to Fleury cottage.

Around six o'clock that evening, we had an even stronger wind from the west pushing the remainder of the clouds off to the east and causing the waves to fling themselves up on shore with a resounding boom. The crashing waves sent bubbles and spray high into the air. I sat on the sand for a few minutes looking straight out into the liquid gray-green eyes of the water. Even that wonderfully loud roar didn't mitigate my anger against people like the Binghams or their narrowness over the deafening bells. Other times in the past I had also fled to the beach when the electronic bells started. Down a few feet from the foaming waves was the only place where the shrill sound was partially cut off.

I was deeply depressed. What was the sense of traveling hundreds of miles to a lovely place like this every summer if the mewing of the gulls, the alarms of the sandpiper, and even the freighter boat whistles sounding forlornly through a fog were constantly inundated, overpowered, by electronic bells? One might just as well stay home in the city and listen to the boom-booms of the radio emanating from the teenager's car down the block.

My morale needed a boost so I phoned my friend, Enid that evening.

"How's it going?" she asked.

"Badly. I have only one signature and none of the people I canvassed today will go with me to see the priest at the church." I complained bitterly to Enid about the rudeness of the Binghams, then I laughed and added "Too bad cats can't sign."

"What on earth do cats have to do with bells?"

"I heard noises under the porch of a vacant cottage up the beach west of here and found four baby kittens. Maybe I'll go back to check on them again tomorrow...to make sure the mother cat hasn't abandoned them. I'd bring them back here to our cottage but Pillage would make life miserable for them."

"Sounds typical of you...always caring for some stray animal or... hey, remember that college friend who ran out of money and you insisted that we give her a free meal for a week? What was that jingle?"

"Silly Sally spent all her savings."

"That's it. Actually I think she spent her money on those mini pecan pies that were so popular. Abruptly, Enid changes the subject. But you were right to help her. I've been going through some of my notes on noise pollution. Listen to this: The word 'noise' comes from the Latin word which means 'nausea'."

"Don't I know! So appropriate. If you find anything else of interest that will help me, let me know." We talked a bit more about the bells and her coming vacation in August and then I told her, "I promised Tommy a wild game of Monopoly this evening, so I'd better say goodbye for now."

"Keep in touch and keep thinking positively. Bye."

Half way through our Monopoly game, which Tommy appeared to be winning, Pillage began to bark. It wasn't his usual lackadaisical friendly one either. He actually got off his lazy haunches and ran to the back door.

"Did you hear footsteps?" I asked Tommy. He shook his head and kept on stacking up his paper money. "Time out," I said, as he was about to roll the dice again.

At the backdoor, I peered out, but saw no one. The screen was hooked, though I had left the door open because it was a pleasant evening and not quite dark yet. Stuck in the screen was a white folded paper.

"Who was it?" Tommy called.

"I didn't see anyone," I answered as I unfolded the note and read it to myself:

> *Stop your canvassing against the bells. The bells are a sacred part of our church. He who defies the church, defies God, and will pay a horrible price.*

I tucked the note in my pocket, then closed and locked the back door. Nor did I tell Tommy anything about the threat, just went back to playing the game with him. After Tommy had gone to bed, I reread the note carefully. The last few words of the note upset me the most. I read it once more: *He who defies the church, defies God, and will pay a horrible price.*

Who would carry out this wrath for God? Obviously, it would be someone right here in the beach colony or in the village of Tatterack. Upon rereading the note, it sounded to me more and more like a threat from a religious fanatic, a threat that the perpetrator intended to carry out himself, or herself, because it was destined by God.

CHAPTER 16

*E*ven before my feet touched the floor the next morning, I was jolted by the memory of the Binghams and their vitriolic behavior towards me...and towards the idea of lowering the volume of the electronic bells. Then I remembered the folded note stuck in our screen door last evening, which now lay on my nightstand next to my bed. I picked it up again. Could it have been written by the Binghams? They seemed narrow-minded... perhaps even mean people, but they didn't raise a great deal of fear in me. They thought themselves to be Christian believers. But they didn't live their belief.

Again, I read the note: *Stop your canvassing against the bells. The bells are a sacred part of our church. He who defies the church, defies God and will pay a horrible price.*

It was an out and out threat. Was it to be carried out right now... or later, sometime in the future? One thing was clear: Someone would be hurt. No, not just hurt... *horribly hurt.*

This second reading of the note did raise fear in me. The fear wasn't for myself though; it was for Tommy. What if I couldn't protect him? Was it even safe to leave him with Mavis for even one more day? All during breakfast I went over and over the same question: was it safe...was Tommy safe?

Half way through our breakfast, Tommy began to complain, "I'm tired of staying in this same spot every single day waiting for you to come home. We never go anywhere or do anything anymore."

"This will be the last day, I promise, except when I go to visit Father Ciconni at the church. You couldn't have been too lonesome though. Didn't Mavis invite you over for cookies and milk at least twice?"

"I suppose." Then he whined, "When's Peter coming back?"

I was half ashamed to admit to myself that I had kept careful track of the exact day when Peter might return. *Might*, being the key word.

"Maybe he'll come at the end of next week if nothing delays him." I wasn't that secure in my belief that Peter would actually come back and pick up our friendship exactly where it had left off.

Because of the threatening note stuck in the screen door last evening, I approached my first cottager of the day with far more trepidation than usual. A Mr. Fleener came to the kitchen door. Immediately, he told me that he was going to return to his winter home in Lima, Ohio, either today or tomorrow. I could see the cardboard boxes stacked in his kitchen and a suitcase as well.

"I can't go with you to visit the Father, but I will add my name to your list of those who agree that the bells are too loud. His signature made a total of two signers: Mrs. Sjoberg and Mr. Fleener, neither one able to go with me to speak to the church Father in person. I thanked him and asked the name of the people in the bright blue cottage next door.

"Mr. Selveich. New paint." Mr. Fleener's pursed lips conveyed skepticism over the paint job.

"Gorgeous color," I told Mr. Fleener. He appeared slightly disappointed at my lack of color taste, which obviously wasn't the same as his. "Thanks for your time," I smiled and walked to the back of Mr. Selveitch's radiant blue cottage.

I could actually see Mr. Selveich through the window of his back door when I tapped on the door, but he didn't respond. I knocked louder. Finally, he glimpsed me through the glass and opened the door. I explained to him my need for his signature because of the loud bells.

"Since I attend that church from time to time, it might not be expedient for me to sign anything against the bells. Besides," he added in a booming voice, "I haven't noticed that the bells are especially loud." I looked around the kitchen and soon spotted a hearing aid lying on the counter just to the right of the sugar. The electronic music probably didn't sound very loud to him because he forgot to wear his hearing aid. After he closed the door behind me, I hurried on home to see if Tommy was safe. In retrospect, I should have taken him with me this morning because my worry over his safety cut my patience short.

I found Tommy and Mavis sitting on the Harris' back porch sorting through a large bowl of pinto beans. It brings back a memory of how I, when about Tommy's age, was helping my mother do the same thing. Only I couldn't resist the beautiful colors of the beans and kept eating my favorite colors, which at that time were violets and pinks. Later that same day, I got sick and threw-up all the raw beans. I asked Tommy if he had eaten any of the beans, but he exclaimed, "No, they weren't mine."

After lunch, I planned to go no further than the Ostler cottage nearby. This time, I took Tommy with me. I was far too anxious over his safety to leave him alone again, and besides I felt too much in debt to Mavis for all her help.

I knew slightly more about Mr. and Mrs. Ostler, though they were certainly not close friends. They lived in the sixth cottage west of my father's. I guess I shouldn't term it a "cottage" any longer because I'd heard that it had recently been winterized. By now the Ostlers were elderly and retired; but once a few years back, they had a thriving business in the area. They sold rustic bird feeders, window boxes, bird houses, even bat houses. Those charming driftwood pieces were what the tourist liked to take home as souvenirs. Besides, they were souvenirs with an actual use. As I recalled, each piece was prominently stamped with the Ostler brand name.

Tommy lagged behind as we walked up the road. "Mom," he whispered as we approached the Ostler cottage, are you sure we should stop here?" Evidently he remembered how Mr. Ostler behaved so angrily towards us last summer when Pillage made a mess beside the road in back of his property. At the time Mr. Ostler must have been hiding behind his evergreen hedge watching as Pillage squatted beside the road in back of their property. Suddenly, Mr. Ostler stomped out from between two red cedars and confronted Tommy, me, and the dog just as we were about to walk onwards.

"I don't want dog messes on my property," he shouted. "Never let your dog make a mess here again!" Then he added sharply, "Have him do it somewhere else."

I had been peeved at the cold, mean tones in his voice, so I retaliated by saying, "The mess is actually on the road right-of-way and not on your property at all." Of course in thinking about it later, I had to admit that it would be far better if everyone cleaned up after their pets, especially here at this highly populated beach colony. After all, it was on this road where everyone strolled, jogged, and rode their bicycles.

Because of that confrontation with Mr. Ostler last summer, I felt a lot like Tommy did, not too keen about approaching that cottage and asking for help with the bell problem.

Today, I cautiously peek through the opening in the hedge and spot Mrs. Ostler's figure slightly hunched over tending her hostas and impatiens, which thrive so well in their shady back yard. It's with great relief that I don't have to mount the porch steps and knock on another door. Though, by now I have knocked on over a dozen doors, experience hasn't lessened my reticence. I dread bothering other people, even nice ones, but especially the more explosive Mr. Ostler. Today I had gotten lucky, at least thus far.

Mrs. Ostler's eyes reflect her keen interest in having visitors and she proudly shows me around her yard from flower bed to rock arrangements, not leaving out a single detail.

At first, Tommy follows closely on my heels, still keeping an eye out for Mr. Ostler. Suddenly, his interest is caught by something up a nearby tree trunk. "That's a strange looking birdhouse."

Mrs. Ostler smiles, hearing Tommy's interest. "That's a bat house. There are lots of bats around here. I'll bet you've seen them flying around in the evening when they sweep out over the water to catch insects.

"Oh, like the one flying around my bedroom one night. It woke up the dog and me too,"

"You didn't kill it, did you?"

"No. My mom caught it with a piece of cloth net. What was it…I forget what it's called."

"' Tulle," I said.

"After catching it, she laid it on the back porch. The next morning the bat had flown away."

Finally, I guided the conversation around to the subject of the electronic bells. "I can't understand why someone besides me hasn't already complained about the harshness and the…" Even before I had finished my sentence, Mrs. Ostler began to shake her head, her little fox face alert.

"Oh, we did, we did!" She interrupted. "We tried, but listen to me. I want to warn you." She lowered her voice. "My husband and I had a good business here in the village, remember?"

I nodded, recalling that my mother had bought one of their bird feeders. It still hung in the back yard of my father's house back in Holland.

"Well, we complained to the village council about those loud bells. That was about five or six years ago. Very soon after our complaint, we, my husband and I, were told by some of the stores up town that they wouldn't buy our craft products any longer." Mrs. Ostler lifted her chin defiantly. "Now what do you think about that?"

"Stores wouldn't buy your crafts just because you wanted the volume of the electronic bells turned down?"

"That's right. I hated them, the loud taped hymns; fake bells I called them, but now that we have an insulated cottage and my hearing has deteriorated, I don't mind them quite so much. When they start to blast away, I just go inside and close the door. But I thought I'd best warn you."

Tommy was getting bored by now and left us to check out the beach.

"Stay in sight," I cautioned him; "we're going very soon."

"Thank you, Mrs. Ostler, I appreciate your warning, but since I don't own a business here in town, or even try to sell my paintings up here in the gift shops, what could anyone do against me to retaliate?"

"Doesn't matter. They can find ways of making life extremely uncomfortable. We used to get weird phone calls in the night. Usually no one was on the line...just breathing. Workmen were slow in coming to fix the crack in our cement steps...things like that. People simply shunned us for a long time afterwards."

"Which people?" Couldn't she be more specific?

"The town people. They stick together, you know."

Where had I heard those exact same words once before? Oh yes, from Beatrice Tullman.

"So, be careful what you say to folks. In this town everyone has extended families, uncles and cousins, even second cousins. There's lots of overlapping of married cousins as well."

"Would you be willing to sign my petition or go with me to speak to the Father at the church?"

"No, I don't think we had better get mixed up in that again, especially now that we live here year-round... not at our old ages." She began to laugh and ended up with a rough sounding cough that alarmed me. "If we got sick and called an ambulance, they might forget to come... on purpose."

She was still laughing, and coughing intermittently as I left her garden.

"I'm going home the shore way," Tommy claimed and ran off before I could stop him. I heard him chanting... "the shore way... the shore way."

I did believe exactly what Mrs. Ostler had told me about the poor treatment she and her husband had received, yet wondered if there could have been a secondary reason for the snubbing. Again, I recalled the incident regarding our dog, which had so easily raised my ire against Mr. Ostler. Could it have been the undiplomatic attitude of the Ostlers that the people in town had resented and not the complaint over the bells?

I didn't want to believe that the people I greeted and smiled at every day in the grocery, the bakery, or the post office were so narrow minded, and especially not the church people I knew. I wanted to dismiss Mrs. Ostler's warning even more readily than Beatrice Tullman's dire predictions.

Surely, good church people wouldn't stoop so low as to give the Ostlers the silent treatment. Tommy and I were church people. I frequently attended and always tried to get Tommy to Sunday school so that he would be exposed to the morals and attitudes of which I approved. Approved? I absolutely did not concur with the narrow-minded treatment supposedly leveled at the Ostlers. The church people I knew couldn't be blighted with a myopic attitude like that, could they?

No, I answered my own question. Beatrice and Mrs. Ostler couldn't have been referring to good church people. Naturally there were always a few, a minority, in every church who hadn't progressed very far up the ladder of "do unto others."

"Oh!" I muttered out loud as I headed back to Fleury Cottage, "How pompous I sound even to myself." But I did believe that each person had to develop their Christian behavior at a different rate. Not everyone reached the same level of moral rectitude at exactly the same time. My own good behavior wasn't so high up on the ladder that the air had become rarefied. No indeed.

Now it became quite clear to me that I had more or less failed in my attempt to gather signatures, with the exception of two, or to persuade people, as previously I had been so sure I could, to visit Father Ciconni with me. Either people simply did not care enough over the imposition of the loud bells to make a complaint, or was it fear? Yes, I decided, it's fear of being ostracized by the church if they are caught signing.

Are just two people and myself going to be enough to convince Father Ciconni to lower the volume of the bells? I shrug doubtfully. There needs to be a lot more people, a lot more leaded weights on the scale, to even-out the chances of success.

CHAPTER 17

I actually have a spring in my step now that I am approaching the end of my mission—so reluctantly started—to lower the noise level of the bells from the church. After today, I think to myself, I'll be free… free to paint again, free to enjoy the remainder of the summer with Tommy and maybe with Peter as well if we are still friends.

In this promising mood, I retrace my steps to Mr. Delbert's door, the older gentleman who has promised to go with me to speak to the Father at the church about the bells. When I knock on the door, a middle-aged woman opens it instead of Mr. Delbert.

"Is Mr. Delbert here?" I asked politely.

"Yes, but he can't come to the door. He's having a severe attack of arthritis." The woman further explains that her brother can't go with me to visit the church Father either. I already know that the man is rather bent over and walks with difficulty, so I believe what she tells me; yet, I also have a strong suspicion that she or some of his many relatives may have talked him out of going with me to face Father Ciconni.

"Oh, I was counting on him." My keen disappointment, which must have been clearly visible on my face, is met with an abrupt, "Sorry."

"Wait!" I call through the rapidly closing door. The door opens just a crack to reveal an impatient face. "If you think Mr. Delbert might feel more physically able next week, I'll delay the appointment at the church."

"It's not likely. My brother isn't going to get much better from now on."

"Oh, I'm sorry to hear that." I was too, and not just for my own sake.

Now the chances for success at getting the volume lowered are much less with just Mr. Lumus to accompany me. True, it is Mr. Lumus who has spoken out the most vehemently against the electronic bells using defiant, harsh words, but because of his brash responses, I'm less sure that Father Ciconni will find him quite as convincing as Mr. Delbert. Also, I'm less confident that Mr. Lumus will stand firmly against the noise pollution. When I return to Fleury cottage, I phone Mr. Lumus and tell him that I am going to make a Thursday afternoon appointment with Father Ciconni. His answer comes after a brief moment of silence, "Well, sure."

On Thursday, fifteen minutes before one-thirty, which is the appointment time, I rap on Mr. Lumus' heavy plank door. When he finally comes to open the door, I notice that he is neatly dressed in a clean striped shirt and pressed khakis. Obviously I think, he has dressed up for our visit to the church since at other times he frequently wears stained work clothes.

"Are you ready?"

"Huh? Ready for what?"

"To go and see Father Ciconni."

"Guess I thought it was next week. I've got a job to do right away hauling brush to the dump in my truck for someone up the beach. I'm going right now." I note that he isn't appropriately dressed for that type of job, but I say nothing about the discrepancy.

"I'll be glad to change the appointment." That's what I tell him out loud, but inside I am terribly disappointed. I try not to show it. "I can go any day you can go, or that the Reverend Father will see us. Just tell me which day is best for you."

"Well, not today." His eyes slide past mine and down the road as though he is hoping someone or something will whisk me out of his presence. His mind also seems scattered. It certainly isn't on the subject of the appointment.

"Will tomorrow be better for you?" He nods. "Now are you absolutely certain?" Intuitively, I feel that Mr. Lumus is trying to wiggle out of his commitment. I suspect that all his bluster and boasting about how he will confront the Father and tell him a "thing or two about those damn bells" is simply bravado put on for my benefit. Now, when he has a chance to go face to face with the Father, he is vacillating. Standing there, I observe how deflated his manner is, wholly unlike his former cocky behavior. He spoke so resolutely earlier in the summer—so adamantly against the loud bells. Now his resolve appears to be as dilute as the coffee in the local bus station.

Once again I phone the church and fortunately I'm able to reschedule the appointment for the next day at eleven o'clock. I leave a note to that effect stuck with masking tape on Mr. Lumus' heavy door.

I felt relieved that I needn't face an interview today. On the other hand from past experiences I had learned that the anticipation of a job interview or a visit to the dentist, both dreaded ones, were often more difficult by waiting than getting them over with immediately. Naturally, I wanted the chore over and done with so that I could get back to my private life and not this highly public one of knocking on the doors of cottages belonging mostly to strangers.

At this point I never had a single doubt that the good church Father would understand and give-in to our wishes of curbing noise pollution. If he didn't seem immediately convinced over lowering the decibels, I planned to invite him to walk back to our cottage so that he could hear for himself how dreadfully loud the electronic bell sounds were.

During the noontime bell concert, actually more organ than bells on this particular tape, a loud militant "Onward Christian Soldiers". was played. I sighed and contemplated happily how the music would be much more subdued by tomorrow evening. I told myself the same thing during the brassy six o'clock hymn, T<u>hyne Is The Glory</u>, a familiar hymn woven in among a medley of several unknown ones. The loud rendition brought forth a picture in my head of a long ago movie where the organ was being played by a man in flowing black robes, wind blowing his wild hair and bats flying around his head. Or did I make up that last part? Perhaps it had been an old cartoon.

At fifteen minutes before eleven the next morning, after first asking Mavis to keep an eye on Tommy and staunchly assuring her that it would be the very last time, I knocked on Mr. Lumus' door once again. There was no response. I knocked a second time and waited. Then I softly called out his name. I looked around and realized that his pickup truck was missing. Just as I suspected, Mr. Lumus had scampered. I checked the time on my watch... five minutes before eleven. It was so close to the exact time of our appointment with Father Ciconni that I didn't have the nerve to phone and cancel the meeting a second time. I realized that I had no choice but to go ahead and face the Father alone.

It seemed unbelievable... all those beach people I had approached and none of them, including Mr. Lumus, had the gumption to walk a block to the church and help me confront the Father concerning the loud electronic bells. Why? Was he such an ogre? Or was it because those people felt the power of the church establishment hovering over them? That could hardly be a comfortable way to feel. That they would feel reverential I could understand, or perhaps awed, and of course inspired by a church. But instead, were they feeling out and out fear? And what about all those people in cottages who didn't attend that church denomination at all? Their attitude was even more of an enigma to me.

"How unfair," I muttered out loud. At first I shuffled my feet and looked expectantly down the road in both directions, hoping to see Mr. Lumus' red truck appear. Here I was, left with the burdensome duty of fulfilling the appointment all by myself, and I was absolutely the wrong person. I would probably appear there in front of the

Father, get flustered, and forget the salient points of my protest. But at this juncture I simply had no choice.

I rechecked my watch every second or so hoping that by some legerdemain, Mr. Lumus would suddenly come driving around the curve in the road in his pick-up truck. He didn't.

CHAPTER 18

*B*ecause I was already late to my appointment with Father Ciconni at the church, I cut through Mr. Lumus' backyard and picked my way on tiptoe through the patch of poison ivy, wishing it were tulips as in that old familiar song, to the back of the church's property. On my way I passed the flower garden of tall, stiff gladioli, hollyhocks, and Canterbury bells. The buff colored brick edifice didn't look like a rectory but I reasoned that it couldn't be anything else since it was attached to the church and there were no other buildings anywhere nearby except for the little store where religious books and crosses were sold.

The windowless heavy door was opened by a woman of perhaps forty-five years of age. I guessed that she was either the housekeeper or a secretary. "Good morning," I said. "We, I mean I, have an appointment with Father Ciconni." Already I was getting flustered. Not greeting me cheerfully with a return "Good morning" or even a smile, just added to the tension that I already felt. Soberly, the woman nodded and led me into the Father's office.

Just off the hallway, I found myself stepping down into a concrete-floored room with cinder block walls. Father Ciconni, a small older man on the thin side, sat behind the desk facing me. He looked harmless enough in his black suit. Yet, there was no more of a smile of welcome on his face than there had been on the woman's face, the one who opened the front door. He didn't rise up to cordially greet me nor invite me to sit down, but after introducing myself, I did sit down anyway. I was nervous and sitting gave me the stability of the chair's armrest to grasp. Aside from the chair, there seemed to be very little sign of comfort in the gray bunker-like room. There were several carved crosses and an icon of Mary, Mother of Jesus, on the walls. That was all. The room felt cold and barren.

I explained my mission and gave Father Ciconni the facts about the dangerously high decimeter readings.

"Many people in the beach colony, including myself, would be most grateful if you considered reducing the volume on the electronic music." I paused, but saw no nod of comprehension in return, so I continued. "You see, now that you've added those huge speakers to the tower, the decibels are far too loud, especially for your own ears. Also, some of your concerts—I don't mean music for funerals or official church doings—are very long... some as long as twenty minutes. Obviously you like music or..."

Before I could continue with the facts gleaned from the decimeter, which I had prepared ahead of time, he interrupted, "I haven't heard anyone else complain."

I swallowed, hoping to loosen up my dry throat. "Several have, Mrs. Sjoberg is one, though many are reluctant to speak out against the church... and,..."

"... I don't know her. She does not belong to my church."

"... also Mr. Delbert and Mr. Lumus have asked me to..."

"Oh, him." His tone of voice dismissed Mr. Lumus with spit-on-the-floor disdain. "No, I can not change the volume."

"Why not?"

"Come, I'll show you." I followed him into an even smaller cinder block room across the hallway where a bank of electronic equipment was stacked on shelves across one whole wall. "See? It's all set. The dials are all set. It can't be changed."

I gestured towards the equipment. "Why can't you just twist the volume dial lower?" It seemed simple enough to me. The Father ignored my question completely.

"The music is beautiful! In my home village in Italy bells are rung all the time... day and night... night and day... so lovely." His wily face became softly sentimental for just a moment.

"But those were genuine bells back there in Italy at that time, not the harsher electronic music that you play here. The quality is far different from genuine bells. And," I continued before losing my nerve, "those churches, though they rang the bells often, didn't ring them for long periods at each time... or play long concerts as you do." Then I repeated my former evidence in what I thought was a firm voice, considering how unconfident I felt. "Sometimes you play the tapes as long as twenty minutes at a time."

The little man stomped his foot. "Don't argue with me!" He flounced and puffed up like a prairie chicken only it wasn't to attract a mate. "I am not going to shut down the bells!" he proclaimed loudly, nearly shouting, and flung his arms outward as though to sweep away any disagreement. His voice had risen in decibels, and I began to feel unsafe. I felt threatened. I took a step backwards and then two more. "Perhaps then," I swallowed and took another step backwards, "I should write to the diocese and get their opinion."

"Do what you like!" he bristled. I watched him push a button on the electronic equipment, heard a whirring sound, and had a vision of all the doors sliding shut sealing me inside the small cement-block room. Instead, a large reel of tape came slivering out. He thrust the reel of tape into my hands and pushed me with gestures out the door and down the hallway. I was too stunned to resist. From the angry look in his eyes I was sure that he was going to throw me out bodily.

With the reel in my hands, I literally backed down the hallway as quickly as I could to the heavy outside door. Father Ciconni was right in my face as I backed. He kept gesturing to keep me moving along the hall until I turned my back on him to facilitate the opening of the door. My agitated mind noted a young boy of ten or so sitting below me on the cement steps.

"You, Jimmy Jay." Father Ciconni pointed decisively at the little boy. "It's time for you to go on home now."

My breathing was coming in quick short spurts as I stumbled over the doorsill and made my way down the steps. I turned around again and tried to hand the reel of tape back to Father Ciconni.

"No," he snapped, "you take it back to the Tribners. They donated it to the church. Go ahead, tell *them* you don't like their music!" Before I could protest, he stepped backwards into the hall and closed the door with a slam.

At the bottom of the steps I froze in position. My body and my mind were both stuck in one gear—consternation. In my bewilderment I barely noticed the little boy who looked up at me from the steps. He quickly got up and ran off.

Slowly, I moved away out the driveway to the road. I felt utterly confused... completely befogged. With help from some inner automation, I did arrive back at Fleury cottage, though everything between the church and the cottage was a complete blank in my mind. It was as if a pleat in time had taken place.

My daze didn't seem to wear off even after I got back inside the cottage and sat down. I kept repeating out loud, "The little man actually stomped his foot at me! What kind of a man of the cloth would behave like that?" I glanced at the fat reel of tape that lay on the corner of the kitchen table where I had dropped it. "Now what should I do with that?"

How stupid that I hadn't had the presence of mind to leave the tape on the steps of the rectory instead of bringing it back home with me. "Will the Tribners think I have stolen it?" Should I walk back to the church and leave it with the housekeeper? "Oh! But what if that little hornet of a Father should come to the door instead?" The very thought started my hands trembling. I had to calm myself down before I could do anything. Perhaps, I thought, a cup of tea would help.

I made the tea and took the cup into the living room where I could look out the window at the soothing water and also watch Tommy who seemed to be putting the finishing touches on a little ditch that he had dug from the overflow of the artesian well. Mavis's ample form appeared on the beach nearby much to my relief; she was keeping a close eye on Tommy for me. "Bless her."

After slowly sipping about half of my tea, I came to a decision: No, I would not take the chance of facing the little mad Father again. I decided to take the tape to the Tribners instead. After all, it belonged to them. I put on my sun hat to protect me from the hot noontime sun and walked up the road with the tape in my hand. It was merely a half block to the Tribner cottage, just across the street and not far from the library. All I knew about the Tribners was that they were an older couple who played bridge with my neighbor, Fred—that is, Frederick. I approached the front of the cottage slowly, not expecting any sort of problem. I would simply place the reel of tape in the hands of whomever came to the door and quickly head back home.

CHAPTER 19

*I*t took only a minute or two to walk the abbreviated block down the road to the green shuttered cottage directly across from the Kramer cottage. The Tribners' cottage was one I had previously stopped at twice before in my canvassing, but no one had ever come to the door, though I always saw a car parked in the driveway. There was a car parked there today.

I tapped on the screen door of the porch. A white-haired woman still in her bathrobe, though it was now nearly lunchtime, came hurtling through the cottage door and across the porch to open the screen door. She yanked the reel of tape out of my hand and yelled, "Why you stealing little bitch! How dare you take it?" I was so swept away by her accusation that I stood there mute.

Finally I garbled, "I didn't... the Father at the..." I tried to explain, but was immediately cut short by the woman's husband who had come striding out right behind her, a glass of pale liquid in his hand.

"What kind of a person are you to steal from a church?" Mr. Tribner shouts. "That tape isn't yours. Why did you take it? You're a thief!"

Again I attempt to explain, but the woman keeps interrupting me by shouting in my ear. "I'm surprised there's people in this nice beach colony like you! You go on home now. We don't want to see your bitchy face ever again!"

At last the woman's boozy breath reaches my nose, assaults me as much as her words. There really is no use trying to explain anything to two people who have been steadily drinking. I quickly step down from the porch with as much dignity as I can muster. I feel sore and battered even though no one has actually laid a finger on me. I fervently hope the Kramers, who live across the corner, aren't listening to this rowdy, disgusting shouting. The ruckus has taken place right out in the open air where several neighbors could witness my humiliation.

How embarrassing... how humiliating I think... to be mixed up in such a trashy scene... to be called a bitch and even an outright thief! Thief... thief... keeps reverberating in my head. If people in other cottages have been listening, will they believe that I really did steal the tape? Probably. I groan out loud at my lack of foresight. Anyone with half a brain would simply have laid the reel of tape down on the steps back at the church and fled. Now, much too late, I do exactly that. I flee from the Tribners' cottage. My walking pace is almost a running one as I rush down the road...to hide inside Fleury cottage.

As I hurry away from the Tribner cottage a numbness grips my mind; then, when I'm nearly home, anger and embarrassment send waves of heat to spread across my face. My damaged pride is taking precedence over everything else. To imagine that I have been accused of stealing like a common thief! Would the "thief" label spread all up and down the beach? Very likely. The Tribners are well known as bridge club enthusiasts and what little society our beach colony retains, musters from its' humble beginnings, has developed around the Tribners and Mr. Harris, my neighbor. Would the socially aspiring Frederick rally to uphold my reputation? That I doubted.

The hurt and anger scorch me as thoroughly as if I'd been in a roaring oven. The closer I get to Fleury cottage, the harder it is to keep from crying. I lower my head and run up the porch steps and through the door of the cottage.

I am utterly humiliated over the public accusations. In my mind I live through the shouting match over and over again. Anyone walking along the road past the Tribners or even sitting on their porches nearby could have overheard the rowdy, embarrassing scene…could have heard Mrs. Tribner loudly calling me that foul word…,."bitch!" How I wish I could run down to Peter's cottage and hide away in that closet he had offered. To think that just recently we had laughed and joked—I had even giggled—over such a thing as hiding in a priest's hole.

In the living room at Fleury cottage I sit down again in a rocking chair and yank my sun hat down to cover my face. Next, I find myself nervously clutching my hands to keep them from shaking. As I sit there, the situation begins to clarify itself in my mind.

Father Ciconni must have phoned the Tribners to inform them that I had taken the reel of tape. In fact, he must have strongly implied that I had actually stolen the tape. That in itself was a mean, childish thing for anyone to do, but a Reverend Father? Surely that was not the proper way for a man of the cloth to behave.

Suddenly I remembered Tommy. "Where is he?" I jump up from the chair, freeing it to rock wildly. Out the front windows I could see him setting sticks afloat in his newly dug canal to rush like rafts down the twists and turns to the open water. Tommy was perfectly safe.

At the edge of the shore two people doddered along trying to avoid the freshwater clamshells with their bare feet. They each turned and one of them gestured towards the cottage. "So soon?" I muttered. Were those people pointing out the cottage where the woman had stolen the tape from the church? No. Word couldn't have spread so quickly. Anyway, people wouldn't openly point like that, would they? I was just being overly self-conscious…acting guilty even though I knew I wasn't guilty. Suddenly, I felt a primitive urge to run down to the shore, yank Tommy off the beach into the cottage, lock the doors, close the shutters, and pull up the drawbridge, though I had none to pull up. Better still, I wanted to close the cottage and run all the way home to my father in Holland. Instead, I sat down again in the rocking chair and began to sob.

A few minutes later I calmed myself enough to look at the situation more realistically and talk myself back into some semblance of normalcy. "In the first place, Leah," I lectured myself, "it isn't your fault. Try to get that straight. Then why do I feel so guilty? Because you were meant to feel guilty. That little man, the priest, did it. He had no right to treat you the way he did, or to slyly imply to the Tribners that you had stolen the tape. Maybe, when the Tribners sober up, they'll realize that. Maybe." I sniffled and dabbed away at my tears.

"Open up a window, let in some fresh air," I staunchly command myself out loud, "and then maybe you'll feel better." I do exactly that, and the northwesterly wind sends the white sailcloth curtains sailing and flips the magazine covers up and keeps them flapping. The wind is also beginning to pile the waves up on the shore and Tommy's carefully built series of canals are being inundated. He doesn't seem to mind though. He has taken off his sneakers and with his bare feet is stomping around gleefully to help the waves wash away his diggings.

Fluffs of clouds billow on the horizon, their whiteness contrasting sharply with the blue of the sky. The water out in the distant freighter channel is rapidly changing color from glassy yellow-green to a deep jewel-like blue-green. It's turning out to be a gorgeous afternoon, and the weather inside me can't help but respond to the lovely picture outside the cottage window. It's worth copying on canvas, but I doubt that I can keep my mind on painting at all. I feel too edgy and strained.

I make a few Pepperoni and cheese sandwiches and pour milk for our lunch.

Later that afternoon Tommy and I ride our bicycles along the beach road behind the cottages. To reach the main road into town, we have to pass both the Kramer and the Tribner cottages. As we pass, I look neither left nor right, but straight ahead with a stiff smile on my face in case anyone is watching.

CHAPTER 20

I held my breath, almost literally, but there seemed to be no
further repercussions from my visit to the church nor from the
Tribners over my alleged stealing of their tape. Neither was the volume
of the bells reduced by even one decibel. Mr. Lumus stayed out of
sight and I certainly didn't care to seek him out. Now, of course, after
discovering first hand what Father Ciconni's tempestuous nature was
like, I understood why Mr. Lumus appeared to be such a coward.

If Mr. Lumus had gone with me to voice his complaint over the
loudness of the bells, he doubtless suspected that Father Ciconni
would resort to retaliation against him... not necessarily a divinely
accepted code of behavior for a church Father. Mr. Lumus was afraid
that the unpredictable Father, with just a few caustic remarks, could
make him feel permanently uncomfortable in church by setting him
up as an example, a bad one, and doing it right there in front of the
entire congregation. I, of all people, knew what criticism could do
to one's self esteem. I had gone through a slightly different version
of the same thing with Roger, though in my case the sharp little
innuendoes never happened to occur in church... just everywhere
else or so it seemed.

A couple of days after my visit to Father Ciconni and the Tribner
embarrassment, I happened to glance out towards my garden of
orange lilies and noticed a multitude of white stones protruding
from the garden. Oh, our soil was stony enough on its own account

but these stones were different. They were large white limestones collected from somewhere further west along the shoreline.

"Tommy," I asked, "did you throw stones into the garden?"

"Why'd I want to do a dumb thing like that?" He ran over to the garden to get a closer look. "Wow! Looks like someone threw the stones in from the road. Who'd want to do that?" Tommy looked at me to see my reaction. "Maybe some kid like me, huh?"

"I don't know who did it." But Tommy was probably right. It wasn't the sort of petty thing an adult would do, not even an angry one. To me it seemed like a child-type action... a flailing out in retaliation, though I didn't say so to Tommy.

Long ago—it seemed like ancient years ago—when I was around ten years old, a little neighborhood boy and I had done exactly the same thing. Oh yes, now I recalled it with chagrin. We didn't like the woman who lived in the corner house because she yelled out her window at us to keep off her lawn. It was a very lush, velvety lawn with very few weeds and we liked to cut across it instead of using the sidewalk. My friend, Sid, and I gathered small stones from the gardens in our own backyards nearby and threw them helter-skelter into her lawn.

In the midst of our crime Sid was spotted by his mother and she made him pick up every single stone. My mother knew nothing about the incident so I didn't help Sid. Instead, I stood safely on the sidewalk nearby watching the bent-over Sid as he picked up every single stone and dropped it into a basket. I remembered taunting, "Do you always do everything your mother tells you to?"

Now a vision, an indistinct periphery scene, returned to me and I remembered the little boy sitting on the steps of the church last Friday when I retreated out the door as Father Ciconni continued to threaten me with his angry gestures. The boy probably had no idea exactly what the problem was between Father Ciconni and me, but he did believe that anyone who caused the Reverend Father to be so upset must be at fault for some reason or other. Who else, if not that little boy, would do a childish thing like flinging stones into someone's garden?

At first, I was going to ask Tommy to help me pick-up the white stones from the garden. Then I decided that it was about time for me to do what I hadn't done all those years long ago... pick up my share of stones. So I did.

On Sunday I took Tommy to Sunday school as usual, but I didn't attend church myself. There was an undercurrent working in me, a deeply troubling one. I knew that my problems with people over the electronic bells should not have had the effect of discouraging me from going to church—shouldn't have kept me from having the faith to see around my current troubles—but it did. It had subtly undermined my feelings towards religion in general.

My mind kept repeating the same niggling question: would the people in our Presbyterian, Methodist, or Congregational denominations behave just as narrowly as some were doing in the other church, the church with the electronic loud bells? And quite logically the answer was weighted towards the affirmative. I knew perfectly well that narrow mindedness and retaliation were not attributes confined to any one church, any one town, or any one country.

Cynicism had inundated me and a wedge of fearfulness slid over me, even though I could almost hear my father repeating, "Everything's going to be all right." Still, it failed to soothe me. I needed some distraction to wipe the bell problem clear out of my mind for a while. As a diversion, my first thought was of Peter, but he wouldn't be back in Tatterack until the coming Friday. I sighed and wished he were present right here, right now this minute. Maybe I'd even allow him to put his arms around me to assuage my fears. The daydream of Peter cuddling me in his arms was a powerfully soothing one.

In the afternoon, Tommy and I drove over to Fenville to attend their small carnival. We both rode on the camel and nearly toppled off when it folded its front legs to kneel, and we ate bratwurst on buns and buried our faces in pink cotton candy. Getting away from Tatterack and the beach colony was good therapy for both of us. Gloomily, I reminded myself, our relief wouldn't last.

Early in the evening before darkness fell, we started back for home. I liked the rolling hills around Fenville where the farmer's fields were all up down and the cows had to climb their way back to the barn to be milked.

"Look, Tommy," I said, "this road is almost like riding a roller coaster." When our car came to the top of a hill, we had a sweeping view of woods and fields, then immediately our stomachs felt the sudden drop as we swooped down again and drove back up the road to the top of the next hill.

"Let's do it again," Tommy begged.

So we did. Twice. Later, as I told Enid on the telephone, after spewing out all my troubles to her sympathetic ears regarding my clash with Father Ciconni and the Tribners, "I almost felt like repeating that hilly drive a third time simply as an excuse to put off going back to the cottage in the beach colony."

"Sorry you feel so depressed. Wish I could take the time off to drive up there to console you. I'd even leave dirty notes on the Tribner's doorsteps if I thought it would do you any good." Enid laughed at her childish idea. "I have some more environmental information to feed you. Want to hear?"

"Sure."

"It's kind-of long so I'll just read the first sentence or so and then E-mail you the rest. Here goes: *Sound evokes much more than the sensation of hearing. The sound signal is transmitted, via the brain, to almost every nerve center and organ of the body. Therefore, sound influences not only the hearing center of the brain, but the entire physical being.* That's from Baron's book: <u>The Tyranny of Noise.</u>"

"Thanks, Enid. Even though I'm finished with the canvassing, I'll need some persuasive material if I decide to write a letter to the church diocese."

"That's a good idea, kiddo. Do it. Bye."

No sooner had I finished talking to Enid, than the phone rang again. I presumed Enid had forgotten to tell me something more about noise pollution or that it could be a call from my father; so I picked up the receiver with alacrity. But it wasn't Enid and it wasn't my father.

"Hello?" There was no answering greeting. No one answered at all. I could tell that the line was still open and I thought I could hear breathing, but I wasn't absolutely certain, so I hung up. "Probably a wrong number or telemarketing," I rationalized, and dismissed it from my mind until later when I looked at the clock. Telemarketing calls never came this late in the evening.

Fear begins to strap my chest tightly again.

This was exactly what Mrs. Ostler had warned me about.

CHAPTER 21

*E*ven by the first week in August, I was no closer to finding out who was responsible for the petty retaliations that were happening to Tommy and me, or who had left the threatening note jammed in the back screen door one evening.

It had been Saturday when we found the white stones in the garden and Monday when we discovered that the garbage, which was meant to be inside the metal can, was missing. "Who would bother to steal garbage?" Tommy whooped with a laugh. He soon solved that part of the mystery by discovering the bag of garbage in the lower branches of a birch tree near the road. I'm fairly certain that the rocks found in the garden and the garbage prank could be attributed to the young boy...the one I'd seen sitting on the church steps on that embarrassing day when the Father at the church behaved so badly towards me. The Father had called the boy Jimmy Jay. Neither the stones thrown in the garden nor the garbage incident had been so hurtful that I couldn't handle them with a shrug and a laugh. Soon, the boy would run out of ideas for retaliating on behalf of the Father, or time would soften the boy's feelings towards me.

Still fresh in my mind, was the chilling note found in the screen door on the back porch one evening. It claimed, no not just claimed, actually threatened that the person who protested against the bell music would *pay a horrible price.*

That evening, Tommy and I walked the dog along the road behind the cottages in an easterly direction. There weren't too many places to walk Pillage in the evenings unless we wanted to take him up to the main road past the church. Perhaps the church grounds might be the perfect place to let the dog do his duties if I wanted some kind of symbolic revenge, which I didn't, though the idea tickled my sense of humor. This time, I brought along a plastic bag to gather-up the dog's leavings if it became necessary.

We passed most of the cottages where I had canvassed lately including Mrs. Sjoberg's, which was now empty until she returned this coming Friday. About five cottages later we crossed to the opposite side of the road and were heading back to Fleury cottage when a man began yelling from the opposite side of the road. I wasn't sure if he was calling to us, so I stopped and turned around.

"Are you calling us?" I asked.

"That's my property your dog is on," he shouted. He must be joking, I thought, and started to walk on again. Though I didn't actually know the man's name, I recognize his face and knew that he lived in a cottage we had already passed on the opposite side of the road from where we were walking right now.

What could his problem be? At the moment, I was keeping Pillage on a short lead close to the edge of the road so that he wouldn't get into the poison ivy, which was rampant right here next to a weathered old garage. Out of the corner of my eye, I watched as the man made his way across the dirt road towards us. He halted his bulky frame smack in front of me, effectively blocking my way. Pillage sniffed at the man and wagged his tail as though recognizing a long lost pal. Why oh why, couldn't Pillage act more like an attack dog once in a while and let out a low threatning growl? How gratifying it would seem, particularly in a case like this.

"I own property over here on this side of the road too," the man stated.

"Well," I answered, "we're not on it." I could sense trouble brewing. "Please take the dog, Tommy, and walk on ahead while I find out what's bothering this... gentleman." Obviously his behavior was not intended to be gentlemanly at all, so I admit that I might have sounded a bit sarcastic.

Tommy walked on ahead of me, but I could see his head turning every now and then, curious to see exactly what was going on between me and the peculiar behavior of the man.

"What's bothering me, lady, is that you want to cheat us out of our bell music, don't you?" His tone was cheeky and angling for a fight. Evidently my reputation as someone anti-music had spread way up to this end of the beach, far beyond where I had canvassed for signatures. Either the little Father or the Tribners had been busy spreading the word.

"No," I answered, looking the man straight in the eyes. "I just want the volume turned down." The man took another step towards me and pushed his bristle-chinned face and his beer-breath further up under my nose.

"That's not what *I* heard," he shouted loud enough for the entire neighborhood to hear. "You want to cheat us out of our music. Well, you'd better not try. And if you do, I'll come down to your place, that swamp you live in, and fix you good including your whole family and your dumb dog."

"Don't threaten me, Mr!" Now I was really boiling. I started to walk on.

"Don't walk your dog back this way again," he yelled after me.

"This is a public road, Mr. I'll walk my dog here if I want to."

Further up ahead I can see that boy called, Jimmy Jay suddenly jump out of the bushes from the side of the road. He began to follow Tommy. He was the same boy I'd seen before at the church. He was older than Tommy, and a half a head taller.

Jimmy Jay took a quick glance back at me, then yanked the dog's lead out of Tommy's hand and flung it down on the road. When Tommy bent to pick up the dog's lead again, the older boy grabbed Tommy by the arm and yanked him off to the side of the road.

Why was Jimmy being mean to Tommy? I asked myself. I began to walk faster to catch up. Then, fear induced me to begin to run. I watched the boys disappear between a cement block garage and the Kramer cottage on the left side of the road.

"Tommy!" I shouted. "Wait for me!" But the boys had disappeared. I couldn't see either boy, but then I heard the dog barking from the small patch of woods just behind the library. I worked my way through the trees to the rear of the library drive. No boys!

"Tommy," I yelled as loudly as I could with my hands around my mouth to better direct my voice. There was no answer. I noticed that the library was dark. It wasn't open tonight so they hadn't run inside the building. So instead, I dashed through the empty parking area to reach the sidewalk in front of the library where I quickly looked up and down the walk. No boys. Next, I looked across the street into the tennis courts and over to the ball field, and then across to the entrance of the school. All empty.

This had been my worst fear right from the beginning... that someone, angry at me, would harm Tommy, yet Jimmy Jay was not a grownup. He was just another young boy. How dangerous could he be and how could the boys disappear so quickly? But they had!

A dog barked a second time. This time I was more certain it might be Pillage. "Tommy, are you inside?" I yelled as loudly as I could. Faintly, I heard Tommy's teary voice. "I— can't get loose!"

"Don't cry. Is Jimmy with you?"

"No. Heeee... tied me up and raaan away." I tried to calm Tommy, though I didn't feel at all calm myself. I'll find someone to get you out. I ran to the next house and pounded wildly on the door, then to the picture window where I also pounded, and then back to the door to pound again. "Alright! I hear you!" a shouted voice answered, and the door was suddenly flung open.

When the woman opened the door and was faced with a wildly distraught me, she knew something was terribly wrong. "What happened?"

"My son!" I tried to lower my voice below panic level. "He's locked inside that machine shop house next door! Please, please, can you phone the police for me?"

She nodded. I saw her pick-up a cell phone on the table and punch-in some numbers and with relief the switchboard operator answered. "She thinks her son is locked inside this vacant house here in Tatterack. It's next to the library. She's quite distraught." The operator wants to know your boy's age.

"Seven, just seven! He's crying."

"Yes... just a child." The house next door to the library I heard her retell the operator. "Only seven." She repeated. Then she turned to me. "The only policeman on duty this evening is dealing with a fender-bender. He's nearly finished, though." I groaned in disappointment. My stomach was heaving. Nerves of course.

"Ohhh!" I utter in disappointment as I rushed back next door with the woman following right behind me and still carrying the phone in her hand.

"I don't see him through the window." She said doubtfully.

"That's because Jimmy Jay tied him up. Tommy is further back among that mess of horrible machinery."

"Did you say, Jmmy Jay?" She must have heard me. "That boy! He's gotten into some other scrapes lately. Guess he doesn't have much of a home life since his mother began working. She's the housekeeper for Father Ciconni."

I immediately remembered the unsmiling housekeeper who opened the door to me when I visited the Father just recently. "Where does Jimmy live?"

"He and his mother live at that motel across the street, close to the school. By the way, I'm Claire and I know you must be Leah Frary."

"Yes, hello, Claire." Then I added, "that motel is closed...has been for years." I, myself, remembered staying there overnight once when the cottage was full to overflowing with relatives. It was a nice motel back then."

"I think it's Jimmy Jay's aunt who lives in the house nearby."

"Tommy, I called through the closed door. A man is coming to help you get out." Tommy was sobbing harder now.

"I cut myself on the wire around my waist!"

"Oh, my God, I muttered under my breath. I tried to stay calm, but warned Tommy, "Don't pull on the wire and maybe it won't cut as much. Is the blood actually dripping?"

"No, but it's messing up my T-shirt."

Claire touched my shoulder to alert me that the policeman had just driven up into the library parking area next door.

"Now how did the young man get locked in the house?" The policeman had his note pad out. The neighbor standing next to me interrupted. "The little boy is only seven years old. It was Jimmy Jay who locked him inside."

"Oh," I groaned, feeling my stomach kick up again "My boy, Tommy, has been crying. Didn't you bring a tool to break this padlock?"

The neighbor spoke up. "It was Jimmy Jay who locked him inside," she repeated.

"Where is this Jimmy Jay right now?"

"We don't know. Try the motel next to the school." You didn't bring any tools to break the padlock?" I accused. "Absolutely nothing to open the door?"

"No, but I'll get something if we can't find that boy right away who evidently has the key. You called him, Jimmy Jay?"

"Oh" I groaned. "My son is crying. Now he's bleeding. Can't you speed things up somehow?"

"Doing my best." Again he asked, "Where does this Jimmy Jay live?" Both the neighbor and I spoke at the same time. "That motel near the school."

"Or," I added, sounding distraught, "at the church where his mother works."

"If I can't locate him right away, I'll get a tool from the hardware store. I don't think there's a locksmith here. Too small a town."

I called through the door to Tommy, "The policeman will soon get you out." But what would reassure me? I was far closer to completely breaking down than Tommy.

My new friend, Claire, and I waited. She brought out two beach chairs for us, but I couldn't sit down... not while Tommy was crying inside. I paced.

The policeman soon returned with Jimmy, but Jimmy's mother sat in the patrol car and waited.

"Where is the boy's mother," I demanded, feeling anger that the woman cared so little about what happened to my son that she didn't even get out of the car.

"You may be sure," the policeman said, "I'll talk to Jimmy's mother and ask lots of questions afterwards. The policeman began to fit the key into the old padlock.

The neighbor woman asked Jimmy, Why did you lock the little boy inside?"

"Cause I knew Father Ciconni would like me to get him."

"Get him? Why? Did he do something bad to you or the Father?"

"No, not him; his mother upset the Father."

"No doubt, I did." I explained to the policeman, "I asked the Father to lower the volume of the loud bell music."

The neighbor spoke up. "That would do it! I tried that once myself."

"I get the picture." The policeman said. "Jimmy, we'll talk this over with your mother, afterwards. You could have hurt the little boy badly by chucking him in with all that rusty old machinery," Besides, he's much younger than you." The neighbor interrupted again. "That was a mean thing to do Jimmy Jay. Shame on you."

"Please! Could we get my child out of that dirty trap?"

I could hear Tommy crying again. The policeman turned on his flashlight and we both stepped cautiously just inside the door. "You wait here," he told me. No reason for two people to get in that mess." He blocked my way.

"But he's crying and he says he's bleeding."

"Besides," the man lowered his voice to a whisper, "he'll be braver if his mother isn't right there."

I backed out of the doorway. The neighbor woman spoke up for me. "The boy is only seven so naturally she's terribly worried."

The policeman turned on his flashlight and made his way through the tangle of junk. I heard him say, "Hey there," greeting Tommy in a cheerful voice. "Tommy replied with a sob, "I'm bleeding!"

"You'll be just fine in a minute. Let's get this wire off. It's old and tangled."

The neighbor left, but quickly returned with a bottle of alcohol and a box of cotton swabs.

I was so anxious to see how badly Tommy was bleeding that I almost bumped into the policeman who was guiding Tommy out the door. I wanted to hold Tommy closely in my arms and sooth him, but knew the policeman had the right approach. If I over-reacted in any manner, so would Tommy. He would cry harder and be less brave.

It took only minutes for the policeman to come out leading Tommy by the hand. I gave Tommy a quick hug... not the kind I would have given if others hadn't been there watching.

"See Mother,' the policeman said, "We have a brave boy here."

I was sure Tommy felt like crying, but seeing Jimmy standing right there watching, he pressed his lips tightly together allowing only a small sob to escape from his throat.

The policeman told Tommy to hold his arms out. "Let's see how badly that wire tried to bite you. Well, not so bad as I thought." He gave Tommy a pat on the back."

"They're very small nicks," Claire said, as she touched several with her swobs dipped in alcohol. Tommy jerked a bit but otherwise didn't cry out."What about the dog?" Tommy asked.

"We'll tend him at home and give him a bath," I said. I thanked the policeman and also my new friend, Claire, and I invited her to stop by the cottage soon to allow us to get more aquainted. "I'll never be able to thank you enough," I said, and felt the grateful tears escaping.

CHAPTER 22

*T*ommy didn't ask to go anywhere alone today, nor would I have let him. He remained inside the cottage all morning while I painted, but after lunch we both went down to the beach in front of the cottage. We left Pillage tied near the back porch so that he could alarm us by barking if a stranger came near the cottage.

Tommy dug up a bucketful of clay while I sat in a nearby canvas chair trying very hard to keep from falling asleep. The wild night of banging shutters plus my fears over a possible intruder had kept me awake part of the night and little progress had been accomplished at my easel today because I felt more and more fatigued. Anyway, my mind is too scattered; mostly, if I think at all, I dwell on the recent incidents, the faux attempt at kidnapping, and our insecurity. My painting has become unimportant in relation to everything else, especially to Tommy's safety.

The gulls circle and dive above us in the blue sky, watching and hoping that we have come down to the shore to feed them. Though naturally I need to think of getting Tommy back to Holland in time for the beginning of school, I wonder if, because of the recent scary incidents, it might be a smart idea to send him home earlier than planned...just as a precaution of course...perhaps a whole week earlier, maybe even two. Far too many scary things are happening here lately including the mean man incident, the breather calls, and the Jimmy Jay prank. Yet, if I send Tommy back to Holland, how would it feel to be here without him? Lonely, of course, but I also know that

I'll get a lot more painting done if I don't have his well-being nagging at my conscience.

It wouldn't be fair to foist Tommy's care onto his grandpa for too long a period, so I realized that I couldn't prolong my stay here at the cottage much beyond a week after Tommy was sent home. Also, I had commitments. On the way down state to Holland, I needed to veer off my usual route to pick up two of my paintings, one in Lansing and one in Grand Rapids, unless by some lucky chance they had been sold and the checks were on their way to me in the mail.

As Tommy continues to dig clay out in the shallow water, I simply doze off until he accidentally splashes cold water on my legs from his clay bucket and wakes me up. "Hey, be careful."

"Sorry, Mom. Can we sift out the sand now?"

Together we try to get as much of the sand out of the clay as possible by pouring off the top water and letting the heavier reddish clay sink to the bottom of the bucket. The clay isn't pure enough to make commercial products but that doesn't matter to Tommy who only wants to create funny animal shapes and bake them in the hot sun on the beach. It's soothing to my spirit to squeeze and pummel the reddish clay through my hands as I compete against Tommy to make my animal figures funnier or more grotesque than his.

Later, after we finish, our clay figures and leave them to dry, in the sun near the back porch, Tommy asks if we can go swimming and take Stevie.

"Good idea."I want to leave Tommy on an upbeat note. "I'll wait right here by the road for you.

"Mom, couldn't you come a little closer to the front porch? I don't want to go alone."

"Yes, I can do that." I concede willingly, knowing the fear that still lurks in Tommy after the kidnapping.

I listen to Tommy's footsteps as he runs up on the Lewis' front porch and hear him knock on the door. Then I hear Stevie's voice telling Tommy that he can't play with him anymore.

"Oh. Not ever?"

"That's what my mom says."

Only seconds later Tommy comes running back down the porch steps to tell me, "He says he can't play with me anymore."

"Not at all? Maybe he has to go somewhere today with his mother."

"No, he says he can't play with me anymore, not ever."

"Did you have an argument or a fight last time you saw him?"

Tommy shook his head. "We didn't fight or nothing."

Then a thought occurs to me. "Which church do the Lewises attend?"

"Heck, I don't know. Not ours I guess. At least I've never seen Stevie in Sunday school."

Can it possibly be that my reputation as music-killer has traveled this far up the beach, west, as well as east? What has that ornery little priest been doing... broadcasting an announcement about me and my canvassing against the loud music straight from the pulpit every Sunday? Poor Tommy. Stevie is his only playmate up here at the beach this summer.

"Mom?" Tommy is still looking at me, waiting for an answer to the puzzle of why his only friend doesn't want to see him anymore.

"I'm sure it's only temporary. Stevie is still your friend. Let's go swimming anyway. The high waves will be lots of fun today." Perhaps, I tell myself, we'll be lucky and find someone Tommy's age already at the beach. I make Tommy a placating offer. "We can take some orange soda with us and stay a bit longer than usual." Tommy isn't allowed soda very often, so I hope to cheer him up with this promise of a treat.

"All right," Tommy agrees, but his voice lacks its usual bounce of enthusiasm. Longingly, he adds, "I sure wish Peter would hurry back."

I am wishing exactly the same thing, but for an entirely different reason.

After swimming with me, Tommy does find some children close to his own age to play ball with on the shore. Perhaps he's a bit more subdued after yesterday's trauma, yet he seems to be enjoying himself.

After returning from the swimming beach, Tommy hangs up our bathing suits and towels on the clothesline while I get supper and listen to a short newscast on the radio. The news is all about some Slovakian commanders who are on trial for slaughtering over two hundred prisoners and leaving them in shallow graves. "My God," I think, "just because the people are Muslims?" Naturally I do not concur with some of the radical, religious groups, but those prisoners of war in Bosnia, as far as I knew, were just family folks trying to protect their homes from the Slovak aggressors.

Hundreds of years of supposed civilization and still people were unable to tolerate someone else's ethnic background… much less their religion. Obviously, the smattering of history that I studied in college never sank in very deeply or I'd be less surprised by the present conflicts. Staunchly, I tell myself, religion is supposed to stir up people to become more Christ-like or Mohammed-like, Buddha-like, or whatever. It's supposed to make us more tolerant and loving. Instead, it riles people up to hate or, as in Tommy's case where his friend Stevie's mother was concerned, a narrow-minded avoidance.

By eleven o'clock, usually my own bedtime, it became even windier outside. The air became cooler and crispier, almost fall-like. Shutters squeaked and bumped, waves drew back from the shore with a loud, rattle-bones sound and then boomed back in again. It's what I always termed "two-blanket" weather and usually my favorite…but not this night. Tonight I wanted to be able to hear a car or footsteps approaching the cottage, that is, if there were any. Unfortunately I couldn't hear anything over the constant pounding of the surf and the straining of the old shutters against their metal hooks.

I kept my light on until nearly one-thirty. I'm reading an Anita Shreve novel but the plot of the story isn't making too much sense, and it's not the author's fault. The words are recorded by my eyes as usual but they leave no imprint on my brain, because at the same time that I'm reading, I am also listening with my ears for the sounds of a car stopping in the road or the stealth of footsteps near the cottage. Who could have predicted that a simple little request to have the volume of the bells lowered would whip-up so much senseless animosity in others... and so much fear on my part. I simply could not get to sleep.

Suddenly there is a tremendous bam! Pillage, sleeping in Tommy's room, howled-out once followed by a long drawn-out whimper. I felt like I'd swallowed a rubber ball and it had become stuck somewhere just above my stomach.

I looked at my bedside clock. One forty-five. My legs were stiff from fear, but I slowly lower them like landing gear from the high bed to the rag rug on the floor and forced myself to creep slowly down the hallway. I listened at the top of the stairs and then ventured a bit further down to the first landing were I peered into the dark living room. A black image with straight edges loomed up clearly against the window at the bottom of the stairs. It was a shutter. It had come unhooked from its eye. What a relief!

Rather than put on my jacket over my pajamas and go out into the windy, branch-beating night, I decided to let it go until morning. I doubted that the bumping sounds of the loose shutter would waken Tommy. Satisfied that it was not an intruder, I tiptoed back to Tommy's door, avoiding the place in the wooden floor that creaked so dreadfully. "It's all right," I whispered in a soothing voice to Pillage through the door. Finally, about two in the morning, I fell asleep.

CHAPTER 23

*T*ommy performs his usual morning task of taking Pillage out to the road and along our cedar tree hedge so that the dog can do his duties. Suddenly, Tommy returns running. Immediately, I become alarmed by the strange expression on his face.

"Mom, the trees... something's happened to them. They're all crooked."

Those cedar trees by the road had been planted years ago by my father and kept trimmed to a fairly regulation height of six feet. Earlier this year I had climbed a ladder to help him clip the long green branches that reached too close to the road. The blue-green berries that clung in clusters had been so lush and numerous that it seemed almost a crime to trim the branches back so harshly. Sometime I thought, I'll get around to painting those berries in one of my paintings. I might mix yellow azo and hooker green with a pinch of blue to make the berries look tender and translucent.

Together, Tommy and I hurry out to the road. "Oh!" I hear myself gasp. Suddenly I understand so well that old cliché, "wringing her hands." It's exactly what I find myself doing, as well as crying out in anger. "How could someone do this?"

Several of the trees are bent completely over; one is totally snapped off. What happened is plain to see. The deep ruts made by a car or a pick-up truck are clearly visible in the soft dirt of the road. The slaughter of the trees had been done deliberately. Whoever did it shifted into forward, and then intentionally backed up into the trees again and again. Finally, the person must have straightening up the vehicle and headed down the road in the opposite direction from which they had come.

It hurt me to see the white tree roots so meanly snapped in two pieces, after being wrenched from the moist earth.

"Up here, too," Tommy shouts to me from the other end of the tree hedge. Even though I'm standing at the opposite end of the row, I can see two more mutilated trees. No sane person would choose this sharply curved section of the road to turn his car or truck around... and no one would do it twice. The incident had been intentional... a planned act of vandalism.

Tommy shakes his head; his voice sounds disdainful. "Someone sure doesn't know how to drive! What're we going to do, Mom?"

"Get some sticks and prop up the trees."

"This one's broken into two pieces."

"We can't save that one, but maybe the rest can be propped back up."

"I'll get the sticks," Tommy says.

"Bring the shovel too." I begin stomping the earth back around the roots of one tree while Tommy puts the dog back inside the cottage, then runs to the shed for the shovel and sticks.

Up until now, I have been certain that the resentment towards me over the bells would run down like the mechanism of gears and weights in our old-fashioned cottage clock. None of my actions recently should have begun winding up the clock weights again, figuratively speaking, but the harassment obviously continues. Propping up trees with sticks is one thing, but my growing apprehension needs far more. What about the possibility of broken bones, not roots? What about the chilling idea of a rock thrown at Tommy's head? I look around furtively, wondering if, even now, Tommy and I are being watched and judged.

That same evening after Tommy had gone to bed around ten o'clock, the telephone rang. Surely, it would be my father, I thought, since I hadn't talked with him for several days. Anyway, I should have called him earlier to tell him about the damaged trees. Of course, dreading it, I put-off telling him the bad news. Now I must face-up. I pick up the phone. "Hello." There is no cheerful fatherly voice on the line. No voice at all.

"Hello?" I repeat again. Dead silence comes across except for light breathing. Then the caller clicks down the receiver at the other end. I no longer try to placate myself with the simple explanation that the phone calls are just wrong numbers or glitches from a cell phone. They aren't.

Am I being overly paranoid? No, I don't believe so... not after all the other mean things that have been happening lately.

I shiver and slip my arms into my sweater. But, of course the chilly air has little to do with my sudden shaking. The cause of my huddled body, arms across my chest is unadulterated fear. I am fear-struck... as immobilized by the recent occurrences as Tommy was during his kidnapping a few days ago. If last night someone backed into the trees along the road without my actually hearing it happen, what further acts will that person or persons think up to keep my adrenaline high? Something even more damaging than broken trees could happen tonight unless I am more vigilant.

Could the purpose of the spook phone call simply be to discover whether the cottage was still occupied before striking out at me again? Thank goodness Tommy is in bed because I'm not good at fooling him. It wouldn't take a divining rod for him or anyone else to detect that something more had happened to instill fear in me.

Now, right tonight, I'm in a quandary... what should I do? What is the expedient thing to do? Should I stay up all night with the fireplace poker by my bedside? How defenseless we are! For the first time I wish I had Roger's shotgun or something to scare away intruders.

It's only a bit past ten o'clock right now and still not solidly dark on the water-side of the cottage, but I can only guess at the unknown shapes in the back yard. Are the black humps really bushes or is one of them a person? I become more and more jittery as the hours pass and it grows closer to midnight. I can't circle the cottage with a stockade wall like the nearby fort or man the ramparts with guns. I feel so vulnerable—totally exposed to some unknown person, who could be mentally ill or just temporarily out of control. He could be making plans right this minute to take us by surprise.

I speak firmly to myself. "Leah, you must not panic." That command is about as useful as telling Tommy not to be afraid of lightning. Finally, when I do go to bed, I decide to sleep on the couch in the living room for the night with the heavy black encrusted fireplace poker handy on the floor at my side. I know that I won't get much sleep.

CHAPTER 24

"Are things getting more and more out of control?" I ask myself. Naturally I am deeply upset over the ruined trees and also the mean behavior of Father Ciconni and the Tribners, but now my greatest fear is the pugilistic man, the one who accosted Tommy and me along the road two evenings ago. The man is big and mean. I take his threats seriously. His wrestler's body and jutting chin alone promote the feeling of danger. It happened the same evening that Jimmy Jay tried to harm Tommy by locking him in the dirty old house next to the library. I'm not worried about Jimmy Jay interfering again since supposedly the police chief had a candid discussion with him and his mother over the treatment of Tommy.

The telephone call that came last night also raised my anxiety to a new higher level. Still, I quickly attempted to reason with myself. There were no threats... none at all... made by the phone caller. Even so, I'm not going to take chances. I don't want Tommy and me to become religious martyrs, not over the issue of noise pollution, which should have absolutely nothing to do with one's choice of religion. "The harassing incidents are definitely accelerating though. I whisper out loud to the empty room, "Someone still might try to hurt Tommy just to get even with me." That's exactly what terrifies me most...my son being hurt. I make the firm decision to send Tommy home two whole weeks earlier than planned.

All day long, after discovering the torn trees, I had wasted time by running to the back cottage windows when I heard people walking along the dirt road behind the cottage. The rest of the time I spent looking out the windows on the beach side of the cottage to make sure of Tommy's whereabouts.

Between bouts of running to the windows, I think about doing a painting that's a clear departure from my usual ones. I'm heeding what Lin Yutang, a Chinese philosopher, said about art: *Art should be a satire and a warning against our paralyzed emotions, our devitalized thinking and our denaturalized living.* None of my paintings fulfill that idea and perhaps never will. Still, a new idea does enter my head. My next picture might depict just a shell of an old church, and torn hangings attached to a remaining arch or two.

In the middle of the morning, Tommy calls upstairs to tell me that he's going to ride his bicycle up to the beach store. I was happy to see that it hadn't taken very long to restore Tommy's confidence after the trauma of being locked up. I, however, still didn't feel at all secure.

"I wish you'd wait until later, Tommy." I put down my brush and picked up a palette knife. What can I say to dissuade him? I don't want to promote fear in him, yet I'm reluctant to let him out of my sight.

"Why wait?" Tommy argues from half way up the stair landing. "You've always let me ride my bicycle up the road to the beach store before. Why can't I do it this time?" I perceive a new tendency of Tommy to argue.

"Just wait a minute," I try to stall him and then decide that I could use a break in painting even though I've accomplished very little today. "I'm going with you." In my haste I flip the sharp palette knife against the side of my hand and draw blood. Quickly I grab a paper towel and wrap it around my hand and drop my brush into a jar of water. As I slip off my painting shirt, I call down to Tommy, "I need some…" but what excuse can I think up? I check the small bleeding cut on my hand. "Well, some bandaids for one thing and some milk." I had used our last band aids on Tommy's waist where Jimmy Jay had wrapped the rusty old wire around him.

Tommy and I rode our bikes the quarter-mile to the store without meeting even one person. For that I was thankful. I no longer felt comfortable meeting people. They could so easily be the very folks who were harassing me. How am I to know? This situation wasn't the same as a movie where the good guys and the bad guys were clearly scripted.

At the little store with its narrow aisles and limited merchandise, Mr. Perkins, the storekeeper whose garrulousness is usually about baseball, doesn't even smile at us. I am tense, perceiving or imagining the heavy atmosphere of bad feelings pushing against me. I already know that Mr. Perkins attends the church with the obnoxiously loud bell music, but even if I did not know, I could easily have guessed it from Mr. Perkin's disapproving, sparse-of-speech attitude.

"Mom can I have a licorice?"

"Yes." I pay for the overpriced milk. There are no bandages of any sort on the shelves. Tommy pays for his own candy, and then I fairly drag him away from the rack that's displaying sports cards.

"Hey, what's the big hurry?" he asks.

"I want to get back to work on my painting. OK? Let's go." I urge him out the door.

On our ride back we are just approaching the Ostler cottage when Mr. Ostler jolts us to a stop by popping out from between his tall hedge just as he had done once before. He even repeats the identical waving signal of his arm.

Now what nasty thing have we done, I wonder to myself? For no logical reason I feel anger erupting even before I know why he's waving us to a stop.

"My wife told me about your petition against the bell noise..."

"... not exactly a petition."

"Anyway, I reminded her that the rumor about the old bell cracking might be just that...only a rumor. It was never proven, so I thought you might want to talk to the caretaker, Bill Growgood, an Ottawa Indian. Only now they like to be called Odawa Indians,

I guess. Last I heard, he lived over in the Indian Village. You know where that is?

I nod. "Do you have an address?"

Mr. Ostler shook his head. "But it's merely a village. Everyone knows everyone else. Just ask."

"Thanks for the information. I'll check it out." In fact, I feel spurred-on to doing it right this afternoon. Then my depressed mood takes over again and I sigh. Why get too excited. The caretaker probably doesn't know anything that will prove the rumor one way or another.

On the half block back to the cottage after talking to Mr. Ostler, I mull over the new information. What if the retired caretaker actually does know something? Just suppose the rumor about the cracked bell is absolutely untrue and the bell is still intact. That would mean that someone at the church was being less than honest simply because they wanted an excuse to install the electronic system. It could mean that someone has purposely lied to the diocese.

Tommy has gone ahead of me and is waiting on the back porch for me to unlock the door and let Pillage out. "Tommy let's go to the Indian Village for lunch."

"Yeah? Great! I'm sick of peanut butter. Do you think that store where they had the beaded Indian belts might still be there?"

"Maybe." I recalled the last time we were there and how Tommy had teased for one of the expensive belts. Oh dear. What was I letting myself in for? Obviously, major, big time teasing.

The village had a French name, L'Arbre Croche, but everyone I know simply called it the Indian Village. We travel part of the distance on the same road we had taken to the Fenville carnival, the one with its delightful roller coaster hills and woodsy scenery. When we pass the cemetery with its tilted memorial stones, I know we are close to the village outskirts. We haven't visited the village this year so I look forward to the view over the bluff and across the water to the Beaver group of islands in the distance.

We have lunch at a tiny café and afterwards ask the waiter where Bill Growgood lives.

"You can't miss his place. In fact you must have passed it on your way into the village. It's a trailer, painted on one side with a scene of blue sky or water. Ask over at the filling station or the art gallery if you can't find it."

"There's an art gallery now?"

"Oh sure. We've got a lot of tourists coming here now."

Tommy interrupts. "Growgood? How could someone get a name like that?"

"He got tagged with the name because generations of his family probably grew corn or other produce and sold it in the towns nearby, maybe even to the fort over there in Tatterack way back in the seventeen hundreds."

Tommy lost interest in the name and immediately asked, "Is that store, the one with the Indian stuff still here?" He wasn't going to let me off the hook.

"That's gone now," the café owner said. I heave a sigh of relief until the man adds, "... but the art gallery might have a few Indian crafts."

"Thanks, we'll check it out." I speak firmly in Tommy's ear, "First we find the caretaker." We drive back to the filling station and they verify that Bill's trailer is the one with scenery painted on it and hang gliders for rent. We find it easily. Bill is outside kneeling on the grass patching a colorful sail. I could easily imagine the thrill of jumping off the top of the sand dunes located a few miles up the shore and drifting slowly down over the beach. The trailer is painted in vivid shades of sky blue and depicts a person sailing across it under a hot pink and green glider.

Bill looks short and sturdy, not anywhere near retirement age. Do Indians age less obviously, I wonder? Intermarriage has probably long ago sifted out most of the expected Indian features because I don't see any except the long dark hair. I apologize to him for not being there to rent a glider.

"Something else you want?"

"I heard that you no longer work at the church in Tatterack, but maybe you remember that rumor about the bell?"

"Maybe." he sounded cautious.

"About six years ago there was a rumor about some boys cutting the bell rope in the church tower and letting the bell drop. Was it true?" It seemed like I waited a long time for him to answer.

"Just rumor. You live anywhere near Chet?"

"Chet? You mean Mr. Lumus? Yes, how did you know?"

"Just guessing. Him and me belong to the same band. He plays guitar and I play..."

I watch as Bill digs in his jean pocket, pulls out a harmonica and waves it.

"Chet and me, we're recording band music and scary voices for entertainment at the Vets Halloween shin-dig."

I try to bend the conversation back to the bell subject. "Then that old rumor about the bell rope being cut is false?"

"Yeah. The bell still hangs in the tower. Back then I climbed the ladder to check on the bell. Took a flashlight with me...didn't see any crack...didn't see why the bell couldn't be rung. I told the Father so. Of course, it could probably use a new rope by now."

"Did you tell your friend Chet?"

"The Father said to keep my mouth shut, but that was years ago. Don't expect it matters now."

I asked again. "Did you tell your friend?"

"Might-of."

"Thank you, Mr. Growgood." Inwardly, I feel like crowing. Now I really have some grist to put into my letter to the archbishop. I feel an urge to rush right back to the cottage and write my letter, but Tommy has to be placated first so we go back down the road and stop at the art gallery for a few minutes. The gallery has no beaded belts, thank heavens, just some of those miniature birch bark canoes, each one about an inch and a half long. They immediately catch Tommy's eye.

"I can use them to float down the canals I make on the beach. I'll need at least two." Tommy said, "Three would be even better."

"Two will have to do." The rest of the gallery has watercolors, some very good, some fair, a few glass paperweights, porcupine quill boxes, notepaper, Maple syrup and maple candy, and various other homemade items. It's worth viewing more carefully, but I am in a great hurry. I am so fired up by this new slant on the bells that I give the gallery far less attention than it deserves.

"Let's come back again soon," I tell Tommy as I urge him closer to the outside door.

"We didn't have any dessert after lunch," Tommy complains.

"You're right, but you have two canoes instead and you have some licorice at home."

"Yeah, that's true," he concedes, but... I..."

I hustle him past the maple candy on display and out the door.

On the way back to Tatterack I write the letter in my head—between Tommy's chatter—to the diocese. After we reach the cottage, I quickly put this new slant regarding the undamaged bell on paper in a manner of minutes. Then I reread it several times just to be sure it clearly states the facts as I have just learned them. Then Tommy and I ride our bikes uptown to mail the letter. Surely this letter will convince the diocese to pressure the church into either lowering the volume or in reinstating the old bell. I hope for the later.

CHAPTER 25

*T*hat night I move permanently into the spare bedroom facing the south side of the cottage. It has two windows; one faces the east side of the cottage and one looks out over the back yard and the road. In my usual bedroom on the front of the cottage, I can hear only the in and out rhythmic movement of the water, a sound I dearly love. No longer though, because the sounds of waves ramping up tonight will cover-up all the other night sounds.

From the back bedroom I can monitor cars on the road if they slow down and I might be able to hear stealthy footsteps across the back porch or the crackling of bushes near the garden. Pillage sleeps in Tommy's room, which is also on the waterside of the cottage, so I can only partially count on him as an alarm if an intruder should enter the cottage from the back.

I wait until Tommy is asleep to make my move into the other bedroom, because I don't want him to suspect how worried I am. There is no need to alarm him unduly. Again, I can't get to sleep until nearly dawn on Friday. Then I oversleep until Pillage's barking wakes me with his need to be let outdoors.

I blither through the day on cups of coffee. My eyelids are swollen and red, and my thinking is as slow as a recovering stroke victim's movements. At four-thirty when I should have been thinking about fixing supper for Tommy and myself, I accidentally doze off in the rocking chair in the living room. That's where I still repose at five-thirty when Tommy slams the back screen door and jubilantly announces: Peter is back! Not only has he come back, but he saunters into the room and smiles down at me. I am only half awake so I don't smile back, but Peter doesn't seem to take it personally. Instead, he sits down in a chair opposite me.

"Thomas has been telling me about some unusual things going on around here. Something about being tied up in a house, the one next door to the library, a red faced man shouting at you and broken trees along the road?"

Pulling myself out of my lethargic state is like trying to pull my feet out of a sucking clay hole in the lake in front of the cottage. A sudden quickening in my stomach reminds me of Peter's close physical influence.

"Want to talk about it?" Peter asks sociably.

I nod again. Do I ever! It will feel like such a relief, like sliding my fears down the off-ramp of a highway if such a thing were possible. But should I? Hadn't I learned from past experience that *telling all* was tantamount to giving Roger license to direct me... to plot my course? Roger had always told me what to do whether I liked it or not. Along with his gratuitous advice there always came an equal obligation to follow his directions explicitly or he would become short tempered with me. Be reasonable, I tell myself, Peter is not Roger. Peter is quite different. Finally I give him a belated weak smile.

"Tommy, check out the beach, will you please? I think I hear a flock of geese, and you know what messes they make. Scare them off. Do you think you can?"

"Poop patrol on the way! Be right back." Tommy bounces out of the room and I take the opportunity to quickly tell Peter about my disasterous visit to the church and the drunken Tribners. Finally I tell him about the latest incidents: the angry man and the broken trees and how Jimmy Jay had tied Tommy up. I skip telling him about the strange phone calls because none have taken place today, not so far. I wait for Peter to give me advice, to hear him say firmly, as Roger would under the same circumstances, "You should give up your fight against the loud bells," but he doesn't say that at all.

"You've had a rough two weeks."

I expect Peter to give me pejorative advice, to hear him say firmly, as Roger would under the circumstances, "You should give up your fight against the loud bells," but Peter doesn't say that at all.

"You did report all those incidents to the police, didn't you?" I nod, but of course I hadn't told the police about every single one.

"Why should you feel guilty about the Tribner incident? You know perfectly well that you didn't steal the tape. None of it was your fault." Peter stood up and gave me a gentle pat on the shoulder. "Right now let's help you get your mind off those narrow-minded people. Mother and I want to take you and Thomas out to dinner tonight."

I start to demure. I am so very tired.

"Now don't' turn me down. I'm only going to be here for the weekend, and I'm determined to make the most of it."

"Now exactly what does that mean?" I ask in a teasing voice? Already I feel better.

"It means that I'm going to hang around and take up ever single minute of your time. No one else will even get a chance to get near you. Not the bad guys or the good ones."

Peter's declaration warms me and I even manage a hesitant smile. "Thanks for the dinner invitation, but maybe you'll have to prod and pinch me every now and then to keep me awake. "Where is Tommy? Why didn't he come right back?" I spin out of the chair and turn to the window facing the shore. Suddenly I am fully, completely awake.

Peter laughs at my display of panic. "Because he's engrossed in skipping stones. Relax. He's coming up the path right now."

"Sorry. I'm easily spooked these days. Someone could hurt Tommy just to get at me... to retaliate." Tommy comes back inside the cottage and promptly besieges Peter, begging him for another sailboat ride.

"That's a good idea, Thomas," Peter quietly subdues Tommy, "but let's see how the weather is first. Right now, you and your mom need to spruce up for dinner."

I push at the hank of hair that keeps falling over one eye and look down at my paint-splattered shirt. Suddenly I realize how unkempt I must appear to Peter. Actually, except for the addition of circles under my eyes, it isn't much different from the way I always look at the end of a day of painting. I bend over to retrieve my shoes, which have been kicked off under the chair.

"Pick you up in half an hour?" Peter asks.

"We'll be ready... unless I fall asleep again."

During the course of our whitefish dinner at the Darby Inn that evening, I remark to Peter and his mother, "Tommy and I did some detective work at the Indian Village yesterday by interviewing Mr. Growgood who was once the caretaker over at the church. According to him, it was just a rumor about the bell being cut down. He claims the bell wasn't damaged at all, but Father Ciconni had told him to keep it hush-hush."

"So the rumor might have been started just so the Father could have a good excuse to install the electronic bell system?" Peter quickly drew the same conclusion as I had.

"Just a rumor?" Peter's mother looks inquiringly at her son. "Didn't you know one of the boys who said they cut the rope?"

"You mean, Jason? No... well, it was his younger brother I knew."

Had Peter been holding out information? Besides not telling me that he personally knew one of the boys whose older brother claimed to have cut the bell down? Was there more he could have told me? Did Peter know all along that the bell wasn't cracked and just let me go on wasting my time with the door to door canvassing? If he even guessed that the rumor was false, he should have confided in me.

Bluntly, I ask, "Were you also one of the boys who climbed into the tower?"

"Me? No. Those were boys four or five years older."

"Some friends!" his mother retorts.

"But you weren't living here then, so how could...."

Mrs. Sjoberg interrupted, "... for years we rented that stone cottage near the stockade before buying Summer Place," she explained.

On the way back from our dinner Peter stops the car at his mother's cottage. I note with pleasure how many Hosta blossoms are still in bloom in her garden even though fall is approaching. Mrs. Sjoberg invites Tommy and me inside, but I decline. "Thanks, some other time perhaps." Peter then walks with us the half block onwards to Fleury cottage. It isn't quite dark outside yet, just dusky now at eight-thirty, whereas a week earlier it didn't get dark until nine. Peter doesn't really need to see us safely to our door, but I am greatly appreciative of his careful attitude.

"How about a hike tomorrow morning out on Follow Tree Point?" Peter suggests.

"Me too?" Excitement comes alive in Tommy's voice.

"You too, absolutely."

After Peter says goodnight and leaves, Tommy drags out our backpacks and eagerly plans exactly what each of us will carry on the hike. "I'll carry my own bottled water, a compass, and the first aid kit," he declares.

There really is no need for the compass since we will be following the shoreline and can't get lost, but I don't discourage him. After all, carrying a compass is an excellent habit to promote. Tommy allocates the carrying of the sandwiches and towels to me in case we want to go swimming. We assign Peter, though he doesn't know it yet, the job of carrying the small cooler for the juice and beer.

"Isn't Pillage coming, too?"

"Dogs aren't allowed out there, at least not during plover nesting season. I'm not even sure that people are allowed. Anyway, it's best to leave Pillage home. You wouldn't want Pillage to frighten the baby birds, would you?"

"Guess not."

"Off to bed, you go. You'll need all your energy for tomorrow." I have no trouble convincing Tommy about an early bedtime because he's so eagerly looking forward to our hike with Peter; I would be too ... except ... I have strong suspicions over Peter's failure of communication concerning the bell.

Why hadn't Peter been more forthright, more open about his friends, the ones who evidently knew something about the bell? Were there additional things about the church and the rumor about the bell that Peter wasn't telling me?

CHAPTER 26

*P*eter stops by the cottage to pick us up the next morning at eleven o'clock, and we drive about ten miles out to the park office where Peter pays for a one-day permit to hike in the area.

After we pass by the small fishing village, we leave the paved section of the road and follow the long winding dirt road the remainder of the way. It's dark in the dense woods of tall pines, birch, oaks and many fallen and uprooted trees. Tommy quips, "Will someone please turn the lights back on?" Peter switches on the car headlights and we creep slowly down the single lane road. There is no room to meet cars coming from the opposite direction except where a turnout has been cleared between fallen trees and stumps for that purpose. We edge along slowly, quietly, and peer into the deep woods as though trying to make out shapes in a night scene.

I tell Tommy, "Keep watching out the window for deer. Sometimes we see them along here." Finally we reach an open sunny area with fewer trees, and the land begins to thin out and truly become a point projecting out into the water. This is where Peter stops and parks his car. There's a wooden outhouse nearby so I ask Tommy if he needs to use it. He shakes his head, so we make our way through the deep sand towards the shore ahead where we begin our hike.

"Let's try to get all the way out to the end of the point this time," Tommy urges.

"I'm not sure we can," Peter tells him doubtfully. "Sometimes there's an island at the very end. It all depends on the height of the water each year. Also, the current may be too swift for us to wade to the very last section."

"Awww, we never get very far."

"We'll go as far as we can," I placate Tommy. Then I ask Peter, completely forgetting to take into consideration his male pride, "Will it tire your ankle to walk so far?" I recall how white and fragile his bare ankle appeared on the day we went sailing.

"It's strong in spite of its appearance," Peter replies stiffly. After a pause he adds, "I don't like to be worried over. That's what my mother has been doing for years ever since the polio."

"Sorry." I didn't dare broach the subject again for fear of hurting Peter's feelings.

"It's all right. By now I shouldn't be so touchy on the subject. I apologize."

I nod my acceptance of his apology. We begin trekking along the sandy shoreline. Just inland, behind us, are more sand rills backed by wild juniper bushes and a scattering of grotesquely shaped evergreen trees. The trees, though shorter and smaller than most along the Michigan shore, seem to thrive in spite of being swept by the harsh winds and bitter cold which sweeps across the narrow piece of land in winter.

My son keeps forging on ahead and at first refuses to slow up, but Peter and I finally prevail and Tommy stops, reluctantly, to take a lunch break with us. Already, we have walked over a half-mile. The cool weather is perfect for hiking but trudging through the heavy sand makes it more tiring. We find one of the numerous washed-up logs to sit on and eat our lunch.

I let Tommy explore the shore nearby while Peter and I rest a bit longer. I watch the sunlight flicker and dart, quick as little silver minnows, across the shallow lake bottom. When I drag my hand through the cold water, it literally nips at the tips of my fingers.

Tommy fills his fists with the stones he finds and brings them back for us to admire. I myself fail to resist the pretty stones and pebbles in the edge of the clear, icy water. These are different from the white limestones so prevalent in front of the cottages. These are more varied, colorful, tossed around and smoothed down by the fierce gyrations of the water, the scrubbing action of the sand, and also by the stones themselves rubbing against each other. Follow Tree Point sticks out into the vast open water of Lake Michigan and takes the full brunt of the wind and wave action.

Soon both Tommy and I give up trying to keep our sneakers dry in our hunt for the most unusual stones. Tommy is grabbing all the red and orange stones and I'm collecting the green ones. Peter removes his hiking boots, ties the laces together and slings the boots over his shoulder, then joins us barefoot. An occasional grimace on his face attests to his tender feet as we head on towards the point, mostly walking in the shallow water where there are now more stones than sand. Tommy's backpack is becoming heavier and heavier with the weight of his favorite stone specimens. Peter and I stash ours inside the cooler where they rattle around loudly as they joust and bang against the empty cans of beer and juice.

We stop to rest a second time, but Tommy with his excessive energy keeps right on going. "Stop now and wait for us," I call out, trying to sound firm without sounding overly bossy.

"It's been years since I've been out here," Peter tells me, looking around at the land behind us. "Once, two other kids and myself camped out here overnight. Back in there somewhere," Peter points inland, "somewhere near a group of scraggly trees. Our fathers brought us out here and picked us up the next day. None of us slept at all. There were so many noises."

"Noises, way out here?"

"Owls, cracking of the brush, deer, maybe bear, and also what we imagined as footsteps of ghost Indians. We lay there awake all night in our sleeping bags holding our flashlights ready and our hunting knives within reach."

"So has that early experience quelled your camping enthusiasm?"

"Hardly." Peter laughs. "Every fall a group of friends and I go hiking and camping. Peter's voice exudes enthusiasm, "This year we're going canoeing up on the Boundary Waters near Ely, Minnesota. Up there, folks have long been fighting another type of pollution…a critical one. A certain faction of people want larger power boats on the Boundary Waters and the other faction, folks like myself, don't want the solitude spoiled by the noise or by oily emissions from the motors. Most of us go up there to get away from urban noise and smells."

"Will you try to do something about it?"

"Write letters to influence people. Also, give money where it might help."

"It's obvious that you like boating. I noticed all those model boats in your mother's cottage. It must have taken a lot of patience putting all those small pieces together. Is that what you do in your spare time?"

"Make model boats?" Peter laughs. "I wish! Those models were made years ago. Seems like there's very little of that 'spare time' commodity anymore." Peter sighs. "Besides the job, I'm also on the Allegan town commission. More meetings… more decisions."

I smile knowingly, remembering the pattern of how Roger always joined everything. Making contacts are important, he always claimed. In fact, I don't want to know any more about Peter or his personal life. It really doesn't matter whether I approve of Peter's activities or not since I'm not in the market for a new boyfriend. Nor do I consider myself, like some women, just treading time between marriages… hoping to meet a man who can fill a void. I am far more fortunate than many divorcees who have a child to support; I have a home. My father is delighted to have Tommy and me board with him. We take turns cooking and caring for Tommy. With the exception of a half-dozen vivid explicatives that my father uses from habit and have been assimilated by Tommy, all runs smoothly. I have a roof over my head so I assiduously avoid asking myself if I need anything else in my life right now.

Peter interrupts my thoughts. "Forgive my probing, but I think it's quite normal for a guy like me to wonder why a woman like you—extremely nice looking and very personable—decides to part ways with her husband?"

His question, though asked in a low-key non-challenging tone of voice, is like dust scuffed up by a shoe. It circles and stirs up all sorts of things in my head that are better left dormant. It wipes out the camaraderie and ease I had enjoyed just minutes before. Still, I should have anticipated the question arising sooner or later. "I... we... I made a poor choice, that's all."

"And you absolutely do not plan to let that happen again." Peter's facial expression is not hard to read.

"No, never again." Is Peter passing judgment on my present lifestyle or what?

"You plan to live the rest of your life with your father?"

"Possibly." I look at Peter's face and wonder if he is admonishing me.

"No father for Tommy?"

"He has a male roll model in his grandpa and occasionally in his own father." Actually, Roger has invited Tommy to visit him at his apartment less and less often recently. Does that mean Roger now has a girlfriend? Oh, I do hope so... fervently.

"No companionship for yourself; I refer to organizations, charities, boyfriends?"

I shrug and leave the question unanswered, though I could have told Peter quite definitely that there were no boyfriends. Naturally there are art organizations to which I belong and I do have a few companionable women friends. Enid is just one. I wish Peter hadn't broached the subject, because it makes my life sound like a desert when the cacti aren't blooming. Also, I feel guilty for not mixing socially with more married couples who have children, so that Tommy could have more friends his age.

In one swoop, Peter has hit upon two of my weaknesses: my reluctance to get involved in social functions and my wariness where men are concerned. But because of my crippling experiences with Roger, I believe the latter is more than justified.

Carefully, I avoid thinking too often about myself in regard to the future, but now that the subject has been opened, I ask myself: Will I be living the remainder of my life with my father? My father's total sphere is the two "C's": computer every day and cribbage every Saturday night. Years of hearing about both, is not too exciting a future to contemplate.

"Aren't you coming?" Tommy calls from further up the shore, and I realize that Peter and I have been standing here talking far longer than just a few minutes.

"Time moves on, and so has Tommy."

Holding Tommy back any longer is like telling Pillage not to chase a squirrel. We hike on, my soaked sneakers making squishy noises at every step. Before catching up with Tommy, I try to explain to Peter in defense of myself, "When one gets bitten, one tends to stay away from dogs."

"No," Peter states emphatically, "it's better to get over your trauma and meet a new dog, a nicer one."

I laugh, "Oh? And who is suppose to be a nicer dog?"

"Woof, woof," Peter retorts, brightly smiling.

In answer I also smile and quickly forge on ahead in an attempt to catch up with Tommy, or is it to put space between me and the evermore tempting *new dog?*

At last we face the swift current that runs between the last point of land and the island at the tip of Follow Tree Point. Tommy is elated that we have hiked this far. The seasonal height of the water this year seems very high so Peter and I see no point in taking a chance in attempting to wade through the gap of swift moving water that faces us.

Except for the momentary shadow cast by Peter's probing into my past and my future plans, we have a lovely, sometimes funny, day. All my anxiety over the electronic bells and the subsequent retaliations against me and Tommy have been left behind; even the headlines about Bosnia and Afghanistan are temporarily forgotten, washed away by the beautiful surroundings and Peter's cheerful company.

As we turn around to hike back along the same shore that we just followed a few minutes ago, I caution myself against becoming too complacent over having Peter around. Having his affable personality at beck and call would be a comfortable state in which to settle and also wonderfully habit forming. I suppose it's natural for me to depend more heavily upon Peter's kindness simply because folks in the beach colony are behaving so narrow-mindedly towards me. Yet, in the long run, wasn't it far safer to remain self-reliant? Besides, these associations never stay at just the "companionship" stage. They tend to either stop completely, causing an emotional rift, or go forward and become slippery and unmanageable affairs.

Later, back at the cottage, Peter sets the cooler on the back porch where we make two piles of our stones, his and mine. Then Tommy empties his backpack and makes a third pile of stones three times as high. "Don't you want to take yours home?" Tommy asks Peter.

"Just a couple of stones as a memento of a great hike. Our cottage doesn't have a wide back porch on which to stash treasures like yours."

I can hear Pillage barking and fretting inside the cottage to be let out, so as soon Peter leaves, I unlock the back door and Pillage immediately comes bursting out and begins jumping all over me, unusual behavior for him. Then, instead of running out into the yard to pee, he followed me back inside the cottage and around from window to window as I open them. "Let's get more fresh air in here," I mummer as I fling open the door on the beach side of the cottage. That's when I discover the damaged screen.

It's a long jagged slash. The cut is nowhere near the location of the hook, which would have allowed the person to release the screen door. From that fact I assume it wasn't anyone actually attempting to get inside or burglarize the cottage. Rather it appears to have been done for the sheer pleasure of maliciously destroying. It might also have been done to raise my fear level. That it has certainly achieved.

"Should I inform the police? But why bother." I hadn't called the police about the broken trees either because there were no clues, that is, no way for them or anyone else to trace the person who had done the damage. Maybe in a fictional mystery story a detective would have tried to match the tire treads to someone's pickup truck, but not here in Tatterack. As for the slashed screen door? There would be no clues left behind there either.

What had prompted the vandalism? I hadn't done anything further to anger anyone at the church or in the beach colony except to talk with Mr. Growgood. It certainly couldn't be the letter I had written to the diocese in which I had quoted what the former caretaker, Mr. Growgood, had divulged: *the rope on the bell had not been cut and he, after climbing up to the bell in the tower, had seen no cracks.* I had concluded the letter with the questions: *Why had the expensive electronic equipment been installed resulting in a waste of church money and also resulting in a much higher level of noise pollution?* There could be no repercussion from my letter, not yet. It had just been mailed two evenings before this one.

What a letdown after our wonderful, carefree day. I didn't tell Tommy anything about the slashed screen. Why frighten him. Now I am more determined than ever to send Tommy back to the safety of living with his grandfather in Holland, even if it is several weeks before school officially begins.

CHAPTER 27

*O*n an otherwise gorgeous morning, rich with evergreen scents and clean watery smells, the electronic music begins at eight forty-five. Because it's Sunday, the taped music begins fifteen minutes earlier than usual because of the nine o'clock mass. The medley of hymns blasts forth renting the curtain of morning for ten minutes. It seems far longer. than ten. At eleven o'clock the same medley is replayed. One hymn sounds much like *Go Tell Aunt Roady*, a Burl Ives folk song and another recalls the folk song, *On Top of Old Smokey*. Both are unlikely genuine hymns but are not unpleasant, but the decibel level is extremely high. It's at splitting headache level. I shudder, knowing that there will be at least two more of these exact renditions at noon and at six in the evening. Later, I discover that I am entirely wrong about the noon and six o'clock electronic music.

In the middle of our Sunday breakfast of waffles, Tommy clamps his hand over his sticky, maple syrupy mouth. "I forgot! Dad phoned last Friday afternoon while you were sleeping in the chair."

"You mean Grandpa?"

"No, I mean my dad, Roger. He wants to come up here some weekend. I told him all about our great sailboat ride and about Peter, too."

"But Tommy, you must not..." Abruptly, I close my mouth. How can I tell my son that he should not divulge anything of a personal nature about me to his own father? I can't, and I stop myself just in time. This news about Roger coming up to Tatterack is extremely upsetting. I don't want Roger visiting me at all, though he does have a right to see Tommy. "Did you tell your father that you have to return to Holland next week?"

"I do? Already?"

"Yes. It's almost school time again."

"Then I won't see dad?" Tommy's disappointment is obvious.

"I'll phone and tell him to visit you in Holland instead. It will be a much shorter drive for him than coming way up here."

"But he said he wanted to meet my new friend, Peter?"

"Peter might not be here next weekend. I'm not sure." I have to think of a subtle way to keep Roger from coming up here to the cottage. But exactly what?

Don't I have enough to depress me right now with these alarming retaliations going on without also having a visit from Roger as well? As far as our "new friend, Peter" is concerned, the humane thing to do is to insulate him completely from someone like Roger.

Oh how well I know Roger! As soon as he hears even whispers about another man in my life, he feels the immediate urge to get in touch with me…especially after learning from Tommy about the good times we've been having. What can I do to keep Roger from driving up here to the cottage to visit? Exactly what?

"Time to get dressed," I tell Tommy. As he heads for the stairs, I pick up my coffee cup and walk down to the shore to do my thinking alone and to see if anything new has washed up during the night. The sand has tiny dimples on it from a light sprinkle of rain early this morning. I sit down in the beach chair, nearly dry by now, to digest Roger's threat to visit and spoil my last few days of vacation. Perhaps if I tell Roger that I am sending Tommy home to Holland right away, it will undermine his excuse for coming up here to Tatterack to spy on me. The ploy is certainly worth a try.

Roger and I may be divorced but a mere legal document hasn't put a stop to his possessiveness. It's part of his innate nature to be jealous. Maybe after he finds himself another woman, I will be released from his web. I fervently hope so. Don't I have enough problems with Father

Ciconni and the retaliations to harass me right now without adding Roger to the list?

Just this last spring there had been an uncomfortable incident, a confrontation between Roger and me when Roger had unexpectedly shown up at a gallery exhibition in Holland where I had a one-woman show of my paintings. Roger had walked around the gallery chatting…introducing himself as my husband even though we were no longer married. He told everyone that he was the only person in my life who had inspired and guided me into painting, quite ignoring the fact that I had chosen my art major at the university long before we had met each other. Being sequestered in the same room at the gallery that evening with Roger had been a total embarrassment. Why, why couldn't he stay completely out of my life?

Today the noon concert from the church runs into overtime. It lasts nearly fifteen minutes instead of ten. The additional music is a complete surprise: *Yankee Doodle Dandy* and *America the Beautiful.* During the latter tune an unusual stuttering sound occurs. Either the electronic system is breaking down or the tape is wearing out. Both ideas give me a secret hope of squashing the fake bells.

That evening I phone my father and discuss with him my plan for sending Tommy home early. We agree to meet on Tuesday in the town of Cadillac, slightly more than half way down to Holland, a good place to transfer Tommy and the dog and also save each of us from making the full round trip.

Right after speaking to my father, I put in a call to Roger. Seldom do I communicate with him without misgivings. Roger answers the phone in a cheery drawl, "Helllooo." His tone of voice is equivalent to adding a creamy topping to his hello. I suppose not knowing who is going to be on the other end of the line, he answers in his most gracious manner. Now that he knows it's just me phoning, his voice quickly reverts to his normal one with a touch of sarcasm. "So," he begins before I can tell him about my plan to send Tommy back to Holland, "you've made yourself a new conquest."

"Not that I know of. Tommy is quite keen over Mr. Sjoberg because of the sailboat."

"And are you keen over him as well?"

"He is Tommy's friend." It's a partial lie, but I'd prevaricate a lot to keep Roger from getting his possessive streak into gear and whipping up here to snoop around in my life. Finally, I get a chance to tell him about sending Tommy home early. "He won't be here the weekend you're planning to come, so there's no sense in making the long drive up here to see him. You can just drive over to visit Tommy in Holland instead. It's a much shorter drive."

"Oh, I'm on to you, Leah. Why are you sending Tommy home early, more than two weeks before school starts, if it's not to get yourself a bit of leisure alone with your new beau?"

I ignore the baiting. "I have some paintings to finish up. Also, there won't be much room in the car for Tommy and the dog after I pick up additional art work from various galleries."

"I'd still like to come up there just to see the old place. It's been three years, though I don't suppose the cottage has changed much."

"It looks exactly the same except for a fresh coat of white paint." I wait, holding my breath. Have I been successful in discouraging him or not?

"I can see Tommy in Holland any time. It doesn't have to be that particular weekend. I'd rather see what's going on up there in Tatterack."

"Tommy will be very disappointed. I already told him that I was positive you would want to visit him in Holland as soon as he returns home."

"Well... if not that weekend, maybe the following one."

"Roger, I want all this coming week as well as the next one to paint. Remember, painting is how I make my living right now. I don't want company."

"Is that an order, fair lady?" Roger teases.

"I'll see you back in Holland, Roger."

"Or a lot sooner."

"Good bye." I hang up the phone in exasperation. Of course, slamming down the receiver is exactly the wrong thing to do because cutting off Mr. Big Power-mover before he decides the conversation is over, will just make him angry and even more determined to defy my wishes.

As I prepare a new canvas by stapling it to the stretchers the next morning, I glance out the upstairs window and see Stevie coming along the beach. Evidently he has sneaked away from home to play with Tommy. "So much for parental rules." Naturally I realize that I must phone his mother so that she won't worry about him, but I decide to wait fifteen minutes or so. It makes me feel more optimistic to know that young kids haven't absorbed all the prejudices of their parents, at least not yet.

The next time I look out the window, I see Tommy and Stevie dragging old lumber from beside the shed down to the beach. Soon afterwards, Tommy calls up the stairs asking where to find the nails. "Gonna make a raft," he announces happily."

"Nails are on that shelf in the closet under the stairs," I call back. I doubt that their raft will actually float, but why disillusion them? I will now have to keep a closer eye on the boys in case they do succeed to float the raft out too far in the water. This is one of those times when I wish Tommy had a father...I mean a full-time father, one who could help him build things. A few minutes later when I do telephone Stevie's mother, all she says is an abrupt, "That's what I suspected. Tell him to come straight home."

After I have gone out to the beach and quoted to Stevie what his mother has said about "coming straight home," but in a much milder tone of voice, I go back to stapling canvas on the stretchers. From the upstairs window I can see that the boys continue to work on their raft. I also notice that Stevie isn't in any great hurry to go home. I finish the stapling and begin to brush gesso over the canvas. By Wednesday I will be ready to begin another painting. Maybe this painting will help me keep my mind focused, or rather unfocused, on my latest problem which is Roger.

It has been almost a week since my confrontation with the burly man who threatened me, the one who lives at the east end of the beach, and also the incident of the broken trees and the slashing of the front door screen which Tommy still hasn't noticed. Though I realize the kidnapping of Tommy wasn't the accomplishment of a "sicky", merely a boy misdirected by the church Father, I am extremely suspicious if anyone approaches the cottage. Also, I keep a much closer eye on Tommy than I ever did before.

Even at night I am on guard duty. A full night of uninterrupted sleep is something from the past. The least little noise wakes me up and I drop out of my warm bed to the wooden floor and peer out the back window. Each time it happens, my bleary eyes try to penetrate through the dark, checking the bushes and shadows for furtive movement.

As yet there has been no answer to the letter I wrote to the church diocese, so doing anything to modify the volume of the electronic bells is temporarily out of my grasp. Maybe the diocese won't grace me with a reply at all or perhaps it will simply refer the letter back to the church here in Tatterack. Whatever they do, there could be new repercussions… more incidents of retaliation. My decision to send Tommy home two weeks early before school starts is a sound one. If he is safe, I won't worry half as much.

Our week has begun calmly enough so I start to relax and assume that all the animosity towards me has temporarily run its course, but my confidence doesn't last. By Wednesday, I grow apprehensive all over again. The phone rings and when I pick up the receiver there is no friendly voice on the line. No voice at all. I no longer try to placate myself with the fallacy that the calls are from advertisers who dial two people at one time, keeping the second person on hold while they speak to the first person they contact.

There are two more ominous phone calls in succession on Friday. Now I'm beginning to dread the ringing of the telephone. A breather call turns a perfectly sunny day into a day thick with overcast. On the second call I can clearly hear the breathing, a bit raspy like someone elderly or someone suffering from a bad cold. A chill of worry crawls up my spine.

"Face up," I tell myself out loud after the second phone call, "nothing has changed; the river of hate just keeps flowing along." The calls are just another form of harassment so I have no doubt but what the perpetrator is one of the same people who has already tried to frighten me: maybe it's the Tribners or possibly it's that big-chinned man up the beach... or, I suppose, it could be someone totally unknown to me.

With my nerves set on high alert, pinging like tin pans banging together, I even find myself being impatient with Tommy. My worry changes my attitude towards everything, taints everything. If the checkout girl at the grocery store fails to greet me cheerfully, I am immediately suspicious, and I am often set-faced and curt in my replies to the postal clerk. Yet logic tells me that neither one is likely to have anything to do with the "breather" phone calls.

Several times I've seen Mr. Lumus limping down the road behind the cottages. Has he hurt his leg, I wonder? I'm not curious enough to ask him. Why stir up another hornet's nest?

On Friday there are no breather calls, none at all; so, when Peter arrives for the weekend at his mother's cottage, I don't feel the necessity of telling him about this new twist, this new attempt to scare me. I rationalize that the perpetrator of the phone calls will surely lose interest after a while.

CHAPTER 28

The next day turns out to be too gusty for Peter's small sailboat, so instead of sailing he takes Tommy and me to the swimming beach where we all three jump through the thundering waves, or "surfer waves" as Tommy insists on calling them, though they are small compared to the ocean waves where surf boards are used. Peter raises Tommy up on his shoulders and then lets him jump straight into the turbulent, breaking wave.

"You're getting goose bumps," Peter observes to me just as we are about to dive into an approaching wave.

When I emerge from the foam and bubbles, I answer, "Yes, I am getting cold. I'd better go in and let the sun warm me up."

"I'll go in with you."

"Come-on guys," Tommy pleads over the noise of the breakers, "don't go in yet. Awww, please?"

"You can stay," I tell him, "but on the first sand bar, not way out here."

We all trudge back to the first sand bar with the waves assaulting our backs. They are so strong that they frequently knock Tommy completely over. "Look down, Tommy," I observe. You can actually see the grains of sand on the bottom being sucked back after each wave, and it's destroying the fancy ripple design we usually see on calmer days."

On shore, Peter and I dry ourselves and lay down on the terry beach towels I have brought along. I adjust and lean on my elbow, my head twisted in the direction of the water so that I can see if Tommy's feather-light body is knocked down by a wave or not.

Taking note of this, Peter says, "You're a good mom, Leah." Peter bends closer and gives my forehead a friendly kiss.

"Watching out for Tommy is being a good Mom?" I laugh teasingly. "That's just basic maternal instinct. Just think of the kisses I ought to get for being a good artist."

"Presumably, you'd be drowning in kisses, or would be if we weren't at a public beach where I have to behave myself."

"Peter, you've been so thoughtful, so nice to Tommy and me. We appreciate your attention, but...."

"... Yes," Peter takes a deep breath, and puts forth a long exaggerated and lugubrious sigh, "and it is so terribly difficult. Shouldn't I receive a little reward for all my goodness?"

"Well, you know what the good book says."

"You mean that saying from the bible about doing good deeds but not letting anyone else know that you've done them?"

"Something like that, but here's a small reward anyway." I blow him a mocking kiss.

"Not quite what I had in mind, but I'll take little crumbs like that and give back double."

Before I can turn away, Peter gives me another kiss. This time it's closer to the curve of my lips. This game is accelerating. I shift myself a bit further away, as I realize how serious Peter is becoming. Also, I take into consideration the shivery feeling creeping mercurially up my thighs and acknowledge to myself how easily I could be drawn into kissing him back with a fervor I have never felt in the past towards anyone else.

"It's not a game," Peter says softly. "Of course, if you are afraid of getting too involved with another man..."

Clearly this is a confrontation of sorts, and I'm unprepared to face up to it, at least not right now.

"Are you afraid.... because of your past relationships?" Peter takes my hand and gives it a comforting squeeze.

His succor is so tempting. I want to curl up close to him, though I suspect there is far more to my desire than just seeking comfort. Quickly, before I can become entrapped by my own blossoming urges, I stand up. "It's time to get Tommy out of the water and me out of this hot sun." To myself I add: and the sun of your attention, which is warming me all too quickly.

That night I dream that I am in the bathtub letting the water run on my upper thighs. The water begins as a tiny, soft stream that induces tingling. Soon the trickle of water conjures up all the sensations of fingers touching my most erogenous spots. I begin to feel the coming of warm sexual desire and in my dream have relaxed and opened up my thighs. The yearning is so absolute, so overpowering that it has to be satisfied somehow. I am heading towards an orgasm and it finally brings me to complete wakefulness. I realize that my hips have actually begun moving in a familiar rhythm. I stop. The thin walls and the wooden floors in the cottage can amplify every sound, and I don't want Tommy to hear me moving and groaning.

Now I am thoroughly awake, but the desire still lingers as a lovely warm exciting urge. Reluctantly, I decide that I must thwart that ancient need to consummate my desire, even symbolically. I know the sexual dream has something to do with swimming this afternoon and lying too close to Peter on the warm sand, his kisses and his touching.

CHAPTER 29

I should be urging Tommy to get dressed for Sunday school this morning, but I didn't. My feelings toward churches in general are very tenuous right now. There is some kind of mental barrier in my path. It doesn't take a visit to a professional analyst for me to realize that my problems with Father Ciconni and my reading of numerous newspaper accounts of atrocities... most of them related to religious hatred... have tainted, as surely as iodine in a glass of milk, my desire to attend a church of any religious persuasion.

Also, my feelings against attending church are affected by an item I happened to notice in yesterday's newspaper about another southern church being burned to the ground. It's the fifth or sixth church. Too many people hurt and too many more at risk. Racial differences and religious ones were claimed to be the cause. So much for religion, I decide. I figuratively tuck all the various faiths and all their visible edifices away in mothballs. Anyway, I philosophize; one does not need to have an earthly church, complete with printed creed, to have a relationship with God.

After Mrs. Sjoberg hears from Peter about the insulting words used by the Tribners towards me regarding the allegedly stolen roll of music tape, and also the threats from the blustering fellow up the beach, she phones me and invites Tommy and me to stay at her cottage at night. I thank her but decline since Tommy, the biggest source of my concern over the threats, is going home to Holland on Monday or Tuesday. Also, I resist Mrs. Sjoberg's gracious invitation for another reason. My reluctance over becoming too dependent on someone else asserts itself. I know this is just another residual of having been married to Roger, but my wariness of getting too involved with any man again or even being obligated to his family, is difficult to overcome.

In the afternoon, Peter stops by the cottage and finds Tommy and me giving Pillage a bath in the shallow water just a few yards out from the shore. Tommy holds the dog while I apply the shampoo, but as soon as I get enough lather going, Pillage decides to shake vigorously. The shake starts at his head and ripples like underground earthquake tremors throughout his body to his tail, sending wet suds flying everywhere. One glob ends up on my chin and another on my shorts. Obviously, I should be wearing my bathing suit. I am almost as wet as the dog and probably just as ridiculous looking.

"Bath time?" Peter cheerily calls out to us over the gap in the water where it now takes all our strength, Tommy's and mine, to keep the dog from bolting. I can see Peter's face breaking out in laughter at our predicament.

"Pillage has to get clean before he and Tommy go back to Holland," I explain. "Tommy, can't you hold Pill tighter?" I dip water with an old tin pan and pour it over the dog's curly coat to get rid of the soap. I call out to Peter across the short gap of water, "Our biggest problem is that we can't keep Pill from rolling in the sand afterwards. He's too heavy for me to carry very far to a clean dry place."

"When you bring him up on the beach, maybe I can throw a towel around him and carry him up to your back porch. Then you can tie him up until he dries."

"You'll get soaked," I warn.

Peter looks down at his T-shirt and navy shorts. "It's all right... can't spoil these duds. Where's the towel?"

"Over there laying on top of the canoe. All right, get ready. Here we come." I grab a flap of skin at Pillage's neck and another hunk of fur near his tail and allow the dog to lead me to shore, but it's so fast that I stumble. Peter catches me by one arm to keep me from a splat into the water. At the same time he lassos the dog using the towel as a sort-of loose noose. Then he picks up the dog in his arms and runs with him dripping and struggling to the back porch. Tommy and I follow, slip the collar back on Pillage, and tie him to the nearby post.

"You did it!" Tommy announces triumphantly and then flops himself down on the porch next to the dog. Pillage immediately goes into his dog-shaking dance once more, shedding his fur of its excess water. "Oh, Pillage!" Tommy wipes at his wet face using the bottom of his T-shirt as a towel.

As I rinse off my bare feet under the faucet near the back porch, Peter says in a low tone, "I want to talk to you privately before I leave around five o'clock so I thought I'd stop by your cottage just before taking off for Allegan.

"Yes, all right." Immediately, I try to guess what is so important that he can't tell me right now. Obviously, it must be something he doesn't want Tommy to hear. I still haven't confessed to Peter about the breather phone calls, but he has witnessed my agitation over the other recent retaliations such as the damage to the tree hedge along the road; also, the childish attempt to kidnap Tommy, and the note, the one left in our screen door one evening threatening that someone *will pay a horrible price,* for wanting to lower the decibels of the church bells.

Just before five o'clock Peter returns. Tommy is upstairs stuffing his backpack with stones and other beach treasures. Next week is going to seem pith-less and lonely without either Peter or Tommy. Already, I have that abandoned, left-behind catch in my throat, even though I am the one who made the decision to stay up here alone in the cottage.

Peter speaks softly so that Tommy, whose room is directly at the top of the stairs, won't hear. "I'll phone you Tuesday or Wednesday to find out if anyone else has been harassing you." Peter touches my shoulder gently as though reading my thoughts about being left all alone. It's his way of giving me comfort without being too forward, since his previous attempt to get physically close to me has failed.

"Oh, there's no need to do that because…"

"…. I want to or I wouldn't. I know a phone call can't keep you safe. I guess it just eases my own mind. Also, if you're not going to accept my mother's invitation to stay at night up at her cottage, I wonder if you shouldn't consider the idea of going back to Holland along with Tommy?"

Disappointment temporarily silences me. Doesn't Peter like me enough to want me to stay at least through his next visit? For the first time I admit to myself that it really does matter whether Peter cares for me or not. It matters enormously. I try to keep this new revelation from blossoming out on my face, which must be as readable as a second grade school book. My face has always given me away by revealing far too much of my feelings. Finally I answer, a bit distantly, "The timing isn't right. I have two paintings started and they'll be easier to finish after Tommy has gone. Anyway, isn't running away exactly the same as succumbing to the people who are trying to frighten me into giving up my fight against noise pollution?"

"Going home at the end of a summer vacation is not quite the same thing as running away. Nearly three-fourths of the summer people here at the beach will be leaving anyway, just like Tommy. Isn't that true?" he asks. I nod. "In the meantime you could write letters in an attempt to influence people against the noise of the electronic bells."

Stiffly I answer, "Thanks for your concern." To me it sounds more like Peter wants to hurry me out of town. Does Peter have some other agenda in mind after I leave? For all I know, he could have another girlfriend stashed away in some cottage up the shore. If rejected by one woman why not have another handy? Immediately I reprimand myself for the jealous thought.

Before Peter can respond, Tommy comes slowly down the wooden stairs, noisily dragging his backpack, bump, bump, bump, on each step.

"I'll be seeing you soon, Thomas," Peter smiles at him.

"I wish," is Tommy's grumpy reply. "I have to leave tomorrow to go back to school so maybe I won't see you again till next summer." Tommy is more than just unhappy. Somehow he has gotten the vague scent, like an animal lifting its nose to the wind, that he is being shuffled-off home early. He is right; I sympathize with him. Who would want their summer to end this soon when the weather is still so warm and lovely? Tommy especially doesn't want to miss the attention and sail-boating fun with his newfound friend, Peter.

"Tommy, I'll visit you in Holland if your mother says it's all right. Holland is just twenty-five miles from Allegan. That's where I live. Maybe we can go fishing or biking."

"All right!" Tommy thrusts out his hand for a shake. Peter grasps it fondly and also gives him a friendly thump on the back.

At the door Peter reminds me, "Call my mother if you need help of any kind. Promise?"

Staunchly I reply, "Nothing is going to happen." Actually, I am worried, but I decide not to let Peter know exactly how anxious I am. Call it whatever one likes, false pride or stubborn independence; I certainly am not going to bother his mother.

Perhaps at the last minute I should have told Peter about the breather phone calls. I could have made a joke about them so that he would think I'm very unconcerned; or I could have laughed and told Peter that the breather, whoever he or she was, definitely needed a nasal spray. Perhaps I should have, but now I've missed my opportunity because Tommy is back in the room, and I don't want him to know about the calls. He might tell his grandpa.

CHAPTER 30

I pack Tommy and Pillage into the car and drive about a hundred and twenty-five miles south to the town of Cadillac where we meet my father in the park beside Lake Cadillac. I let Pillage out of the car to do his duties, then transfer him to my father's Chevy van. From the park we all walk a block and a half up to the main street of town and eat lunch in a nearby café called: Cadillac Café, for want of a more original name.

When Tommy weaves his way between and around the bulky pine tables to visit the restroom, my father takes the opportunity of being alone with me to advise, "Maybe you should be coming home too, before something worse happens than a slashed screen door and broken trees." He touches my arm to make sure he has my undivided attention. "Just think of all the tragedies that have occurred in the past where religion was involved... still is happening in some places."

"I know." I think again about the burned churches in the South. "But I never meant religion to have anything to do with my protest against the noise pollution of the electronic bells."

"Well, someone or several someones do. Why else are they making far too much over your stand against the bell noises than you contemplated, if not because of religion? Best forget it and come on home."

Why does everyone want me to give up, even Peter? Fortunately, I have yet to tell either Peter or my father about the breather phone calls, or they probably would tie me up and haul me away bodily from the cottage.

I try to reassure my father. "I will be coming home very soon. My staying has nothing to do with the electronic bells. I want to finish some paintings and..." Should I confess to my dad that a major part of my reason for staying is Peter? No, I tell myself, not quite yet; it's too soon. Besides, there may be nothing to tell. My few short weeks of knowing Peter seem more like a series of pictures flicking on and off across a computer screen. What do I really know about Peter except for the short eclipses of time when we're been together, other than the fact that I like him and he makes me feel sexually alive.

"Dad, can I borrow a few dollars against a painting that I just learned sold at the Priam Gallery in Lansing but which I can't collect on until they send me a check?"

"Sure." He pulls four fifty-dollar bills and a couple of twenties from his wallet. "Will this be enough?" I nod. "Get yourself a haircut, too. I like the way you used to wear your hair... sort-of Joan of Arc style, shorter, just below your ears." He makes several clipping gestures around my neck to indicate the length.

"Maybe I'll do that." It surprises and pleases me that my father can remember even one of my hairstyles from another. Now I can see Tommy threading his way back to our table, cutting short any further private conversation between me and my dad.

We walk back to the cars where Pillage is thrusting his head out the van window with tongue slobbering. Tommy gives him some water from a paper cup he has brought from the restaurant.

"We'd better get going now," my father urges, then adds, "before Pillage slobbers up so many windows that I can't see to drive home. See you in about a week, God willing." I shake my head in mock disgust. His "God willing" is just another of his annoying platitudes.

I give Tommy a quick hug of goodbye before he can protest. Mushy behavior in public is not well tolerated by Tommy now that he's almost eight years old. But before breaking away from him, I can't resist brushing back his straight hair from his forehead with my hand.

That motherly touch is more to sooth me than Tommy. I will miss him very much. "Be nice to your grandpa," I tell him.

"But will I be nice to him in return is the question?" My father grabs Tommy and locks his arm across his shoulders in a mock display of force.

As I wave my final goodbyes, I question my decision to send Pillage away with Tommy. Wouldn't it have been wiser for me to keep Pillage for the two weeks instead of sending him home? Pillage certainly wasn't an attack dog, but at least he would bark and make a loud whimpering fuss if an intruder dared to sneak inside the cottage.

According to the calendar it is still the month of August, yet I notice on my way to the nearby Tatterack Post Office that quite a few leaves on the maple trees have already turned a mottled red. The reds are all the more vibrant because they contrast with the darks of the evergreen trees. I remind myself of how early the fall season evolves up here in the North.

At the post office, the clerk hands me an envelope embellished with a crest; clearly it is from the diocese in Morsey. Does the clerk noticed as well, I wonder? As I become acutely aware of the close web of related people in this town and the manner in which news is shuttled from one person to another, so also have I become more and more suspicious. Instantly, I suspect the post office clerk will tell his wife about my receiving this clearly marked letter from the diocese and maybe she will tell her sister and the sister will tell a cousin and so on and on. "You're verging on the paranoid," I warn myself as I drive back to the cottage.

Even before I get out of the car, I read the letter signed by the administrative assistant to the Bishop. My first reading of the letter leaves me feeling at least hopeful. *You were misinformed about Mr. Growgood's retirement. He is still one of the grounds-keepers. Inspite of Mr. Growgood's opinion, we have great faith in the accuracy of Father Ciconni's report on the state of the bell.* The letter says nothing about my complaint against the high volume of the electronic bells except in the last sentence. We *do not have jurisdiction over each individual church matter; however, we will broach the subject of the high decibels to the church board there in Tatterack.*

My optimistic attitude over receiving an answer to my letter is immediately doused. My fear rises. Once the whole church board in Tatterack knows about my request to lower the volume of the electronic bells, so will exactly that many more people be disgruntled towards me. Of course, I hadn't thought of that obvious downside before writing the letter.

When Peter phones me around eight o'clock that same evening, I tell him about the letter from the diocese and especially their statement about Mr. Growgood who had led me to believe he had a retired status. "Why did he lie to me? Or is it the diocese that made an error?

"To avoid blame for something else perhaps? I don't know. At least your letter was answered, but don't let your hopes rise too high. I've been hearing about a similar case where a whole neighborhood of people tried to sue a church because the preacher's sermons were being broadcast outdoors and could be heard throughout the whole resort. I'm afraid the people lost the court case against the church."

"Thanks for that uplifting message."

"Sorry. Now remember your promise."

"What promise?"

"To phone my mother about any threatening things that might happen."

"No unusual things have happened." It's true. The breather hasn't even phoned today, so it isn't an out-and-out lie. I never told Peter about receiving any of the previous breather phone calls either.

"I sense a reluctance in you to let someone else share some of your problems. Right, Leah?"

I keep silent. He is right, though. I'm not going to let myself get entangled in a relationship just because it's so comforting to have someone on "my side" ready to provide a soft cushion between me and the bumps in the road... especially if those bumps are my own fault.

Peter laughs and teases, "Not talking much tonight, are you?"

"Not much." This time I also break down and laugh over our one-way communication.

"If anything seems threatening between now and Friday when I come, will you please call my mother right away or better still, phone the..."

"I wouldn't think of bothering...."

Peter's sigh interrupts me. "Mother wouldn't consider it a bother, and the police certainly wouldn't."

"Your concern is noted." I am quickly thinking of stronger words to use such as: Why do you men always think you are more capable of solving problems, when Peter interrupts me again.

"If I had my way about it, I'd attach a thread to you, a springy silver one that would stretch all the way to Allegan."

What a lovely, fairy tale sentiment. "Dear Peter."

"Will you please repeat that?"

"Good night, dear Peter."

"Ahhhhaaa, maybe I have finally slipped through that barrier you've constructed to keep friends and would-be admirers out. Good night, my dear."

Peter's words touch me. My mind cannot help but linger on his idea of a silver thread. I can almost see it catching flashes of light as it waves in the sun or the moon at night. Some men could spout the same phrase and it would have spun out as nothing more than romantic drivel, an opportunity to soft-soap me into sharing a bed, but from Peter it reads differently. The expression about the thread seems to come so naturally and sweetly from his innermost feelings. Undoubtedly, it's a good thing that he is unable to see my face and the softening effect his words are having on me.

For several minutes afterwards, I sit by the telephone at the kitchen table and think about Peter's silver thread. Am I being naive all over again? Isn't it possible that Peter, with a slicker line than most, means to win me just for the sake of winning the game of a night in bed? There are guys who actually make monetary bets with each other over their ability to get a girl into bed in a set length of time. But Peter? No. Immediately I sluff off the idea as ridiculous. Furthermore, I confess to myself, I simply don't want to think of Peter in that way, not ever.

About an hour after Peter's phone call, as I am sitting at my mother's desk in the living room writing a note to a newly married girlfriend, the phone rings again. Immediately, I feel apprehensive and take my time about walking into the kitchen where the phone sits on the table. Should I, or shouldn't I answer it?

"Hello." There is no voice on the line, just breathing.

"Who is it?" I ask, calmly at first. "Who are you?" With a rush of anger I almost shout the second time, "Who are you?" Then I remember the advice given to me on how one should react to harassers. A wild reaction like mine is exactly what titillates them and spurs them on. Their whole purpose is to panic the person they are harassing; it gives them a "high," like sniffing glue. I hang up.

From that moment on, the whole atmosphere in the cottage changes. The half darkness outside the cottage now seeps inside. It causes me to feel completely separated from other humans. I feel more isolated and alone than ever before. The once familiar reflections in the windows caused by lamps, chairs, and the wall clock take on weird wavy forms. I hastily pull down all the shades and caution myself to stay completely away from the window in the kitchen door because it has no shade or curtain of any sort to keep a stalker from observing my every move.

Just an hour later, though it is still fairly early, I am already in bed and have just picked up a book to read when the phone rings again. I hesitate before answering but decide that it might be my father returning an earlier phone call from me. I want to find out if he and Tommy have arrived safely back in Holland so I pick up the portable phone by my bedside. Again there is no voice, just breathing. I am more disciplined now, though the urge to shout something terrible into the phone is almost unsurmountable. I hang up the receiver and begin to shake so violently that the headboard rattles against the wall.

After this second breather call, there is no possible way that I can get to sleep. Clutching my terry robe tightly around me, I slip back downstairs using my flashlight instead of turning on the lights, and fix myself a hot drink of chicken bullion. I turn off the flashlight and stand at the window sipping my drink and gazing out into the dark backyard to check for moving shadows. Nothing, so far.

Surely this person who is harassing me must be twisted in his or her mind... sick. Exactly—that's got to be the type of person I am dealing with here—a religiously twisted person who might do all kinds of terrible things to others... to me.

I lie down on the sofa, hoping to sleep. But first, as I have done once before, I place the grimy, ash covered fireplace poker down on a newspaper nearby where I can grab it in a hurry.

CHAPTER 31

I am unable to sleep at all during the night on the old sofa, which has a strong mildew odor, so I am up as early as six o'clock this morning. I recall my jitters of the night before. After checking the yard and screen door for signs of malicious damage and finding nothing more unusual than a new trail of ants. I am somewhat relieved. Still, I need reassurance and advice. I restrain myself from bothering Enid with a phone call so early and wait until two hours later. Enid's shoulders are broad and she has been endowed with a vast supply of common sense. Also, like viewing a piece of art with fresh eyes, she will look at my situation with a new prospective. I count on her to give me good sound advice.

I dial Enid's phone number several times. She is the one person in whom I dare to confide my panic over the breather phone calls. It's only after my third failure to reach Enid that my sleep deprived brain recalls that she and her husband had planned to visit Mystic Seaport in Connecticut this week and then travel on up the Eastern coast to Mount Desert Island. I have her cell phone number, yet I hesitate to use it. This really isn't an emergency and she has a right to take her vacation free of someone else's burdens, mine.

I sputter futilely at Enid, "Why did your vacation have to be this week. . .just when I need you?" Fortunately, Enid can't hear my frustrated appeal for help. Now I have no one else to confide in except my father who will naturally overreact to the breather calls, that is if I decide to tell him. His elderly age, seventy, is a factor to keep in mind as well. No, I tell myself. I'm not going to disturb his peace, at least not quite yet. Neither am I going to confide in Peter. He is seemingly a loving, yet still an untried friend. Instead, I console myself with the hopeful idea that the breather will soon tire of the game.

Peter's mother, Mrs. Sjoberg, phones me around ten that same morning to invite me to come to dinner on Friday. "We'll have it a bit late in the evening just to make sure that Peter arrives in time before we eat.... about seven, if that's all right with you?" I snap up the offer with such alacrity that Mrs. Sjoberg is silent for several beats.

"Is everything all right there? Your voice sounds more like you were just granted a parole, not a simple invitation to dinner." She laughs, knowing how overly dramatic her statement sounds. "Are you sure you're all right?"

Since my friend, Enid, isn't available on whom to unload my fears, it's a losing battle for me to keep from dropping them into the lap of the first friendly being I speak to on the other end of the telephone line. Finally I succumb to telling Mrs. Sjoberg nearly everything. I suppose there is something about my being alone and her outgoing personality, a ready receptacle, which bypasses my previous resolve to manage my own affairs and remain independent. In my relief at being able to spill my problems onto someone else, it completely slips my mind that Mrs. Sjoberg will naturally pass the information on to her son, Peter.

"Really, I wish you would stay up here at my cottage, especially at night. Have you called the police yet? If you get even one more call, I would," she advises firmly. After I have once more turned down her invitation to stay at her cottage, she urges, "Don't forget to come running if you're frightened. Don't stay in that cottage alone." There is a pause before she says, "Have you thought of calling the phone company? Maybe they can put a trap on your line. Or is it called a *tap*?"

"I've never heard of such a thing."

"Yes, They have ways of checking to discover who is repeatedly calling on your line; they'll need your permissions first."

Some of my tension is relieved by Erma's renditions of her own experiences with crank callers. Perhaps she even enlarged upon them just to make me feel calmer.

"I've had some callers who sounded so muffled that I swear they must either have been drunk or had their beards caught between their teeth. And once, a child, who meant to frighten me by just breathing loudly, accidentally hiccupped instead and politely said, 'Excuse me,' just from the sheer good habit instilled in him by his parents."

I end up laughing with her. Erma Sjoberg is such a combination of opposites, of incongruities. She is elegant appearing, almost stately, yet the words and ideas that flow from her mouth are often warm and funny, edging on the outrageous, quite belying her dignified appearance.

Another nuisance call comes the same afternoon. This time when I pick up the receiver I hear more than just breathing; it's a chanting voice, low and whispery. "You'll burn in hell-fire... you'll burn in...." I hang up immediately. Is the voice familiar, I ask myself? Maybe it's that mean-sounding man from up the road or Mr. Tribner having imbibed too many drinks. Obviously it must be someone who belongs to the same church that broadcasts the electronic bell music. Can it be the little Father himself? I shiver, recalling some of the TV movies I've seen where the "breather" eventually breaks into the house of the woman he is harassing and tries to stab her. This vivid mental picture of someone being stabbed springs me into action.

I immediately contact the phone company and ask them what to do about the nuisance calls. They offer to put a tap on the telephone line and then proceed to explain how it works. When a call comes, I am not to hang up the receiver until the caller is completely finished breathing, speaking, or chanting, as the case may be. The longer the phone call, the better the chance of trapping the caller. Immediately after hanging up the receiver I am to punch in an eight hundred number, give the recording my case pin number, my phone number, the date, time and length of the call. I write down all this information and post it beside the telephone in readiness.

Just taking this one positive step against the frightening phone calls makes me feel less insecure. I tell myself with a sigh, "Thank goodness, Tommy isn't here." I have sent him home just in time.

Each morning I work on my two paintings. After the phone calls, which generally come in the afternoons and evenings, I no longer feel relaxed or carefree. The insinuating and ugly intentions of the caller are in direct contrast to the ideas I am attempting to include into my pictures. The urge to continue becomes as dried-up as the clay figures Tommy and I have left abandoned on the porch.

That same evening I hear the bells, accelerated in volume by strong gusts from the direction of the church, shrilling forth louder than ever. Again I ask myself, "Is our family to spend the rest of our lives each summer listening to that trite, false music instead of the soothing sounds of water music coming from the shore?

The harsh, mean words spoken by Mr. Bingham filter back into my mind. *If you don't like the bells, why don't you just go home?* Too late, I now know exactly how I should have responded to his mean taunt: Because this beach belongs to me, my father, and to Tommy just as much as it belongs to mean people like you.

Soon after I finish dinner that evening, the jangling of the phone begins. I dread answering it. I fear the violating words, but if I don't answer the phone, the trap set up by the telephone company will never spring.

I lift the receiver cautiously and immediately the voice begins to chant, "You'll burn in hell." I shiver, wishing to cut off the slippery voice but continue to hold my breath and the line open until the caller has hung up. Finally in relief, I take a deep breath. Then I dial-in the information needed by the phone company.

So far the voice on the telephone has never threatened bodily harm, not in so many words. Just the same, the threat is there… it comes across in the voice…in the menacing whispery tone. Its predictions of doom soon to fall upon me make me feel like checking every window and every shadowy corner of the cottage for intruders even though I know they can't squeeze through small holes like mice or bats. The voice is also meant to make me feel as guilty as a stealer of votive candles from a church, but there it misses its mark.

Around ten o'clock that night when I am just thinking of climbing the stairs to bed or camping out again on the sofa, I hear footsteps on the back porch. Next there is a sharp rap on the back door, and a cold stiffness seizes my neck and shoulders. For brief seconds I become an icy statue. Then I quickly move to another part of the living room where I can't be seen from the back door window. I have already pulled all the shades in the living room.

What should I do? This is definitely not the time of night to be answering doors to strangers. I feel all my joints turning into liquid. Since I can't go out into the kitchen to use the phone, which is located on the table next to the back door where I will be seen, I urge my unsteady legs to head in the direction of the stairs and the portable phone in my bedroom to call for help. A second tapping on the door occurs, followed by a soft voice calling out, "It's me, Peter."

Thank God! I let the air out of my lungs, not even realizing that I've been holding it, and hurry to the door to let him in.

"Peter? You're not supposed to come until Friday!"

"Yes, but I began to worry about you after hearing from my mother about the crank phone calls so I drove up after work. I just got here a few minutes ago."

"Oh, Peter, that's at least a three-hour drive. Really, you shouldn't have." In spite of my fear, I play down my helpless feelings in front of Peter. "I'm just fine." Even an idiot, which I'm turning out to resemble, should have guessed that Mrs. Sjoberg would pass on the information from me about the breather phone calls straight to Peter.

"I have to start back about five in the morning. Are you really all right?" Peter takes both of my arms and pulls me into a friendly, soothing hug. Immediately I feel safer, but not calmer. Peter's nearness is stirring me up in other ways, physically. I shut my eyes so he can't see the impact of his body against mine.

"Just a bit edgy," I confess. What an understatement. "It's a good thing you called out my name a few minutes ago because I was just about to phone the police."

"And I would have been arrested as a Peeping Peter," he laughs and changes the subject. "Did you see the aurora borealis?" I shake my head. "It's splendid tonight, a really fine display." Peter takes my hand and draws me out across the back porch and down the path to the beach where there are no trees to impede our view of the sky. When we first look up into the heavens, there is nothing except blackness and stars. Then, quite suddenly, colors split the sky in two directions. One, a pale green keeps shimmering and darting, the other, pale pink moves less. Both have streaked up from the level of the horizon in the north.

"Aaah," I can't help but breath out my wonder at the remarkable sight. We sit down on a log and watch the light show that nature is putting on. After a few minutes I begin to feel chilly and wish I had grabbed a sweater before coming down to the beach. "I'm going back for my sweater."

"Here. Take my flashlight." Peter puts it in my hand. "Do you have one of your own? You know, flashlights are good for bopping intruders in an emergency."

"Yes, I have one and you came very close to being the boppee just a few minutes earlier when you knocked on the door." I make my way across the sand to the winding path and to the back porch.

Just as I am about to step up onto the back porch, I glance towards the road and notice Mr. Lumus' figure outlined by the orange glow of the bug light hanging above his door. What is he doing? Maybe, I decide, he is trying to see the northern lights from way back there since he has no beach property from which to watch. I pretend not to notice him and hurry inside for my sweater. Before I go back to the beach and Peter, I lock the door, as I should have done in the first place.

Peter and I watch the display of northern lights for fifteen or twenty minutes longer. "Time to get you to bed, right?"

Is this a come-on, an invitation to share a bed, the first I've heard from Peter? But even if it is, I ignore it. "And you too, since you have to get up at five to make that long drive back to Allegan. It really was too far to drive for such a short visit. I'm immensely flattered." Then I tell Peter about seeing Mr. Lumus earlier standing outside his cottage door gazing towards the shore.

"There's no way he could see much of the light display from way back there. The trees cut off most of the view."

"Who knows. He's such a strange man. Even though he claimed to be very upset over the loudness of the electronic bells, he let me down because he was afraid to keep our appointment with Father Ciconni. Once in a while I see him limping down the road behind the cottage. He must have hurt his knee or leg."

Peter gives my forehead a light kiss. "Please come and stay at my mother's cottage. Or, if you prefer, I could bed down here on the sofa tonight to make you feel safer."

The temptation is overwhelming. I think how much safer I'll feel with Peter in the cottage. Oh yes, safe in one sense but unsafe in another. Somehow, I have a feeling that we might both end up in my bed with no sleep. "Goodnight, Peter." Those are the dismissive words I use, but at the same time the urge to reach up and draw his head down to mine is almost uncontrollable. I can easily imagine our kiss. It will be long and piercing as though we are each trying to work our way inside the other with our need to connect. Instead, I lean back for support against the porch post. Peter steps down from the porch and then steps back up again.

"Leah, could we talk about us?" I nod. "Would you agree," Peter whispers in case Mr. Lumus is still hovering around somewhere, "that our relationship is heading for a more serious stage?"

"Doesn't have to," I mutter, but without much conviction.

"You don't want it to?" Peter asks.

"I'm... not sure." How I wish he would just stop talking and kiss me on the lips instead of first making me sign on the dotted line with words and signature as a lawyer might. I'm not ready to recommit myself, and possibly get caught up in another entanglement. Maybe I never will be ready. Right now I possess a freedom of sorts. No one, not even my father regulates my hours. Well, Tommy does, of course, but the remainder of time is mine. I like being independent.

I evade Peter's question and joke, "Let me think about it a couple of years." Even in the dim light streaming through the back door window onto the porch, I can see Peter's jaw tighten. My levity isn't going over well at all. Peter is deeply disappointed by my stalling tactics.

"I think you're afraid. One bad experience shouldn't stop-the-clock. It doesn't portend that all your new relationships will be failures. That Roger fellow certainly must have been a rotten one."

"He was. . .is. Maybe I'm at fault too for being so easily fooled."

"And you're afraid that I'm out to fool you as well. Oh, Leah, I'm not an operator, but I warn you, I am persistent. It's one of my faults and I suppose I ought to also admit to you the bar tender I killed, the dog I kicked, the seven or eight women I raped, and on top of all that I may have been a bed wetter as well." Peter is turning the whole thing into a joke.

"Are you a bed wetter?" I pretend to be serious, though not too successfully because I can't stifle a giggle.

"Maybe I was once. Peter laughs and adds, "You'll have to ask my mother."

Of course, I myself have plenty of faults, which Peter doesn't know about yet, and maybe never will. There is my reluctance to mix socially, my dedication to painting which absorbs all my time and leaves little for housekeeping; also, my impatience and my pride in my independence, and plenty more.

Peter steps closer. "Seriously, Leah, could you try to put your fear of getting entangled or entrapped, whatever you call it, behind you? As some Victorian novels would state, I think I'm smitten with you." This time Peter does pull my shoulders away from the post, grasps me firmly against his body with one hand, and kisses me on the lips.

The kiss is close to piercing me with the blade of his whole body, and I wish it could go on and on.

I'd best go now or else you may get a bed partner you haven't invited."

Oh, how I want to invite him. And with Tommy gone, I could. But I don't. I let the moment slip away. "Good night, dear Peter," I call out as I watch him stride, a bit unevenly because of his ankle, up the driveway to his car. I reprimand myself, "Leah, you're an utter coward."

As I lie in bed that night I think how novel it feels to have a male companion around again; how it lends cayenne to the daily-ness of my existence, and how it stimulates my thinking. At first I can't get to sleep at all because I feel so pulsating, so sexually stirred-up. How easy it would be to succumb to Peter. Tonight's intimate kiss even wipes my thoughts clear, at least momentarily, of the obnoxious chanting phone call and the recent reprisals.

"Watch it, Leah," I warn myself out loud, "Don't get too comfortable with the idea of Peter as a lover. Your judgment in choosing men isn't exemplary." Just half awake now, I wonder, "Do I want to lose my single status? Now that I've regained it, maybe I should keep it and hold it dear."

I philosophize on how as a child one is merely a cog in a family instead of an individual. Then just as a person grows older and "finds" oneself with an ability to think independently, the strong urge of sex slips them up, as surely as the proverbial joke about banana peels, into marriage or at least into being classed as a couple. One instantly becomes part of a twosome—wife of so and so—and now everyone thinks of you as a unit instead of an individual. From that time on, every decision has to pass through the sieve of a spouse or significant other person. "Then just watch independence fly out the window."

Right now I am an individual and able to make my own choices, though my freedom is diluted somewhat by Tommy and my lack of money. I cringe, thinking of my married life with Roger. I sternly caution myself, "Don't be too hasty to throw away your freedom and your identity again."

By now I am groggy with sleepiness and begin to doze into a field of half-awake, half-sleep where deep worries get caught up and mixed like a salad into strange dreams. I visualize pictures of married women, big-eyed, anguished, displayed on milk cartons in the grocery store. They are lost identities who need to be found exactly like the missing children.

CHAPTER 32

Naturally, I've let my father know about the ruined trees and the slashed front screen door because those things have damaged his property. He has a right to know. But so far I haven't said anything to him about the breather phone calls. I'm reluctant to bring up the subject and worry him, especially as no actual physical harm has taken place. Still, I reason, after thinking further about it, what if something catastrophic does occur to the cottage because of this new threat? Then I'll be blamed for not having kept him informed. After all, the cottage isn't mine. Reluctantly, I decide to fess up to this new threat the next time we talk on the telephone.

When I contact my father to find out how Tommy is behaving. I also mention for the first time the subject of the crank phone calls, attempting with a light-hearted voice to downplay the seriousness. I am doing my best to sound unconcerned, but my father immediately interrupts me with, "Come home, Leah. Don't take any more chances. It sounds to me like some crazy nut has reached the end of his tether. Someone is out to seriously hurt you."

"Yes, yes," I try to soothe him. "I am coming next week. It's just a few more days. I want to see a friend of mine again before I leave." There. I have confessed to my father one of my reasons for staying longer than necessary at the cottage. "He's coming tomorrow evening. After the weekend, I promise you, I will either come straight home or take a day trip up to Lake Superior with my friend Peter. In either case I won't be here at the cottage where someone can hurt me. I promise."

There is a long pause while my father digests this new revelation. He has previously heard nothing about my interest in another man.

"Who is this guy? Shouldn't you be more cautious? For all you know, he could be the very one whispering threats on the telephone."

Of course this idea has never entered my head before. Peter as the *breather?* Nonsense, I tell myself. I explain to my father, "He and his partner run a pharmaceutical business in Allegan. You can check that out if you want to. Peter comes up here on weekends and stays at his mother's cottage. He's just a friend."

"How do you know but what he's the instigator of..."

"That's ridiculous! He hates the bell noises as much as I do." But no, I admit to myself for the first time, that's not quite true. Peter has never expressed his feelings that concisely. He has never spoken with fervor against the electronic bells, nor have I ever heard him offer, not in so many words, to help me fight the noise pollution. Again there is a long pause in the conversation between my father and me while I quickly mull over this new idea, absurd as it sounds. Finally I change the subject, "Any other news?"

"Well, Roger is planning to see Tommy on Saturday. He claims that he is going to take Tommy to the Ottawa County Fair. As we both know, he doesn't always show up."

"Oh, I hope he does. That should give you at least two or three hours of respite from Tommy. It's a great relief for me too, I think, because Roger can't possibly manage to be in two places on the same day, the Ottawa County Fair and also hundreds of miles further north in Tatterack.

"Tommy is no problem, but he needs his mom so please be careful... watch your back and don't get anyone's dander up... and please come home as soon as you can. Did you phone the police about those threatening phone calls?"

"Not yet, but I will. I did call the phone company and they put a trap on the line. Now don't worry. If the threats increase, I can always stay with Peter's mother. She lives just a few cottages from ours. Bye now." I have no intention of staying up at Mrs. Sjoberg's cottage—my priest hole—but if pretending to do so will ease my father's mind, well; it's only a fraction of a fib and worth it.

After my father's firm urging, I do telephone the police, but they tell me to contact the phone company about the harassing calls, which I have already done. The Police Chief, Mr. Bruckner, does have one further suggestion, "Try recording the calls on a tape recorder if you have one, or I can loan you one. This is a very small community, so there's a chance that I might recognize the voice of your trouble-maker."

"Yes, I do have one. Thanks for the suggestion."

I heard about your son's scary experience. I hope my deputy got it straightened out."

"Thanks for asking. Tommy is very nervous after being trapped in the old house and so am I."

Next, the police chief asks me if I have any enemies, I don't know how to answer his question. How can I say, "Yes, half of the town." So I mutter, "Several, it seems."

The crank phone call that comes on Friday is different. First, it comes in the morning. That is not the norm. All the other calls have come in the afternoons or in the evenings. I ask myself out loud, "Is the caller getting more agitated, closer to the end of his 'tether' as my father has suggested?"

When the next call comes, I turn on the tape recorder and the strange whispery voice begins, "You are hurting the one true religion. You and the bad harmonica man have condemned yourselves to purgatory." Then the voice rants in a louder, angry voice, "But first I'll get you both!"

My stomach lurches, then immediately begins to cramp up. This, for the first time, is a clear-cut threat of bodily harm. But who is "harmonica man?" Could the voice on the phone be referring to Growgood? Did someone follow Tommy and me all around the Indian Village?

I yearn to slam down the receiver to escape from the voice. A pause in the voice follows and then it begins to chant all over again, "Repent or die! Repent or die!" My shaking hand accidentally knocks over the salad cruet and the vinegar spills out onto the flowered tablecloth. For a moment I sit absolutely stunned, unable to move even though I can see a stream of vinegar reaching the edge of the table ready to drip to the floor. Then I realize that the phone is buzzing. The caller has hung up.

With stiff fingers made clumsy by tension, I snap off the tape recorder and grab a paper napkin to sop up the vinegar. Afterwards, I sit there in the same spot exactly, and continue to hold myself stiffly erect. If I move, will I disturb my circle of safety and become vulnerable. . .even spill out of the circle like yoke from a cracked egg? After this threat of bodily harm, will I even have the courage to step outside of the cottage?

As I sit there, my thoughts revert to that afternoon when Tommy and I went sailing with Peter. He and I had a discussion over why some denominations think they belong to the "one true religion." It's exactly as I'm beginning to suspect; this mentally sick person on the telephone is just another fanatic who assumes no other religion on earth, except his of course, is the "true religion, so anyone who questions it is an infidel and needs to be punished.

It is also quite evident that the person who is harassing me, is a member of that very church from which the noise pollution emanates. People of his or her sort want to eliminate, either in words or by actual force, any human being who will not blindly march to their set rules. What a terrible narrowness! If my phone caller is really someone like that, then I am indeed in physical danger. I shiver and continue to sit very rigidly, not daring to move from the very chair in which I huddle.

Finally, I do break out of my imaginary safety shell and report the phone call as required. Then I lock all the doors—something I have never done before in daylight hours—and peek out of the windows from several different locations in the cottage. I see no one; not so much as a dog is walking along the road or along the beach.

How can some unknown person in a quiet little community like this one, remote from the troubles in the mid-east and the known terrorist areas, make me feel so vulnerable, and set me teetering on the edge of panic?

Almost an hour passes before I pump up enough courage to leave the cottage and drive to the police station in the village.

My guess is that the square-cut, sturdy person sitting at the desk silhouetted against the office window is likely that of Chief Bruckner. I am right. I have seen him cruising in his patrol car along the village streets. In my imagination, I can see this competent-looking police chief placing my phone harasser behind bars even though, as yet, I have no idea what the "breather" looks like. Right now my imagination concocts someone who looks like the beer swigging man living up the road east of here, or a combination of Mr. Bingham and a tipsy Mr. Tribner.

After identifying myself to Chief Bruckner, I play the tape that I have just recorded. "I don't recognize the voice," he claims, rubbing the back of his neck. "So much of it is just whispering, except for that one burst of hatred. Maybe we'll get lucky and the telephone company can come up with the name of the caller."

I fail to admit to the police chief how scared I am. Even if I do confess to him how my stomach churns up...or how my arms shake on the steering wheel as I drive into town, I realize there isn't a thing he can do to protect me.

It seems almost impossible for me to get my mind back into painting again when I return to the cottage, nor does my creative spirit return after relocking all the doors again. The painting of the empty church and steeple has been set aside, but one other painting is complete. I can't claim it is absolutely finished though, because, as always, I put the picture out of my sight for a week or so and then bring it back out to scrutinize it carefully. Usually I discover several things I want to fix or change.

Now I will have much more time to spend with Peter during his vacation, which begins tonight with the festive dinner at his mother's cottage. Tomorrow we can go swimming or sailing, or maybe even take that boat ride to view Pictured Rocks up on Lake Superior that we've talked about before.

In just a very few hours Peter and I will be sitting down to dinner and I can drop the brave front I've been trying to maintain all week and confess to being the coward that I really am, and he will make me feel secure and cared-for all weekend and part of next week too.

Around six o'clock, after changing from my scruffy paint clothes into a slate blue silk shirt and linen slacks, I walk over to the Sjoberg cottage and am greeted warmly by Peter's mother. "It's all right to call me Erma, you know," she says and gestures for me to sit down on the sofa facing the huge fireplace in which she has built a cheerful fire of birch bark logs.

Almost immediate I find it irresistible to ask, "Hasn't Peter come yet?" Erma shakes her head. I am disappointed, yet I know what a long drive it is from Allegan. Even if Peter had left work early, say around three o'clock, packed and then started, he might not get here until seven at the earliest.

"Let's have a cocktail or a glass of wine while we wait. Anyway, my pork roast isn't quite done. Peter will be along soon, I'm sure. What would you like to drink? I have Chardonnay, bourbon and soda, and Vernors ginger ale as usual."

"Bourbon sounds great, but heavy on the soda, please." When Mrs. Sjoberg returns from the kitchen with our drinks, we discuss a book we have both read by Ursu; our conversation ultimately covers the subject of the water level this year, and my paintings which I invite Erma to see before I leave sometime next week. Then quite unaware of bringing up a subject that is going to change my feelings towards Peter from one of beginning trust to one of suspicion, I ask Erma, "Does Peter belong to any particular church?"

Erma hesitates before answering. "Well, he goes to the Congregational Church with me occasionally, but there was a time when he considered joining the Catholic Church because he was dating the Father's favorite niece; then perhaps later studying for the priesthood."

Shock erupts on my face. I find a place to set my drink down before I spill it.

"Peter didn't tell you? Well anyway, he changed his mind."

I lower my head to cover up my reaction. Why hadn't Peter told me? Perhaps, I think, it's because I haven't shown enough interest in him as yet to warrant personal confidences? Or...and I pick up my glass again and swallow a huge gulp of my drink...is it because he's still carrying soft feelings for that girl he met in the church? I swallow down more of my drink instead of sipping carefully, as I ought to, and try to sink all this new information into a deep pit in my mind where it can be ignored or at least ignored until later.

Erma changes the subject abruptly as though guessing at her mistake in blurting out news that her son hasn't yet confided in me. "Have those strange phone calls stopped?" she asks changing the subject.

"No." I tell her about the most recent one... the one that had come this very morning with its chanting threat of *I'll get you first!*. Even in telling about the incident, I feel my hands clinching and my neck muscles tightening. Tension is winding up again in spite of the bourbon and soda. In a further display of my nervousness I do what is by now an unbroken habit: I try to finger back the curtain of my hair behind my ears, forgetting that it's not even possible after my recent short haircut.

"Whoever is making those dreadful calls must be a religious fanatic... someone completely warped... crazy, because, according to Peter, it all started soon after you tried to get the church to lower the volume of the electronic bells. You must be careful, Leah. I don't want to overly frighten you, but fanatics do dreadful things: car bombs, package and letters full of white powder, and...." Mrs. Sjoberg abruptly rises from her chair and crosses the living room to the hall and opens the street door. She stands there for a moment listening. "Are those police sirens or fire engine sirens I hear?"

"Fire engines, I believe." I join Erma at the open door. "By the sound, it's not far away. Maybe just up the road. I believe I'll step outside and see what's going on. Excuse me." I set my unfinished bourbon down on the nearby hall table and head out the door.

Just outside, I look west down the road and see the fire engine opposite Fleury cottage and begin to run. As I race towards the cottage, I spot my neighbors, the elderly Ostlers, the Harrises, and even Mr. Lumus standing out in the road looking in the direction of my father's cottage.

"Is it my cottage?" I call out breathlessly even before I reach the small group standing out in the road.

"Yes," Mr. Ostler answers, "but it's not spreading. Your neighbor, Mr. Harris spotted the smoke almost immediately."

"My paintings!" I hurry past the fire engine and down the sloping driveway to the back door. I can see the smoking hole in the south side of the kitchen and cover my nose against the acrid smell.

"Can't go in yet, Miss." A fireman put out his arm to hold me back. "Fire's out, but there's still too much smoke. Did'ya leave something on the stove?"

"No. Absolutely not! You can see that the stove is nowhere near that wall where the smoke is billowing out the hole."

"Someone may have started the fire on purpose," he finally conceded. "We're checking. It looks like someone stuck cloth doused with turp or paint thinner up under the siding. You're a painter. Maybe they were from your supplies?"

"Yes, I'm a painter. I paint with acrylics. Neither turpentine nor paint thinner is needed to clean up my brushes. Exactly what are you implying?"

"Cottage fires are often started by the owners themselves who want the insurance money. Especially now that property taxes are so much higher."

"I resent your implication!" I snap. "Anyway, this cottage and most of the cottages along this beach will bring in more money by selling than by collecting insurance." Immediately afterwards, I find myself conjecturing, I'll bet I know which church that fireman attends. With disgust, I recognize how biased I have become. Not just biased...out and out prejudiced against anyone attending the church with the electronic bells. I feel ashamed and try to soften my negative tone of voice when I answer further questions.

"I understand from my brother, the police chief, that you've been receiving some threatening phone calls."

"That's right, but no threats to burn down the cottage." What right did Chief Bruckner have to tell his brother about the phone calls? Weren't police matters supposed to be kept confidential? Beatrice Tullman had certainly been right all along. Everyone seemed to be related to everyone else in this village.

"The Chief will be here in a minute. He's just finishing his dinner."

Lucky man, I think sarcastically. He gets to eat his dinner. I am becoming more and more impatient to get inside the cottage and check my paintings. Fifteen minutes later when Chief Bruckner finally does show up, the first thing he asks me is, "Where were you when the fire started?"

"At the Sjoberg cottage. I was invited to dinner." He nods. I know that he will check it out just to be sure that I haven't started my own cottage fire.

"What time did you go up there?"

"About six-fifteen."

"I guess somebody in the neighborhood could have seen you leave the cottage." I nod. For once I'm glad the cottages are built so close together.

Someone, either the Harrises or the people renting the cottage on the other side of my father's cottage, might be able to vouch for me.

A short time later, the firemen allow me back inside the cottage, and they drive away clanging the bell on their truck. Temporarily ignoring the mess in the kitchen, I head straight for the stairs to check on my paintings. They appear undamaged since they are all stacked upstairs. But the odor inside the cottage quickly fills my nose and roughens my throat until a spasm of coughing prompts me to open all the windows. As I take great gulps of fresh watery air, I wonder if the canvas backs of the pictures have absorbed too much of the acrid smell. If they have, no gallery will ever want them and my summer's work will be for nothing.

"What if no one wants my paintings?" I try to gulp down the sobs rising in my throat as the sorry-for-myself thoughts rush in. It takes great effort to squeeze back the tears. I'm unsuccessful. "This is not the time to get all weepy," I tell myself, but end up crying even harder. Again I chastise myself, and again my words come out sounding more like an underwater burble because of my clogged nose and my crying.

"Get a hold of yourself, Leah! There are things that need doing." Maybe Peter will be along soon to help, I think. That last idea gives me some emotional starch and I change my silk blouse and pants for working jeans and a cotton shirt. Both carry the strong aroma of smoke.

When I return downstairs I am again faced with the dirty gray puddles of water on the kitchen floor. The window in the back door. which the firemen had smashed in order to gain access to the locked cottage, is in chunks and splinters all over the floor, and the gaping hole in the outside wall seems larger than it appeared at first. I break down in tears again. I moan loudly as though keening at a funeral for a dead person. I beg futilely for some unknown entity to restore the cottage exactly as it was before I brought on this dreadful mess. "It's all my fault!" I sob.

Now the sun has done its entire disappearing act and the inside of the cottage with its darkly varnished walls harbors gloomy shadows. Finally, I phone Erma Sjoberg to apologize for running off just before dinner. Actually I know my reason for calling her is twofold: good manners but mostly an excuse to find out if Peter has arrived or not. "I'm sorry....."

"... I certainly understand, my dear. Don't apologize. Under the circumstances, I would do exactly the same. I heard from your neighbors, the Harrises, that the fire damage is confined to a small hole in the outside wall of the kitchen, but I suppose the smoke damage is considerably greater."

"Yes," I say, holding back the beginnings of a sob.

"I can't imagine what has happened to Peter. He's usually very prompt or he phones me. Would you like to come back here and eat now that the fire is out? I have all this wasted food, and you do have to eat sometime."

"Thanks, but I'm a bit upset and I have to clean up around here as much as I can before it gets any darker." I know Erma will offer me a place to sleep for the night if I just explain to her about the broken window in the back door, but I say nothing about the lack of security. I don't want her to feel obligated. Anyway, I'm poor company tonight... nervous... angry... but mostly scared. Lately I have grown more and more edgy and suspicious of everyone. Oh, not of Peter's mother, but everyone else. I am like a gun with the safety off... ready to react to the faintest shadow. I literally look over my shoulder every five seconds, especially now that darkness is spilling into the cottage.

Before it grows any later, I hasten to place three of my finished paintings face down in the car with bubble wrap between them for safekeeping. What if someone enters the cottage during the night and slashes my pictures? Those pictures are my entire work of the summer except for the two unfinished one.

Quickly, I add layers of bubble wrap around the garbage can cover and jam it into the burned hole, first checking to assure myself that there are no hidden hot spots in the wood surrounding the hole.

The fit is fairly secure. As the last streak of light on the horizon disappears, I make a decision to pack a small zippered bag with my smoke-smelly pajamas and clean underwear and then drive off to hunt for a motel. This cottage is no place to be, not tonight, not alone... not with a firebug still on the loose.

During the summer season there are at least fifty to sixty motels in and around town to choose from, but I keep my eyes open for a motel on a back street away from the waterfront and away from the glittery Christmas tree lights bordering the main streets where the tourists constantly wander back and forth from one gift shop to another until closing time. Anyway, the motels near the water are far too expensive for me and I don't have a great deal of cash. As it turns out I have to use a credit card anyway. I don't want my old car to be noticed or followed so I drive around for a while before choosing the Gull Motel where the parking lot is behind the motel and where cars can not be seen from the street.

I flop myself supine on the flowered bedspread in the motel room and feel truly safe for the first time in over a week. Then abruptly I sit back up. "How will Peter find me at this obscure motel?" I mull it over in my mind and decide that if he doesn't know where I am, it is likely for the best. Peter didn't consider it important enough to show up at the dinner planned by his own mother so maybe he isn't so terribly anxious to see me as he claims.

There is something strange about Peter's lack of communication with his mother, because I have been assuming all along that Peter is the punctual, reliable sort. Perhaps I'm wrong.

The accelerating interest between Peter and myself has been my prime reason for staying a few extra days at the cottage. Right now as I face myself in the skimpy bathroom mirror, I bluntly tell the reflection: "Be honest. You really don't know Peter that well at all. Look what you just learned about him from his mother about the Father's niece. Perhaps my father was wise to caution me against unfamiliar men like Peter. As it turns out, Peter has a whole spectrum of life experiences hidden from me, including his desire to marry her. Again, I wondered why he failed to be more open about that?

Should I phone Erma Sjoberg a second time and tell her where to find me? No, better not, I advise myself. Calling once is acceptable but if I call again, she will realize that it's just an excuse to find out if Peter has arrived or not. Actually, it's none of my business if Peter is late for his mother's dinner.

This retreat, this obscure motel room, gives me time to unwind. Isn't it exactly because no one knows where I am that I have this feeling of being cosseted as a newborn in a hospital blanket? No crazy person can possibly reach me with frightening phone calls. This room of cheap soft carpeting and rose-colored walls is temporarily my refuge. I sigh deeply. Anyway, I can see Peter tomorrow when I return to Fleury cottage to finish cleaning up some of the mess... that is, if he shows up at all.

I put off my phone call to my father for another half-hour, but finally brave-up enough to tell him the bad news about the fire.

"My God!" he exclaims. "I'm glad you're safe in a motel. Be sure to keep the door locked, just in case someone did follow you. Is there a chain on the door?"

"A double bolt. Don't worry; I'm sure no one saw me come here."

"Now first thing tomorrow let the local insurance agent know about the fire and then come straight home."

"But Dad," I protest, "first I have to get the glass in the back door repaired or at least have a board nailed over it. And what should I do about the hole in the cottage siding? It's large enough for a person to crawl through, and I can't just leave it gaping open to the elements. The September rains come soon and there are usually huge snowdrifts up here in winter. Rain or snow could seep inside and further deteriorate the cottage."

"You're right. I'm not thinking straight...too upset, I guess. All right, I know what you should do. Find out if the insurance agency can hire someone to come in to clean up the smoke stains and ask that builder fellow... what's-his-name?"

"Mr. Cousins."

"Yes, him. He can fix the hole and the glass after you're gone. Just come home as soon as you can before something dreadful happens to you."

"I will. I'm so thankful that Tommy isn't here right now."

"You were smart to send him home when you did. Should I call Roger and send him up there to help you? At least he's good with a hammer and saw." I utter a groan. "No, bad idea. I guess you wouldn't like that and I don't blame you." I hear my father heave a deep sigh over the phone and then he gives me more bad news, "For some reason Roger let Tommy down. He called and said he couldn't take Tommy to the county fair after all."

"Oh, no!" The exclamation is for myself not over Tommy's disappointment. Could this mean that Roger is heading for Tatterack to visit me instead and might in fact show up here at any moment?

"Call me again tomorrow, Leah. I want to know that you're safe."

"Yes, of course. Goodnight, Pop. Love you." I hear a half grunt, half chuckle because I haven't said, "I love you" to him for a long time.

As soon as I hear the bad news that Roger hasn't shown up today in Holland to visit Tommy as promised, my mind begins a frenzied path down twists and turnings, all guesswork of course. Is Roger on his way up here to the cottage to harass me or maybe…could he possibly be here already?

A second idea weasels its way into my tired, overly suspicious mind. Just suppose he has begun to feel the need for my attention; how better to get it than to start a fire and then pose as my hero by helping me cope with the emergency. No, I quickly douse that idea. Roger likes the cottage far too much to do a reckless thing like starting a fire. Besides, he still has vague hopes of recapturing me as in some fabled tale of a lost maiden—or perhaps it is a horse—and reestablishing his ownership of the cottage through me, the horse. Now there's a wild tale! I must be hysterical as well as tired. Still, I have to face the fact that lately Roger has become more and more fanatical about everything, political and otherwise. It sounds unlikely, but maybe he's not above causing a bit of dissension and scaring me out of my wits, especially since he knows that Tommy, his son, is not at the cottage or in any danger.

I realize that my idea of Roger starting the fire is as unreasonable as believing that Peter is the "breather." How can I calm myself down after all that's taken place today and last week as well? How can I keep my brain from going back over and over everything that's happened? All my nervous unraveling over the fire introduces even more weird scenarios. One in particular keeps returning. And it's an especially scary one.

The incident that now forces its way back into my mind happened nearly five years ago, just before my separation from Roger. At that time he became almost unhinged. He locked me inside a closet, swearing that he would keep me there until I changed my mind about the divorce. A spasm of cold shivers, as if I were still stuck in that same closet, attacks me as I relive the incident.

The closet was right there in Fleury cottage, tucked under the stairs just off the kitchen. No mater which way I turned in the small closet, I could feel the filmy dry webs woven by spiders touching my face. I couldn't see them because the closet had no electrical light source as it does now. That dark little closet terrorized me. After a few minutes of sheer panic in which I hammered on the plank door and screamed, "Let me out!" I finally calmed down long enough to recall something useful.

A girlfriend and I had once hidden down under the floor of that same closet when we were kids. We were small then and the sandy crawl space beneath the floor seemed large in proportion to our own diminutive sizes. The conversation of the grownups above us in the kitchen could be heard and that was exciting. We were genuine spies, or so we believed. We had gained access to the snug little space beneath the floor by crawling through an opening in the lattice which skirted the outside of the foundation.

At one time the cool space where we had hidden under the floor had been used for the storage of butter and cheese. This was achieved by lifting up the floorboards in the closet. But also, if one wanted to, a person could actually drop down onto the pristine sand beneath and make their way on all fours in a reverse direction to the lattice panel which opened out onto the west side of the cottage and was well screened by cedar trees. That's how I escaped that day when Roger locked me in the closet.

A few minutes later when Roger left the cottage to check on Tommy, who was sitting in his playpen in the sand down on the beach before Roger locked me in the closet, I ran back inside the cottage, grabbed my purse and car keys, and then hid again . . . this time behind the door to the livingroom. When Roger visited the bathroom, I scooped up Tommy from his playpen, got in the car and sped away. That was a very traumatic event in my life and I wished my mind wouldn't keep skittering back to it time after time. It makes my lungs tighten, and I nearly stop breathing when I relive my incarceration in that tight little closet.

Tonight, in the motel bathroom, I go through the usual ritual of brushing my teeth and showering, but all the time my mind keeps reverting to thoughts of Peter. "Surely he must have arrived in Tatterack by now." His mother had been so positive that he would be there in time for dinner, but she had been wrong. What had happened? An accident? "Please, not that," I beg some unknown entity as I drop exhausted onto the queen-size bed. But the knowledge that caused the sharpest disappointment and trammeled my feelings, was his cover-up about the little Father's favorite niece. Why hadn't he shared that with me?

What if Peter had yearnings to join the church? Though I had just become aware of his previous connection to the same church denomination that I was having trouble with over the loud music, yet I didn't believe that Peter had anything to do with the ominous phone calls. Clearly though, it was most likely that the girl was his excuse for not helping me against the noise pollution. Could his feelings towards the church have changed over the years? It was doubtful.

In spite of my suspicious thoughts regarding Peter and his affinity to the nearby church, I finally dozed off. Realizing that absolutely no one, except my father, knew where I was and therefore could not possibly harm me, caused a deeper, more relaxed sleep than I had enjoyed for several weeks.

CHAPTER 34

$\mathcal{A}$fter an egg biscuit and a coffee at Burger King the next morning, I drove back to Fleury cottage to face up to a day of cleaning and packing. Upstairs I grimaced and sniffed at my smoky clothes and packed the worst smelling ones in plastic bags before tossing them into the car. Some clothes, borderline acceptable, I hung out on the clothesline to air. As I worked, my mind was free to reminisce warmly about my first meetings with Peter.

I vividly remembered the wonderful time Tommy and I had enjoyed when we went sailing on Peter's boat. Also, I recalled my surprise at Peter's thorough knowledge of various churches. I wouldn't have considered it unusual if he had spouted forth about microbes or chemicals since he was in the pharmaceutical business but, instead, he had expounded extensively on the origins of the church. Now I know why: Peter had had to learn all about the history and rituals of that one particular church, the Catholic. He couldn't get married in that church unless he studied for it. I stopped removing clothes from the hangers long enough to ask myself, "I wonder why he changed his mind? Or maybe he hasn't changed his mind?

Just recently, I recalled, Peter had pointed out to me the failure of a lawsuit brought against a church in Fairview, a small resort further downstate on Lake Huron. He had also shown me a newspaper clipping about a group who had tried to put a stop to outdoor broadcasts of sermons by an entirely different denomination. People in the picture were holding signs and walking up and down in front of the church. It was a Baptist church, I believe. Peter had been careful to point out that even though the rally had seemed to be well-organized and publicized, it had failed, "So," he had added, "I hope you don't become overly confident in your protest against the electronic bells and set yourself up for a disappointment."

Why hadn't I been more attuned to those negative hints from Peter before? In retrospect I now realized that he hadn't encouraged me in my pursuit of quelling noise pollution at all...even suggesting that I should go home with Tommy to allow the animosity against me to die down. Surely that not too subtle statement plus the newspaper clippings were clues, and precise arrows, pointing in the direction of his true belief...that churches, especially that particular church, had the divine right to bombard folks with religious music.

All along in my mind I had been assuming that Peter believed as I did about the noise pollution coming from the nearby church. But did he? What if I had been totally blindsided? In fact, it now seemed obvious to me that his opinion would be tainted by his near conversion long ago.

Everyone had at least two sides to their personalities and Peter was surely no exception. Roger possessed even more than two sides. His personality could be represented by an octagon...a warped one at that. What about Peter? Be careful, I warned myself, there are negative sides to every person.

Surely though, I was being overly suspicious. Someone like Peter wasn't warped enough to make those dreadful, frightening phone calls or actually set fire to the cottage as a warning. For it *was* just a warning. There had been no attempt to burn down the whole structure. If that had been the purpose, the rags soaked in paint thinner would have been tucked under the siding all the way around the cottage near the foundation, not just in a few places.

"For shame," I scold myself, "How can you attribute such blatant, devious action, even in speculation, to Peter?" This was the same Peter who enjoyed teaching Tommy all about sailing... the man who became your comforter and also the person who admired your paintings.

"Yet," another little voice, an untrusting one inside me, counters, "if he's so devoted to you and Tommy, where is he right now?"

Stop! I command myself. You are seeing everything about Peter through flawed glass exactly like the wavy antique windows in the cottage bedrooms that make straight lines appear curvilinear. The "flawed glass" is equivalent to my skewed-up vision of things now that I perceived Peter at a different angle. With my changed view, Peter appeared from a disappointing perspective.

All this conjecture didn't prove anything except how confused and scared I was, and definitely more than a little jealous of the church Peter almost disappeared into forever. But, I reminded myself, just because Roger let me down, doesn't mean Peter was made of the same inferior stuff. Besides, Peter had never made promises of any sort to me, nor I to him.

After stowing my metal toolbox of paints in the car along with a bag of dirty laundry, I began packing foods in the kitchen. Though I might not be able to leave until Sunday morning, I could still pack all the groceries, except the perishables, because obviously I wasn't going to do any cooking in this wet, slimy-floored kitchen. With its low beams blackened and festooned with ashes, the kitchen looked like a scene straight from one of Dickens' bleakest novels.

I filled a grocery box with canned goods, plus cereal, crackers, and some cookies, things that wouldn't spoil on the trip home. The perishables I put in a plastic bag to take over to my neighbors living on the west side, the Harrises. I am nearly finished, except for wiping down the inside of the refrigerator and dumping the ice cubes, when the telephone rings.

"Not another crank call, I hope." I pick up the receiver and turn on the tape recorder at the same time. The caller turns out to be Police Chief Bruckner so I switch off the tape recorder.

"I think you'll feel easier knowing that we've found out who started the fire at your cottage. I can't give you his name until we've taken him into custody and double-checked further, but I can tell you that it's someone who lives near you and who has been, shall we say, getting older, bitter, perhaps even a bit senile. He's been behaving oddly for some time. Last summer he was caught peering into a neighbor's window. Still, this fire is the first real harm he has caused. It's best for you to be on your guard until we pick him up later this morning after the sheriff completes some paperwork.

"That's good news. What about the phone calls?"

"Nothing definite on that yet. Keep reporting to the phone company, and they'll let me know if they are successful in tracking down the culprit."

After Chief Bruckner had hung up the phone, I let out a huge gulp of relief. My mind wandered back and forth over the question of "who could the firebug possibly be?" Could the chief be referring to Father Ciconni himself? His erratic, unpriestly demeanor still shook my mind. It's quite unbelievable to me that a priest could have so little control that he would allow himself to stomp his foot and loose his temper as he did in front of me. Or could the breather be one of the elderly Tribners or perhaps the beefy man up the road?

As I finish cleaning the inside of the refrigerator, I glance out the window above the sink and see Mr. Lumus coming down the driveway towards my back door. His shirt is half out of his trousers as though he has dressed carelessly or in a great hurry and I notice that he is still limping.

With his head first turning right and then left, Mr. Lumus appears to be checking to see if anyone nearby is watching him. Very furtive behavior, I think.

My cottage door is already locked, though anyone can get inside by merely pushing against the canvas that I have tacked over the upper part of the door where the windows are broken. I really don't want to be bothered by Mr. Lumus today, so I make an impulsive decision. If Mr. Lumus doesn't see me through any of the cottage windows, he will knock and then quickly go away again. I duck into the closet under the stairs since it is the nearest place to get completely out of sight.

Immediately after stepping inside the closet, I know it's a mistake. I wish I had chosen any other place. I shiver, remembering the awful time I endured once before, the time I had been locked in the closet by Roger. Frantically, I wipe away at something touching my forehead, a floating cobweb probably. The closet has since been updated and now there is an electrical switch. I wish I could turn it on, but the light will surely show a strip of yellow under the bottom of the door and give away my hiding place to Mr. Lumus if he decides to spy through a window before trying to break inside.

It now occurs to me that Chief Bruckner, who spoke to me just a few minutes ago on the telephone about an older, senile man, could easily have been alluding to Mr. Lumus who has always seemed a bit eccentric to me, especially this summer. Or is it simply that I am suspicious of anyone and everyone who approaches the cottage?

What puzzles me is this: If the culprit who started the fire should turn out to be Mr. Lumus and not someone else, then why? It doesn't make a bit of sense. Mr. Lumus has been the first one, aside from myself, to rant and rave against the noise of the electronic bells. We, Mr. Lumus and I, have supposedly been on the same team; we both want to lower the volume of the bells. Then what makes him suddenly reverse his position? Unless of course, he has been psychologically influenced by Father Ciconni. Does the little Father make Mr. Lumus feel so guilty that, along with the "telling of his beads" or wearing a cilice as a penance, he feels compelled to reverse his position on the noise pollution? My theory, I'll admit, does seem a bit stretched.

Mr. Lumus fails to knock on the door, so there is no other sound for several minutes; yet there are no receding footsteps either. Does that mean he is still standing there outside my door contemplating whether to go away or not? Then just as I am about to cautiously open the closet door a crack, I hear the pop-pop-popping sounds of thumbtacks hitting the floor. Mr. Lumus is breaking-in! Surely he must realize that I'm not far away—after all, my car is parked in the driveway—yet he continues to push-in the canvas.

One by one the tacks holding the canvas over the window continue to hit the floor...plink, plink, plink. Next, I hear the sound of his hand and arm fumbling and groping past the stiff canvas and inside to turn the lock. The door opens, catching and scraping on the thumbtacks strewn across the wooden floor. It is exactly at this moment that I begin to feel a shortness of breath, the usual sign of claustrophobia. I must get out of the closet, but how can I? I stop. I'm afraid to come out because Mr. Lumus, having forced his way inside the cottage, can certainly be up to no good.

Why have I foolishly trapped myself in the exact same closet that was the scene of my trauma once before? What a stupid thing to do! I shift my feet cautiously to see if the floorboards are still loose. What if my father has recently nailed them down? But if he hasn't, I can still escape the same way I did four years ago when Roger locked me inside this same closet. I reach my hand down to test the firmness of the boards and realize that the floor is weighted down with a mop, metal pail, broom, and similar household items. There is absolutely no way of pulling up the floorboards without first creating a loud clackity-bang and that will immediately give away my hiding place. But my loud, panicky breathing will *also* give me away.....immediately. I begin to shake against the wooden sides of the closet and dislodge the mop which slides to the floor with a resounding bam.

I tell myself, Leah, get yourself out of here before you panic any further. I begin to cough loudly. Quickly, with the intention of running straight out the cottage door afterwards, I burst open the closet door. At the exact same moment I hear, with unbelievable relief, a familiar voice, Peter's!

"What are you doing here, Mr. Lumus?"

"Just want to see the fire damage."

"Oh? It looked to me like you were breaking in."

"The door's not locked."

"It was locked last night when I tried it. I think you'd better leave before I call the police."

Holding my chest in an attempt to stop coughing, I step further out into the room. Mr. Lumus takes one look at me, turns and runs. Peter and I watch him until he reaches the road and heads directly across to his own cottage.

My relief is so great by Peter's timely arrival that the chills rippling up my neck change quickly to a bolt of warm headiness. Perhaps I have been taking in too much oxygen with my accelerated breathing without realizing it. No wonder I feel slightly dizzy.

Peter leans a piece of plywood against the kitchen counter. Evidently he intends to nail it across the hole in the wall near the floor.

"Your face looks as ashen as that hole...but", he adds kindly with a smile, "not quite as dirty." He gestures towards the ash-lined hole that I had plugged-up last evening with the garbage can cover.

I try to regain my composure and my breath. Then I tell Peter in a high weak voice—as though the closet has been full of helium—about the phone call from the police chief and the subsequent break-in.

"Perhaps Mr. Lumus is the one who is also making the threatening phone calls," Peter suggests as he tosses his cap on the nearby counter.

"But," my voice keeps flaking out into a mere whisper, "how can that be? Remember, Mr. Lumus is against the high decibels. Unless, Father Ciconni is threatening him into doing some kind of penance for his daring to tell people that the bells are too loud." The look on Peter's face tells me that he is dubious over my logic.

"Well," I try once more to adjust my voice to its normal pitch, "the police chief did phone this morning to tell me that the fire bug is someone living nearby and possibly a bit senile and that description could certainly fit Mr. Lumus."

Peter nods. "Next time someone breaks in, and I hope there won't be one, run out the front door and up the beach to us or to your neighbors. Don't get trapped in a closet." I nod my agreement. No more closets for me, not ever.

"Sorry about last night," Peter apologizes. "Mother said you and she were waiting dinner for me when the fire broke out. Very suspicious business. By the time I arrived here after nine o'clock, you had gone off somewhere. The cottage was dark. Where did you go?"

"To a motel."

"A wise decision, though I wish you had told my mother where you were going so that I wouldn't worry about you." Peter takes my hands and draws me into a warm comforting hug.

In spite of the recent stern proclamation to myself about staying independent of further attachments, Peter's "worry about you" statement momentarily gives me a wonderful feeling of security. Then a caution sign flips into my head and I stiffen. Peter hasn't offered to tell *me* where *he* was last night or exactly why he had failed to arrive for the dinner his mother had prepared.

"Well, where were you last night?"

"All in good time," he stalls. Peter has completely failed to tell me about his inclination towards the Catholic Church as a priest and now he isn't even going to tell me where he was last night? I stiffen. In my head I reiterate my father's warning: Shouldn't you be more cautious of new boyfriends? So I tell myself to move slowly, carefully.

Is my relationship with Peter going to turn out to be sincere on one side and a big question mark on the other? Am I going to concede all my independence and individuality to someone who thinks he doesn't have to divulge his own past or even his whereabouts the previous evening or, more importantly, his yearning to marry into the Catholic Church and not tell me. Perhaps then, if Peter is going to treat me like a child or some weak-minded retard, I'd better rethink our relationship very carefully before it's too late.

I push myself free of Peter's arms. "I didn't know I was supposed to report-in to anyone." I must have sounded more like a recalcitrant, pouting teenager than I intended because Peter doesn't pull me back into his arms again. He doesn't even look at me or answer, just picks up the plywood and begins to nail it over the hole in the wall with swift firm strokes of the hammer.

Between hammer strokes, Peter says, "You know very well that I wouldn't expect you to report to me about every move you make. That would be ridiculous... untrusting. I have a hunch that your reluctance to make new male attachments really stems a lot more from your fear of losing your independence than"... blow of the hammer... "from your bad experiences with Roger. Chances are"—another blow of the hammer— "you'll never be able to trust anyone." Peter gathers his hammer and nails from the counter and opens the back door.

Through the door we can both see a police car across the road in front of the Lumus cottage. "There's your culprit." Peter remarks, and walks out the door.

"Thanks for covering the hole," I call after him, but Peter doesn't stop or turn around. He keeps his back to me and simply raises his hand in acknowledgment as he disappears up the road heading towards his mother's cottage.

The tears begin to fall down my cheeks. "You're a stupid fool," I tell myself. I stand on the back porch watching Peter go out of sight. Now it's even too late to call out, "Please come back." What if he doesn't want to come back... ever? Oh, he will... he will, I staunchly tell myself. But I'm not at all sure about that as the tears begin to spill.

CHAPTER 35

*A*n hour later while I'm still wiping the greasy film off my mother's desk with a lemon cleaner, the phone rings. Not another crank phone call! I shiver and don't bother to answer. This morning and the day before have been depressing enough without receiving another threatening telephone call. But then, I ask myself, what if it's Mr. Cousins, the contractor, or Peter calling? Still, I let it ring several more times before deciding to walk across the living room to the kitchen and pick up the receiver. If it should be Peter this is my opportunity to apologize for my strange, alienating behavior when he was here earlier. Cautiously, as though the telephone might explode in my ear, I lift the receiver and hear a familiar voice on the line, Peter's mother, Erma.

"I'm coming down your way and I'd like to stop in to see you before you leave, if you don't mind."

"Yes, of course." How can I refuse her? Her request is so definite. She sounds very determined, a lot like Peter. A few minutes later Erma arrives and parks behind my car. I walk out to meet her so that she won't have to come inside the cottage unless she actually asks to see the fire dmage. After all, the place smells stinky as a swamp due to the large quantity of water the firemen hosed onto the steaming wood. Even the green kitchen rug, which I'm going to throw out, is so saturated with water that it looks more like an algae covered pond.

For some reason Erma has driven the half block from her cottage to this one in Peter's silver Mazda. Immediately, I see the huge dent in the front fender on the driver's side and point to it. "When did that happen?"

"Someone ran into Peter near Kalkaska on the way up here last evening. The garage had to pull the fender away from the wheel. That's why he got here so late. Didn't he tell you?"

I shake my head. "No." To myself I admit that I didn't give him much of a chance to tell me.

"Well, he tried to phone me earlier, around five; I was down on the beach and didn't have the portable phone with me, and I don't have my cottage phone rigged for an answering service. Peter called again around eight o'clock.

Oh, I think to myself, that's just a little after I drove up town to the motel.

"Peter tells me he's not sure when you're planning to leave, so I decided I'd better get these articles on noise pollution to you just in case I didn't see you again this summer."

Erma thrust a magazine and several news clippings into my hands. Quickly, I note that one clipping is from US News and another is from the Chicago Tribune.

"Actually, I meant to give you some of these clippings and articles last evening, but the fire intervened and during all that excitement I simply forgot. Then when Peter finally did arrive, he brought this additional magazine article to give you. It's about the effects of different types of noise pollution on the human physical system. He thought it might give you more facts to use if you decide to write a leter to the diocese about the bell problem. Or you might want to use it to write a news story of your own and try to get it published in one of the nearby towns since Tatterack doesn't have a full-time newspaper." Erma handed the clippings through the car window.

"I was quite disgusted to read," Erma pokes a finger at another magazine she picked up from the car seat next to her. "that the North American Conservation laws haven't set a low enough decibel level to protect us from many sources of noise exposure."

"Thank you, Erma. Thank Peter for me, too." To myself, I wonder. Doesn't this article sent to me by Peter prove that I'm misjudging him? He still does mean to help me. Maybe though, it's too late now.

I note that Erma glances towards my car where the stacked boxes and paintings are visible through the windows, proof that I have been packing to leave.

"When are you leaving?"

"Probably tomorrow or Monday morning. It depends on when I can get in touch with Mr. Cousins, the builder, to fix the hole in the cottage wall. Peter nailed that piece of wood over the hole as a temporary fix."

"Good. That will at least keep out most of the wildlife. I'm sorry you're leaving so soon. Peter seems to care a great deal about you. That's all I'd better say since mothers aren't allowed to interfere."

I flash a smiling message of thanks to her. That she has already interfered is quite evident... bless her. Erma flips the key in the ignition and then she looks back at me as a new thought occurs to her. "How did Tommy cope after his kidnapping?"

"He put on a a brave front for the policeman, but had a nervoius crying jag after we got home. I tried not to baby him too much, but it was difficult for me to remain neutral. I really wanted to hug him and sooth him and do a little crying myself."

"Yes, sometimes it's much harder for mothers to keep a cool head. I'd like to see you before you leave if you have time."

"Maybe I can. Thanks again for the articles."

After Erma leaves, I head for the beach taking the articles with me to read. I reach the sand and sit down in the beach chair, which I have forgotten to fold and store inside the cottage. Everything on the shore seems more beautiful than ever today. It's always so much harder to leave the cottage and go home when the weather is nice. Rain and soggy ugliness, wet feet and damp smelling shoes make the leaving easier, at least emotionally. "No," I amend out loud, "nothing will make leaving Tatterack easy this year simply because of Peter." Now I realize how fervently I want to see Peter again before I go home.

There are misunderstandings to clear up and not just on my part either. If he is truly serious about our relationship, why did he keep his long ago religious plans a secret from me? I can only conclude that he really isn't ready for a serious commitment. Perhaps I'm not ready either.

This afternoon the water slips lazily around the rocks a few feet out from the shore and then washes up on the sandy beach just as placidly. As the first laps of water touch the curve of the beach, others, little tag ripples, flow in seconds later, adding a soft counterpoint sound of shush, shush, sha. How can I get along without this calming water music after I leave?

Emotionally, my life is centered around the water in this place where I have spent so many of my summers, but the water isn't the total picture either. There are the freighters passing the cottage on their way to foreign ports, there are the gulls, selfish and raucous, and also the deep throated croak of the skinny-legged herons. All are part of the ambiance.

For a few minutes I am distracted from the sadness of my thoughts over leaving Peter and this place, and by the antics of the ducks. One slightly larger young duck trails along behind the smaller ones, who in turn are led by the mother duck. The last duck constantly quacks and scolds, even beats its wings against the water as if furious about something. However, the smaller ducks float serenely on, appearing to pay no attention to the disgruntled member of their flock as it continues to splash wildly and fling nasty epithets at them in the form of quacks.

Well, I think, maybe that's exactly how I seem to people in the beach colony... chasing, sputtering angrily after them about the noise pollution of the bells. Like the ducks out there in the water, people are paying no attention to the scolder, which is me. Perhaps I haven't made it clear to them what's really at stake besides deafness...that it's not just a matter of hurting their eardrums. It's also a matter of giving up another one of their freedoms… freedom from noise and air pollution.

Next, I think about all sorts of morbid things in order to push back my thoughts about Peter and my disappointment. I recognize my depression and need to put a stop to it before it gets out of hand.

Right on schedule the twelve o'clock electronic bell music begins. There is no strong wind today to push the electronic sounds in the opposite direction. The disrupting noise blares forth, flaunting over the sweeter water music, literally drowning it. Irritated, I jump up in anger.

What kind of material has Erma brought me? Down I sit again and begin to leaf through the pages of the first magazine article on noise pollution. It had been nice of Peter to find the article with the intention of bringing it up to me. Isn't it proof that he *does* believe in my noise pollution project?

Erma's idea of writing a news type story on how the noise affects people's nerves is another good one. Perhaps I really should stay a few more days up here to write an article, or am I just hunting for an excuse to stay on at the cottage a bit longer? Yes, of course, I am…in hopes that Peter will seek me out again.

Exactly what old notion, Victorian of course, makes me feel that I have to wait for Peter to make the next move? This is hardly the eighteen nineties. I am the one who discouraged him, so why shouldn't I be the one to stitch our relationship back together? Then I answer my own question: because, after my cold, independent and discouraging attitude, he might not want to mend it. He might be completely disgusted and finished with me.

My eye catches on the canoe still lying upside down on the beach, another thing I have forgotten to store away. How could I forget so much? Easily, I grumble, with the fire, the ominous phone threats, and all the other disrupting things happening around here.

"I might as well take one last canoe ride," I decide, and leave the articles on noise pollution held down by a flowerpot on the back porch. I fetch a boyant cushion and the paddle from the shed. Then, with difficulty, because Tommy isn't here to help, I drag the canoe down to the edge of the water. The water is faintly rippled, almost evenly spaced, like corrugated cardboard but in a beautiful yellow-green glassy shade. There is no threat from either the sky or the water. I paddle west, passing several cottages and then decide to go about and head towards my own beach again. After all, there are still plenty of things I need to get done... must get done, like taking the leftover food to my neighbors, Mavis and Frederick. I dig my paddle in deeper at the stern and hold it there until the canoe slowly swings about in the direction of the cottage.

When I look towards the shore again, I realize that someone is walking back and forth in front of Fleury cottage on the beach. It's not Peter, I'd know his gleaming head immediately. Roger? My whole body stiffens with dread. The crank phone calls, the fire, and now Roger!

I don't feel up to Roger's innuendos, his sarcasm, or his ploys to win me back... not on top of all the other things that have happened lately. Tears begin to run down my cheeks and I moan out loud. When Roger shows up back in Holland for his weekends of parental rights, there is always Tommy or my father to act as buffers. Up here at the cottage there is no one to act as a cushion to soften the corrosiveness of Roger's personality rubbing against mine.

Suddenly I am so tired, so discouraged. The tears continue to fall even faster. I have no paper hanky with me so I dip one hand in the water to splash away my tears. Why can't I just lie down in the bottom of this canoe and drift away or stay out here paddling back and forth the rest of the day? Of course, I can't. Roger would soon catch on to where I am ... probably already knows where I am since he is quite familiar with the yellow color of the canoe and can see that it's not in its usual place turned upside down on the sand.

There is no way for me to escape Roger. With my car so visible in the driveway, it must be obvious to him that I am not far away even if he hasn't spotted the canoe. After driving so many miles to get up here to Tatterack, he isn't going to give up so easily. He will wait patiently for his little mouse to show up. Even so, I paddle in the opposite direction for a few strokes, then from the corner of my eye I can see Roger settling down in the beach chair on the sand. It's futile trying to escape from him. Even with two hundred feet of water between us, his very presence there on the beach makes me feel entrapped...my fate sealed as though in a plastic bag. I wipe my wet face with the bottom of my shirt and head back to shore.

When the canoe scrapes against the shore, Roger ambles over to help me pull it up further. "Lee-ah, darling! The way you were paddling, I thought you'd never make it back to shore and I'd have to send the Coast Guard after you."

The confrontation is beginning. I ignore his attempt at humor or is he implying that I am an inept canoeist? It isn't the first time he has used that "weak woman" implication. Usually it's to fuel his own ego. I notice that Roger looks just as he always does, deceptively boyish, clean cut, and so bouncy that one wants to dribble him across a basketball court. I nod to acknowledge him, but fail to meet his smile with one of my own.

"Tommy phoned me about the fire, so I assumed, since you're such a reclusive little lady with few friends, that you could use some help, so I hurried right up."

"So I see. No need though. Everything is under control." Maybe it isn't quite under control, but there is no way that I would admit that to Roger.

"Let's see the damage, so I can judge for myself what needs to be done." We walk to the back door of the cottage and Roger steps inside. Immediately, he wrinkles up his nose. "Wooeeee! pretty awful; you can't stay here. Better come straight home when I go."

"No. I have some things to finish up here before I go home."

"I'm sure your father and Tommy expect you to come home right away. They must be pretty worried. Besides, what about that crank caller I heard about? As long as he's still at large, you need protecting; I wouldn't want you to get hurt. You still mean a lot to me, you know."

As usual, Roger is groping for excuses to stay in my life. He reaches out for my arm as though to comfort me. I react by jerking away. "No, Roger, you're wrong. They caught the firebug. He and the crank caller are most likely one and the same so I'm perfectly safe now and quite able to take care of myself."

"Now don't pull that independence belle stuff, little lady. I can stay and help you scrub away the soot around here." He points to the hanging wisps of gray and black ash clinging to the rafters.

"The insurance company is going to send in some professional cleaners to do the job. Thanks anyway." I try to recall when Roger has ever so much as lifted a broom to help me clean in the past and I simply can't.

"Roger, your son is still looking forward to seeing you this weekend. I believe you were going to take him to the county fair? But you didn't show up. My father told me on the phone that Tommy is terribly disappointed. Why did you let him down? If you leave right now, you might still keep your promise. You could still take him to the fair tomorrow instead of today."

As I talk, I'm also edging myself closer to the back door. I feel an overwhelming urge to escape from Roger. I don't think he will try to corner me and lock me in that closet as he did once before, but I'm unable to control my wariness, my long-standing suspicion. I will never forget the closet episode. He might try something equally frightening. Right now there is this cowardly need of mine to cut and run before Roger thinks up some way to take advantage of my situation.

"I'm not leaving here," Roger states flatly.

Probably he won't. I realize with dread that I might have to contend with his interference all the rest of today and even longer. He is not going to leave, but there's no reason why I can't. Suddenly, I switch directions completely and go back over to the refrigerator to pull out the bag of perishables meant for Mavis next door. Then I quickly head for the door before Roger can catch on to what is happening.

"Hey, come back here; I'm talking to you," Roger calls out as I hurry down the porch steps.

I congratulate myself on evading Roger so deftly. As I cross the back yard to my neighbor's cottage. Roger's voice trails after me, "You're always running away."

After dropping off the lettuce and other fresh vegetables next door, I decide to keep on walking up the road rather than go back and face Roger immediately. Anyway, I need the time to sort out my behavior. Could Roger actually be right?

"Am I always running away?"

CHAPTER 36

"Am I always running away?" The question is on my mind as I continue to hike westward up the dirt road, beyond the beach grocery store, and past the cemetery. Eventually, when the road makes a turn inland away from the water, I leave the road in favor of the beach, which is mostly white limestones at this point making the walking more difficult. Soon, even the cottages are left behind and there is nothing except wilderness. Still, I keep trudging onwards keeping close to the water, sometimes encountering huge up-heaved slabs of limestone pushed by a long ago glacier.

Less sharply this time, I probe myself, "Am I always running away because I hate to face up to things I don't like?" I speak out loudly because along this remote part of the beach there is no one around to see me talking to myself. Yes, it's true. I do hate to face up to Roger, and if it denotes a terrible flaw in my nature, so be it. How many times have I ducked out of an encounter with Roger or shied away from him. Plenty. I justify my past behavior by vehemently shouting loudly, once again to no one but the trees, the rocks, and the water. "Even people with thick skins wouldn't want to stand and exchange sword-words with Roger!"

Am I behaving the same with Peter? Have I been evading his loving overtures because of my "running scared" nature? If I have, it's because I have a good excuse... because of my fear of getting entangled with another man who might have Roger's same character flaws. But no! According to Peter, that's not the reason at all. He claims the problems imminent from my fierce independence. He's implying that I lack the ability to share my life with others, specifically, with a man like him, and so as a result, I'll never have any significant male friends or lovers, and never marry again.

Am I so unbending? "No," I kick at the stones, "it isn't true." Wanting independence doesn't necessarily make me an unloving person. Peter makes me sound like a complete misfit, bereft of the ability to love.

Finally, I sit down to rest. My ankles are lame, not used to the unevenness of the slabs of limestone almost the size of manmade sidewalk chunks, only these were uplifted from billions of years ago. My foot bottoms also hurt from stepping down on the smaller pointed stones in my thin-soled canvas sneakers.

Out in the water opposite me looms the huge boulder that my friends and I used to climb. It was a summertime ritual. There are numerous camera shots of us clowning on the top, documentation of our prowess. Back then we thought it was quite an achievement to reach the top. The boulder is big enough to hold at least four people on the top, maybe five if one is careful not to accidentally crowd a friend off into the water. The rock can be reached during seasons of lower water, which it happens to be right now, by first leaping from smaller rocks that aren't completely submerged.

Why not? I ask myself and begin to jump from rock to rock in the direction of the giant boulder. Sometimes I miss and end up getting my feet wet, but the water depth is shallow here and the lovely coolness permeates my over-heated, sore feet. I remember from the past that it was fairly easy to find footholds to climb up onto the boulder, but in trying to get back down once again, those same footholds were in awkward positions so that one had to slide down in an uncontrolled manner on one's butt, often ending up getting soaked at the bottom.

Today, I manage to climb up onto the boulder, but it feels lonely at the top without my joyous friends of the past. There's no one to share my accomplishment. Well, I scold myself, it's your own fault that you've lost track of Robert, Helen, and other high school friends. Maybe Roger is partially right…about my turning my back on socializing. After resting abit on the top of the boulder, I decide to slide down on my stomach instead of my butt. Even so, I gain too much momentum near the bottom and end up soaking my jeans all the way up to my crotch. I look around almost expecting laughter at my awkward plunge into water at the bottom. There is no one there to laugh. Just the same, I deem my attempt to duplicate the past experience a success.

I decide that it's time to return to the cottage and face up to Roger. "After all," I tell myself in an attempt to bolster my confidence, "you are legally divorced from Roger. Why should you be so afraid of him? He no longer has any real power over you. What can he do to you?" And I answer, "plenty." Roger can act possessive and manage to complicate the relationship between a friend like Peter and me.

The noontime sun is much stronger now and keeps flashing in my eyes. I wish I hadn't left my sunglasses back at the cottage. Maybe though, the sun reflecting off the white limestones is beginning to charge-up the cells in my brain because I immediately exclaim, "Oh, but I *do* want to keep my new relationship with Peter!" In that case I'd better hurry right back to the cottage and see that Roger doesn't make outrageous statements about me to Peter, unless I'm there to refute them or smooth them over again. Roger's smarty tongue can cause a mountain of embarrassment. He can easily dissemble everything between Peter and me.

Thirty minutes later, weary and quite literally footsore because a sharp-edged stone has actually penetrated the bottom of my left sneaker, I return to the cottage. Roger's car is gone and I find the back door key in its usual place under a flowerpot on the back porch. Roger hasn't forgotten that hiding place even though it has been over three years since he last visited here.

I suppose it might be too much to hope that Roger has just given up and gone back home to Battle Creek. That isn't too likely. Inside the cottage, I notice a denim cap lying on the kitchen counter. Is it

Roger's or Peter's? Roger seldom wears hats of any kind so it must be Peter's. Yes, almost certainly. Wasn't he wearing a cap this morning when he arrived to nail the board over the hole in the wall? It seems as though that happened a whole day ago, but it was just this morning.

Hurriedly, I wash my face and change my damp clothes, all the time listening for Roger's car. I pray that I can escape again before he returns. I pick up the cap from the counter, lock the back door, and pocket the key, though Roger can easily get back inside by pushing out the canvas that I have tacked again over the broken window after Mr. Lumus's thwarted attempt to sneak back into the cottage.

Now I tell myself, this is as good a time as any to return Peter's cap and apologize to him for my waspish, untrusting behavior. Maybe then he will confide in me his reasons for wishing to join the Catholic church and why he changed his mind… if he really has changed his mind.

At the Sjoberg cottage, Peter himself opens the door and I spot immediately the deep remoteness in his eyes. The eyes stay the same temperature, cold fiord blue … there is no warming trend. After he invites me inside, I ask him, "Why didn't you come back for your cap?" I look up into Peter's face, but after his first polite greeting, he has wiped it clear of expression. I see no smile, just the kind of formal good manners one puts on for company. Except now I have definitely decided that I want to be more than "just company."

Of course, he and I both know that my return of his cap is just a feeble excuse to get a conversation going. I realize that the reason Peter has not made contact with me again is because of my apparent unbendable, suspicious attitude towards him.

"Sorry, I didn't get the cap back to you sooner. I was going to phone you… but"

"You're sorry about a mere cap?"

"No," I hesitate, "a more important "sorry." I came to apologize for not…." Peter's vacuous expression gives me no help in my choked-out apology. "To apologize for being so untrusting. You have been so kind to Tommy and me." I dab at my cheek where I feel a tear running down and dab at it again. I hadn't expected to become so emotional over a simple apology. Maybe I'm just terribly tired and wrought up over all that has happened... the harassments, the fire, and then Roger's arrival.

Peter's face bursts into a smile. "I accept. Start over?"

I shake my head negatively. "There's something else." The very idea of asking the next question seems so untrusting in itself that I hesitate. Not knowing the answer however, will permanently cloud our relationship. "Did you once desire to marry the Father's favorite niece?" Peter's face reflects complete astonishment.

"Where did you get that strange idea? Oh, my mother." I nod a "yes" and wait for an explanation.

"I was a mere sixteen year-old boy! I would have told you, but somehow I didn't think it mattered; it occurred so long ago." I look at Peter's face expecting sadness over the breaking up of his past ambition, but immediately he adds cheerfully and firmly, "I have no regrets."

"Thanks for answering such a personal question." Now I'm the one to smile.

Peter changes the subject. "Beautiful weather we're having. Too beautiful to leave Tatterack."

"How did you know that I was leaving?"

"I have a spy; the same one you have. My mother told me. I'll help you unpack."

"I'm not sure I can stay. You see, Roger arrived at the cottage about two hours ago. He'll keep hanging around and spoil our chances of doing anything without including him. You see, your high qualifications have reached him through Tommy via the telephone."

Peter's face reflects astonishment. "Maybe if you keep completely out of his sight, he will have no reason to hang around. You can stay up here with me and my mother. We'll put you in the priest hole."

"Oh, thanks loads," I say with a laugh, "but I think I should go back to that motel tonight if I can get my car out of the driveway before Roger blocks it in again." Why, I ask myself, hadn't I been smart enough to move my car earlier?

"No, not this time." Peter's voice sounds assertive. "Stay here at our cottage. You will be perfectly safe... from me too... or are you more concerned about what might tempt you?"

"Is that a smirk I see on your face? I am worried about both of us. There's a powerful force brewing between us."

"Indeed... a natural force and a wonderful one, but we are both smart enough to understand that sex alone isn't the whole answer. There has to be something else to glue a relationship together so that it can stay bonded."

Even though I agree one hundred percent with Peter on this, I'm unable to disguise the disappointment that is surely blossoming on my face. The idea sounds like a complete reversal of his former strong pursuit of me. Does it mean that he has changed his mind about me... about us?

Peter says, "Some of that glue has to be trust... and..." Peter gropes for the correct word... "and a willingness to depend upon each other. Don't you agree?"

"Yes, trust. I agree. But interdependence often comes harder... at least for me. If I work on that fault, what is it in your weakly male character that *you* are planning to improve upon?"

"Since I am already perfect...."

"You're a rotten tease. This is a serious conversation."

"You are right. This is not the time for clowning. I'll work on my patience. I will try to be patient until you become used to the idea of giving up some of your self-determination... but not every single vestige of it of course. It might dilute your personality to skim milk."

"Then it is my considered opinion that we should give our relationship time to season quite a bit longer."

"Agreed, but not too long. I am only human."

Me, too, but I don't say it out loud. Peter reaches out pretending to shake hands on the 'deal' and draws me into a lovely warm embrace.

During dinner that evening at the Sjoberg cottage when the electronic bell music begins its loud six o'clock blast. Erma excuses herself sweetly, rises from her chair with her usual dignity, walks over to the door and slams it with gusto. Peter and I both laugh. Again, I note how his mother is such an amalgam of opposites... of her ladyship manners and what I term "ballpark-fan" behavior.

Peter and I walk down to Fleury cottage after dinner. All the way, I keep praying that Roger will not have returned, but his BMW is once again parked in the driveway right behind my car.

"Oh, I was hoping Roger had gone." I turn around in the road as though to walk in the opposite direction.

Peter catches my arm and turns me back again. "If you and I are going to be together as a couple from now on, it's just as well for Roger to know it right from the start. Why put it off?"

Inside, Roger rises from the chair where he has probably been waiting for hours to pounce on me. "I'm Leah's husband," Roger says. "Just came up here to the cottage to help her deal with this fire catastrophe. You know how these shy artist types are... they tend to forget the practical approach to straightening out a mess."

In horror, I turn to look at the reaction on Peter's face. It carries his cool but polite expression. Roger is making me appear to be a helpless, reclusive dimwit. The sooner Peter and I get out of here, the better. I hurry up the stairs to fetch my shoulder bag which I have left mostly packed from the night before. While I add clean, but smoky, underpants and a cotton shirt to the bag, I can hear Peter introducing himself downstairs.

"Peter Sjoberg."

"Yes, I guessed you were the new heart throb." From upstairs, I can visualize Peter's red-blond eyebrows meeting in a frown over that remark. As I hurry down the stairs to rescue Peter, I hear Roger saying, "You know there are other kinds of harassments, not just phone calls, that the little lady needs to be protected from. I'm here to make sure she doesn't make some unwise choices."

Peter ignores the open insinuation and turns to me. "All set to go?" He doesn't wait for my answer. From the pained expression on my face, it must be obvious how disturbed I am, so he simply holds firmly to my arm and leads me in the direction of the door. Without further words, we walk away, leaving Roger standing there. We have given him no openings for additional snide rejoinders.

"Leah?" Roger calls out, but I don't turn around or answer. In my head I picture his open mouth, figuratively speaking.

Right after returning to the Sjoberg cottage, I phone my father and tell him the news about Mr. Lumus being taken in for questioning by the police and also about Roger's visit.

"Thank God, all that business of weird phone calls may be over and you can feel safe. As for Roger, well, it's just the sort of behavior we've come to expect. If it weren't for Tommy, Roger could get lost somewhere in the remote jungles of the Amazon or he could drop... oh, here's Tommy. He wants to talk to you."

"Hey, Mom. When are you coming home?"

"In a couple of days or maybe sooner. Peter says to tell you, 'hello'." In the background I can hear Pillage barking.

"Yeah, sure." Tommy's voice is loaded with tones of disillusionment. "Hope he keeps his promises better than my dad. He never showed up."

"I'm sorry, Tommy." I thought it best not to add to his disappointment by telling him that Roger was up here in Tatterack, instead of down there in Holland where he had promised Tommy he would take him to the County Fair.

"Mom, can I buy a new computer game? Grandpa says I have to ask you first."

"You wait until I get home and then we'll see. You and I also have to go shopping for some new school clothes."

"But Mom, I need a new game right now. Grandpa says, 'Idle hands make trouble'."

I can't help but laugh. The "idle hands" phrase is just another of my dad's favorite sayings. "You tell Grandpa that I want you to pick up your room before I get home and that should keep your hands from becoming too idle, and also please ask Grandpa to take you to the library for some books and video tapes. Bye now."

"Yeah, yeah. Nuts. Bye."

"Tommy, don't hang up; I want to talk to your grandpa once more."

"I'm here." My father has evidently rescued the phone receiver from my disappointed son just as he is about to hang up. "When are you coming home?"

"That's what I want to tell you. I'm staying here a few more days to contact a newspaper over in Granville. Tommy isn't being too irritating, is he?"

"No, he's fine. What's this about a newspaper?"

"I'm going to write an article on noise pollution."

"That's just going to make more trouble for you... more retaliations."

"But I have to do it. To drop the whole matter of the electronic bells after all my canvassing work would be to capitulate. It would be giving-in to those narrow-minded folks who are trying to force me to stop." I hear a sigh of resignation from my father. "I'll be staying up at Mrs. Sjoberg's cottage, so you don't need to worry about me. I won't be alone at night.

"Yes, got it. Honey, it's difficult to say much because Tommy is hovering around.... but...."

"What is it?"

"Be careful of any relationships you are about to enter into. Know what I mean?"

"Yes, I do understand, and yes I agree with your favorite quote: Look before you leap. Love you, Pop."

CHAPTER 37

*P*eter and I sit in the cockpit of his little sailboat this evening watching the sun go down. This late in the summer the earth has shifted and we can no longer see the sun setting from the shore because a point of land thrusts out into the Straits blocking the view. Peter has attached his father's old seagull outboard to the transom of his sailboat and we putt-putt out into the bay and anchor. There aren't any jet skis around this evening to spoil the solitude so occasionally we can even hear the deep croak of the blue heron standing on a rock nearby gazing down into the water on the lookout for its evening meal.

"Have you ever looked at the setting sun through binoculars?" Peter hands them over to me. "Here. Look carefully at the edges of the sun,"

"They look blurred, like melting red wax." I watch the blue-gray flat water appear to swallow up the hot melting-wax sun and almost expect to hear a sizzle and see steam rising up as a consequence.

"Enough of that." Peter loosens the binoculars from my fingers and leans over to kiss me. All my thirst-deprived longings for love and affection are satiated by that kiss, at least temporarily. I could become spoiled and want more and more of the sweet stuff. I give back to Peter every nuance of that outward symbol of love and affection. Our kisses are reciprocal statements. His gentleness and the tender way he touches my face are pure enjoyment to me. As Peter bends further over to kiss my neck, I groan. My body wants much more than just kisses. No, I mentally pinch myself. I'm not going to slip into any situation that I can't slip out of again, not until I am absolutely sure about my feelings. I'm not going to settle just for this wonderful lost-in-a-maelstrom, sexual euphoria. I gently, but firmly, detached myself from Peter's arms.

The sun has completed its disappearing act now, but it leaves a vast sea of peach afterglow in the sky where it touches the blue-gray of water. We sit there in the cockpit, our hands touching, watching the ever-changing colors in the sky turn from strong yellows, then to vivid pinks and lastly to lavender and mauve.

"Do you think Tommy likes me?" Peter suddenly asks.

"I know he does… especially for your sailboat."

"Yes, but I want him to like me for more than that."

I smirk, "It might take quite a bit of time… for both of us to get used to you. We'll see."

"Now look who's teasing… and what is this 'we'll see' business? That sounds exactly like my mother's favorite phrase. I was brought up on that one."

"You seem to have survived. I'll bet you were a persistent little kid."

"Still am. It's one of my big faults."

I look into Peter's face. He is absolutely serious. "Persistence under the right circumstances is not a fault. Anyway, I didn't imagine you could be anywhere close to a state of perfection."

"And all this time I thought I had you nicely fooled. There's my limp, too, you know. Have you thought about what that means?"

"Your limp doesn't turn me off."

"It's a fault though… especially when I try to dance. It upsets my marvelous rhythm."

"Will it get worse as the years go by? I mean the limp, not your marvelous rhythm."

"Yes, it's possible, especially if arthritis should set in when I get older."

"It seems like an inherent part of your personality." Peter's hand on mine tenses. "Oh, I didn't mean to imply that you project a weak image in my mind. Far from it. It's just that I'm so use to your uneven gait that without it, you would seem a complete stranger, not someone I've become…attracted to."

"Thanks, I think." Peter laughs.

"However," I pause and give Peter a half humorous, half suspicious glance, "like most people, you are probably harboring, unknowingly of course, some additional personality quirks persistence. Maybe you have a dormant, unused imagination, or perhaps you are completely pragmatic." I'm only partially serious because from what I know of Peter thus far, I doubt he can ever be pragmatic to the point of dullness.

"I'm practical enough to earn a living. One does like to eat, you know. Or are you asking if I have broader tastes than just my job?"

"Yes, that's exactly what my probing is all about."

"Well, let's see if I can qualify in your eyes. But keep in mind that if I don't come up to your expectations, I'm sure there is some young lady out there who will appreciate *the real* me."

"I'll do my best to keep that in mind."

"I appreciate natural beauty… sailing and camping… which you already know… art, though I can't paint like you. Oh, and museums, especially on the subject of history. I like music… some jazz but mostly classical, and I can pound the piano if I'm flattered enough. Now let's poke into your soft underbelly and expose your foibles one by one."

"I am utter perfection, naturally."

"Not quite. You do hate to give up your freedom."

I become suddenly wary. So, I sigh, we are back to that old theme again. "I never line my shoes up, straight like soldiers, in the closet or neatly shut all my dresser drawers. Sometimes I don't make my bed for days." I'm exaggerating my sloppiness, hoping to skirt completely around the issue of independence, which has already been raised. How can I make Peter understand how important it is to remain my own mistress?

Like most men, Peter has never lost his freedom. Peter has never been married, but even if he had been married he would never have been asked to sacrifice quite as much of his independence as a women is forced to give up because of child bearing and other domestic expectations. Now I bluntly ask myself whether I can ever again be content inside perimeters set by a marriage? Perhaps not. I have now become too used to handling my own reins.

"Yes," Peter looks thoughtfully off at the still glowing horizon and then back to me. "Your desire for independence could be a toe stumbler, but perhaps it is open to negotiations?"

I nod, "We can talk about it." To myself I think the subject of *independence* shouldn't be negotiable… it should just "be."

"Then there's also a certain kind of magic I could assert."

"Oh?" I wonder at Peter's ability to circumvent the entire subject of women's lib so deftly. "What do you mean by magic?"

"Actually I think I'd better not wait. Now is the time to accelerate my influence."

I can feel Peter's hands reaching under my life preserver and touching my breasts. We both slip off the deck and hunker down in the cockpit as though seeking bodily warmth. Even in the growing dusk I can see the sharp blue eyes fringed in red-blond coming closer and closer. Then I shut my own eyes, yet I can still feel Peter's eyes washing over me, pooling inside of me. It takes so much will power to pull back from the strong physical sensations overcoming me… drowning me right here in the dry cockpit with water all around. Holding myself back is as tough as stopping water from flowing down hill.

"Stop," I almost shout. "I need to think."

"Thinking…that's exactly what I don't want you to do. Then you begin to add up all the bad times you've had in your past married life." Peter appeals to me, "Leah, could you let this be the beginning of a brand new start to your life? Give it a chance?"

"How about a few ground rules to cover this new connection?"

"As many or as few as you like. Whatever will make you feel free and un-trapped. I'm a democratic sort of guy. You get to vote on everything. Come here... please. I want to continue with my persuasion."

"I'm a little suspicious of your 'so called' persuasive magic. Exactly what goal do you hope to achieve, my dear sir?"

"In the short term, it's just to kiss you and feel you close to me. Like this." I find myself sinking back into a lovely embrace with all our parts touching except where the bulky life preservers interfere. "In the long term it's to persuade you to marry me."

"Oh." It's a pleasurable "oh," full of happy relief. He isn't assuming a long, drawn-out, live-in affair. He has just proposed marriage. After we kiss again, I lay in his arms feeling relaxed, even though his arms are obviously symbols of boundaries. I remind myself that they are also symbols of protection. I bask happily in his arms.

Still, I ask myself, will I resent Peter's protective nature sometime in the future when I don't need protection? I am keenly aware of my present state of vulnerability due to this summer's mean little retaliations. The unsettling events have left me in a more susceptible state, churned-up and weakened like fibers after washing with too strong a soap. It leaves me needing greater approbation, far more than usual, after feeling utterly flattened by all the nasty words and the harassments from people regarding the bells.

Later, when this crisis of the bells and the breather phone calls are over, will I cease to need Peter's protection? What about Peter's needs? Am I willing to be solicitous of Peter's needs when they arise?

Perhaps I'm getting a false sense of well being too soon. Once again I sternly reiterate to myself: Go slowly with Peter. It's all too easy for you to let down your guard and forget your former mistake in choosing a mate. You mustn't let Peter's lovable nature overwhelm you so thoroughly that it obliterates the hard lessons you've learned from the past. Perhaps then, I finally conclude, Peter's so called *magic* is too much, too soon.

"Any answer forthcoming?" Peter asks, "or do you have to consult with the Greek Gods?"

"I am deeply honored by your proposal, but at the moment lovely sex is stacked against me. Making an untainted decision right now is impossible." I struggle out of Peter's arms. "Any answer I give right now will be unduly prejudiced. I'm waiting for a cool down, a time when I am more clear-headed. Answer pending, my dear Peter."

CHAPTER 38

*P*eter wakes me the next morning with a kiss and a smiling face. "It's ten o'clock, Lady Friend."

"Oh, I am sorry. Is it really that late? I didn't realize…"

Peter sits down on the edge of my bed. "It's no problem. You must have been very tired. I know you have important things to do today or I'd let you snooze on and on."

Peter's affable face greets me. I'm not used to waking to any face at all, though occasionally Tommy, who finds it difficult to hold back his urgent questions no matter how early the hour, abruptly interrupts my slow awakening. In fact since leaving Roger, I have gotten used to lying quietly in bed thinking about the day to come and almost always feeling a deep reluctance to meet it head-on. I don't have that dread, that negativism, this morning, but still I don't particularly feel like bursting out cheerleader style either. Will Peter expect me to be jovial and perky so early each morning if we ever get married? That "get married" is still a huge *if*. It's a risk. Maybe too much of a risk.

"Yes," I stifle a yawn, "You are right, Peter. I have to keep trying to get in touch with that builder. He ought to be home today since it's Sunday." To myself I wonder if Roger has left Fleury cottage or if he is still hanging around. I dread running into him again. Almost as if I have voiced my fears out loud, Peter's next words bring up the subject.

"Roger's car seems to be gone. I fast-walked past there this morning."

"Good." Now I really feel like smiling. "Go away so I can get back into my smoky clothes."

"Only if you insist upon privacy." Peter gives me a wolfish grin as he moves towards the door. "I'll fix some breakfast for us."

"I can do it," I offer.

"Not this time." I can hear Peter's irregular gait as he walks across the balcony and then down the steps to the room below, the room with the huge stone fireplace. This bedroom has two windows facing the water. I lie there a few minutes longer admiring the drapes which have alternate sage-colored stripes with bands of flowers in between. Finally I get up and pull back the drapes to reveal a clear unfettered view of the water, not the slightly skewered one I see through at Fleury cottage.

The scope of the view from this cottage is nearly the same as the one I have from my own bedroom in Fleury cottage, had I not recently moved into the south facing one so that I could hear better and watch for possible intruders. Now, as I watch from this window, I see a light breeze touching the water and causing ripples like the flutters emanating across my skin when Peter touches me. I can see Peter's little sailboat making jaunty up and down motions as the water slides under her hull.

After I visit the bathroom, get dressed, and straighten the heavy bedspread, which matches the drapes with its ribbons and cheery flowers, I descend to the kitchen where I find Peter whipping up scrambled eggs. I can smell the fresh coffee.

"Your mother isn't here?"

"She's gone to the early church service. Now that she's left, I have free reign to chase you around the sofa." Peter drops the whisk into a bowl soaking in the sink and heads straight for me.

"Threats, threats. Anyway, if I don't run, you can't chase me."

"In which case, I have already caught you." Peter traces his fingers down and across the nap of my neck and then bends to kiss me. I feel the lovely weakness spreading down throughout my body and especially my legs. Immediately I sit down on a nearby stool. As long as Peter is anywhere physically close to me, I'm going to have a difficult time keeping a clear mental balance.

"We're eating in there this morning." Peter draws me from the kitchen stool and moves me through the doorway into a room facing the water, a room that I haven't seen before except for a quick view from the beachside through the window. It's a delightful room, surrounded on two sides by ceiling to floor windows. The third side also has windows and a door leading into a screened porch.

"Beautiful," I exclaim, wishing my father's cottage had a room exactly like this one. In the corners are huge pots of green plants with smaller ones hanging from the ceiling. The white oval dining table is surrounded by straight-backed wicker chairs. The wicker also gives the room a garden appeal. From the kitchen doorway, Peter hands me the silverware and napkins and I set the table.

"It's a great room, but cold in the fall because it takes the full brunt of the winds from the north. Half the time we huddle around the Ben Franklin stove in the kitchen to eat our meals."

After eating breakfast and washing up the dishes, Peter and I walk down to Fleury cottage. Indeed, just as Peter had reported, Roger's BMW is gone. I wonder if he's at a restaurant eating his breakfast, or if he's really gone for good...heading back south to Holland to see Tommy. Even before we manage to unlock the back door, we can hear the telephone ringing.

"Perhaps it's Mr. Cousins finally returning my phone calls at last. I've left several messages on his answering machine." Automatically covering my nose against the pervasive smoke smell about to strike me, I hurry through the back door to pick up the phone before it can stop ringing. I feel alert and refreshed this morning after having nearly ten hours of undisturbed sleep. Also, Roger is apparently gone and Mr. Lumus is now in the custody of the police. There is nothing to fear and nothing to worry me. This morning I feel as light and free as a feather drifting to the beach.

"I pick up the receiver with alacrity and speak with a bright expectant tone in my voice. "Hello?"

"You'll burn in hell along with that big mouthed Indian... you'll burn.....," the voice keeps droning on and on. Immediately a tight lid of fear clamps down over me once again. It's a steel block on my chest squeezing the air out of my lungs. I try to suck-in more air, "aaaauuu". This time I think I recognize the caller's voice though it's more breathless and more in a hurry than in the previous calls. My hands begin to shake and I feel targeted...marked for destruction exactly like someone who knows they are in the cross hairs of a scope. It's an effort to keep myself from behaving like a coward. I want to slip down under the table to hide. Peter takes the receiver from my shaking hand, listens for a minute and then hangs up the receiver. I cup my hands over my face as though to hide from the telephone voice and its threatening words.

Peter draws my hands away from my face so that he can hear my muffled words. "I don't understand? Mr. Lumus was taken off to jail, wasn't he?" Both Peter and I had seen him being taken away in the police car.

"Did you recognize the voice?" Peter asks.

"Y—yes. It was Mr. Lumus' voice. So who were the other voices I heard?"

Even with Peter's comforting figure standing right here close beside me, I sit completely stricken, afraid to move out of my chair exactly as before.

"Aren't you going to make the report to the phone company?"

"Ummmm? What did you say?" I'm too distracted to think clearly.

"The phone company," Peter prompts me. Once more I dial in the information needed by the phone company to trap the caller. I rise from the chair very stiffly, as though it must be done carefully and so very correctly, or some spook will jump out at me with an ax or a knife. I feel the beginning of tears, but check them by lowering my head and swallowing several times.

"Now I see how much these phone calls debilitate you." Peter gently pushes me towards the stairs. "Get all the clothes you need so that you won't have to come back to this cottage for several days. Let's get you out of here."

"I thought all the threats and scary things were over. When we saw the police take Mr. Lumus away, I thought..."

"... So did I." Peter gives me a hug. "Up you go." He actually guides me up several steps and then I begin to climb on my own but keep looking back at Peter. I'm reluctant to leave the safety of his arms.

Upstairs I quickly change my jeans and T-shirt into the same outfit I had worn to Erma's aborted dinner just before the fire. Now, perhaps I won't spread the aroma of a three-alarm fire when we enter a restaurant for dinner. I also add more clean underwear, pajamas, plus clean khaki pants and three shirts to my larger suitcase, then snap it shut. Once or twice I quickly peer out the window to see if anyone is watching the cottage. No one. I ease the large suitcase down as far as the stair landing where Peter takes it out of my hand, then I go back to my bedroom for my smaller case. "Now I don't smell as smoky."

"Let's see." Peter pretends to sniff around me like a hunting dog and ends up by licking the side of my nose.

"Stop it," I gently push him aside before he can distract me by converting his licking into a kiss. "We'd better get out of here in case Roger suddenly returns or there's another crank phone call." To myself I add... or I begin another crying jag.

"Right," Peter agrees. "This kiss is to be continued and....." The phone shrills again and we both halt like criminals trying to escape jail instead of escaping a mere phone call.

I mutter through frozen lips, "Let's not answer it!"

"I'll answer it." Peter picks up the telephone and listens. I hold my breath waiting. My hand goes up to my forehead where a tension ache is building up.

"Here she is. It's Chief Bruckner." Peter turns the receiver over to me.

"Ms. Fleury, we caught your threatening phone caller red handed. As we suspected all along, it was Mr. Lumus."

"But... but you took him away in your police car yesterday. How could he possibly make another phone call today?"

"Yes, well, it's this way. Yesterday we had no proof that he was your crank caller; however, we were certain that he was the arsonist because we found cloth inside his cottage that exactly matched the few pieces crammed under your shingles that escaped the flames. Both pieces of cloth were analyzed and both matched, exactly. Mr. Lumus was consequently charged and jailed.

"Then why was he allowed to make a phone call just a few minutes ago and threaten me?"

Today he asked if he could phone his brother who lives downstate in Jackson; instead, he dialed your phone number here in Tatterack. We were listening-in on him. He became trapped by his own words, which we recorded."

I listened to Chief Bruckner's explanation, and then interrupt again. "There must be more than one caller. I recognized Mr. Lumus' voice on this last call, but not the threatening voices on previous calls."

"We think Lumus recorded voices of other people to use. He and Growgood were rehearsing music and a skit for a Holloween party. From that tape Lumus could have cut and spliced voices to scare you."

Another threat could also have been aimed at Growgood, but I didn't mention that to Chief Bruckner. After all, it was Growgood, not Lumus, who had spilled the truth about the bell being undamaged.

This time the tears running down my face are tears of relief.

"Then it's ended, finally?" I asked the Chief.

"Yes, except you may be called if there's a trial of some kind. I suspect though, there won't be one since it's pretty obvious Mr. Lumus is senile or psychotic. He also has an infected leg just below the knee. We can't imagine what caused it and he refuses to tell, but it's a good thing it was caught in time, because infection has already set in."

I think I could guess. The crusty little Father over at the church must have advised Mr. Lumus to wear a cilice as a penance to make up for his radical behavior... for audaciously advocating that the church lower the volume of the electronic bell tapes.

Chief Bruckner continued, "Give us your forwarding address and cell phone number before you leave Tatterack in case we need to get in touch with you. Your insurance company may want to press Mr. Lumus for the fire damages, but I'm not sure he has any assets available other than that old shack of his or maybe the property it sits on."

"Thank you, Chief Bruckner. I'll stop by the station. Thanks for all your help." I turn to Peter. The immense relief must show clearly on my face.

"It's over. Finally it's all over!" I give Peter an exuberant hug and he swings me around and up in the air with equal joyfulness.

Well I think to myself, not everything is completely over. There is still the noise pollution problem pending until the wily little Father at the church admits that the bell in the tower is undamaged and could be reinstated once again. His congregation needs to know the truth. Mentally, I vow to my friend, Enid: I am definitely not going to run away scared from the commitment I've made to fight noise pollution, at least in this very special place.

Dear Peter is standing here beside me waiting patiently for me to emerge from my euphoria back into a calmer state of mind. I intend to make that metamorphosis in just a minute. I need time to absorb what's happened and maybe another minute to sort things through in my mind. I plunk myself down once more on the edge of a chair.

"Leah?"

"Yes?" I answer vaguely and smile up at Peter. Now that Chief Bruckner has settled the question of the crank caller, I can focus on Peter. I no longer want to sidestep or run away from him. He makes me feel cherished...as though I have finally come into port where my subconscious has been willing me to sail after a long senseless zigzagging. So what if I do lose a bit of my independence by marrying again? Sometimes one has to give-up a little to gain an even greater value, like Peter's love for me and naturally my love for him. Those are far more important than my pride in being self-reliant.

All the same, I intend to thread my way slowly into my relationship with Peter...stepping carefully around the slippery rocks...checking the uneven watery ground where there could be little clay holes that might trip either of us and ruin our chances of becoming a whole family.

It's looks more and more like a home with Peter will be exactly the right place for Tommy and me. Still, I want to be absolutely certain before taking a wrong step.

Peter is as anxious to avoid running into Roger again, as I am, so he asks with some trepidation in his voice, since I appear to be settling down in this chair as a permanent fixture for life, "Leah?" he asks again, "ready to move along?"

"Yes, dear Peter." I take his hand, squeeze it, and smile back secretively, "Now I am quite ready."

CUT GRASS <u>LESS OFTEN</u>

1. Save Money
Mow only roadside front lawns each week… do less seen lawns every other week
2. Noise… Noise… Noise!
3. Less noise is better for all ages. Many elderly, like myself, take afternoon naps. The mowing, as it is now, isn't finished until 5 o'clock. Dinnertime for many. If you think the noise can only be heard exactly where the mower is working, then you are wrong.
4. Mowing period is too long.
5. This year, 2017, you began in March. Last year mowing began in April and ran into October. Last Monday, March 20th there appeared to be no young green grass. The mover near my cottage threw lots of dust into the air.
6. Privacy, privacy, privacy
7. Though men who use mowing machines are very discreet, I feel a lack of privacy especially when I am trying to write a book and need to think carefully.

Jean M. Ponte
2251 Meadowlard Road